RUN!

The man cleared the doorway and in one lunge was directly behind her. She saw his leather-covered hands clench and unclench. She could sense his breath, impossibly hot, as he bore down on her.

Christie's scream pierced the silence . . .

His fist closed around the silky fabric of her blouse. His fingers clawed her skin as he jerked her backward.

"What do you want?" she cried, her voice a hoarse shadow of terror.

"I don't want much of nothing," he said, licking his lips. His voice was as soft as silk, as rough as sandpaper. "I was just wondering, little miss. Does your mama know where you've been?"

WEB OF
SMOKE

ERIN GRADY

AVON BOOKS ◆ NEW YORK

To Rick and Hailey, who have to live with me when I write.

Special thanks to Charles and Betty Grady, for their unwavering faith in me, to Debi Ives-Durham, Leona Pfeifer, Florine Belanger and Miriam Raftery for all the Wednesday nights they devoted to the crafting of this story, and to those first readers whose encouragement will never be forgotten.

WEB OF SMOKE is an original publication of Avon Books. This work has never before appeared in book form. This work is a novel. Any similarity to actual persons or events is purely coincidental.

AVON BOOKS
A division of
The Hearst Corporation
1350 Avenue of the Americas
New York, New York 10019

Copyright © 1994 by Erin Grady
Published by arrangement with the author
Library of Congress Catalog Card Number: 94-94326
ISBN: 0-380-77720-7

First Avon Books Printing: October 1994

AVON TRADEMARK REG. U.S. PAT. OFF. AND IN OTHER COUNTRIES, MARCA REGISTRADA, HECHO EN U.S.A.

Printed in the U.S.A.

RA   10   9   8   7   6   5   4   3   2   1

1

Waiting.

Christie McCoy had spent the entire day in a state of agitated suspense. Waiting. For what, she didn't know.

She cut the engine as the garage door swished closed and sat for a quiet moment in the dimness of the garage while the feeling passed over her again. Pulling her blouse away from her sweaty skin, she stepped from her car.

Blazing hot and dusty dry, the day had started with the howl of a Santa Ana wind blowing in from the desert. A howl that played on her nerves, lacing her thoughts with dread.

She unlocked the front door and went inside, clicking the door shut behind her. Turning her gaze from the silent, vacant living room with its bare windows and walls, and her thoughts from the persistent pulse of anxiety, she started up the stairs. Her hand lightly brushed the blond banister; her footsteps echoed in the emptiness.

At the top, she paused, looking over her shoulder as she'd done countless times that day. Below she could see the front door, part of the unfurnished living room, and the gleaming wooden hallway that led to the kitchen. Sunshine blanketed all in a glowing honey caress.

Hesitating, her body tuned to the slightest change in the house, she listened to the silence. Her ears rang with the effort, but she heard nothing. Nothing to warrant her jumpy nerves or fragmented tension. Nothing to explain the feeling of impending doom. Nothing but a hot wind blowing anxiety through her very bones.

She shook herself, physically—mentally—and continued down the short, open landing that connected the three bedrooms and one bathroom. She entered the master bedroom, unable to prevent one last look over her shoulder.

Which is why she didn't see him until a floorboard squealed under his weight.

The sound rushed at her, spinning her back around to face him. He sprang from the concealing folds of the only drapes in the house and raced at her.

Fear swallowed her in one monstrous mouthful.

Run.

Christie acted on the thought, turning with it and stumbling toward the landing, which suddenly seemed to double, triple in length as her body seemed to shrink. One step. Had it really taken all that time to take that one little step?

Two steps. She had maybe four or five to go. And then what? She glanced behind her.

The man cleared the doorway and in one lunge was directly behind her. She saw his leather-covered hands clench and unclench. She could sense his breath, impossibly hot, as he bore down on her.

Christie's scream pierced the silence like fingernails on a chalkboard as she snapped her face forward. Behind her, she felt him leap, felt the floor sag under the powerful thrust of his deceptively lean legs, and then give like a sprung rubber band as he sailed in the air.

She crossed the bedroom doorway just as his fist closed around the silky fabric of her blouse. His fingers clawed her skin as he jerked her backward.

Her center of gravity shifted, sinking down and down, sucking her under. She hit the floor hard and bit her tongue. The copper taste of blood filled her mouth.

Scrambling to her knees, she scurried toward the stairs. He grabbed her ankle, closed it in a viselike grip, and yanked. She fought him, grasping desperately for something to hold. She clenched the fibers of the carpet, anything to keep her from being pulled back. She gained an inch.

Enraged, he wrenched hard on her leg, dragging her, snapping her nails to the quick. A deep-throated cry burst from her lungs and slammed past her lips.

"NO!" she screamed, struggling against his force. He crushed her ankle in his fist, hauling her to him with a strength beyond his size. Writhing, kicking, she managed to flip over onto her back. Her blouse pulled loose from the waist of her skirt and the rug scorched her bare skin.

Holding on to her leg, he swooped, clamping his other hand in her short hair. He jerked hard.

She felt hot tears on her cold face and panic torched her stomach. Her brain quit sending clear signals of action. Instead, a blistering jolt of adrenaline moved her without thought.

"Let go of me NOW!"

She punctuated the last word with a kick. No time to aim, she drove the heel of her shoe at him. It skidded over his arm, leaving a deep ugly welt in its wake, and plowed into his iron-hard rib cage.

Stunned, his hand opened into a frozen claw of surprise and pain. She jerked her head away just as he realized his mistake. Incensed, he wrenched her still-captive foot viciously.

Her screams echoed one after another through the open foyer, pounding against the walls and doubling back on her. She kicked again and again, frantically back-paddling against the coarse carpet. A lucky shot clipped him on the jaw; a follow-up sent him backward into the bedroom.

Still screaming, Christie scrambled to her feet, fell, hauled herself up using the railing. Behind her she heard him leap to his feet. She took the stairs two at a time, stumbling as she went. Six steps down, his hand connected with the back of her head. He shoved.

Arms and feet waving, she plunged forward. The cream-and-peach ceramic tile by the door zoomed up as her body catapulted down. Instinctively she tucked and curled, crying out when her body slammed to the floor.

No time to catch her breath; no time to check her injuries. His heavy footsteps raced down to her. She launched herself at the front door, yanking it open.

His shoulder caught it halfway and he slammed it closed. Not missing a beat, she ducked under his arm and darted into the vacant living room. She lost a shoe as she rounded the corner, through the dining room to the kitchen.

He'd expected her move, circling the other way, down the hall to the tableless breakfast nook. On opposite sides of the kitchen, they faced each other.

Blood ran from his nose and an ugly gash on his cheek. Watching her with cold blue eyes, he wiped at his face.

He stepped forward, placing himself between Christie and the phone.

"What do you want?" she cried, her voice a hoarse shadow of terror.

He smiled and winked. A chill of recognition teased her memory, then vanished like a puff of smoke in the wind. Who was he? She shook her head in response to her unspoken question.

"I don't want much of nothing," he said, licking his lips. His voice was as soft as silk, as rough as sandpaper. He winked again. "I was just wondering, little miss. Does your mama know where you've been?"

The blood washed from her face in an icy wave.

Eyes riveted on him, she anticipated his intention a second before he charged. Leaping back through the dining room doorway, she hit the floor. She couldn't outrun him but she'd be damned if she'd lie down and die for him.

Braced with her back against the wall, she drew her knees to her chest. Her lips moved over silent words of panic. "Okay, okay, this is it . . . please . . . please, please . . ."

He rounded the door like a charging bull.

Waiting until he was directly in front of her, she thrust her legs out, throwing all her weight and power into them. Her feet slammed into the side of his knee, forcing it to bend in the wrong direction.

Her battle cry came from her gut, reverberating and hammering in her body as it rose up her throat and erupted from her open mouth.

He swayed for a moment, trying to regain his balance. Pulling back, she aimed another kick at his legs. She heard a pop; he hit the floor.

Frozen by terror, she forced herself to attack again. The pointed toe of her shoe buried itself in his abdomen. He groaned, rolled, and gripped his ribs, and, for one split second, left himself totally vulnerable.

Christie pounced, using her one shoe-clad foot to drive the power of her terror and rage deep into his groin. His breath exploded in a squeal clogged by pain.

Gulping, she staggered back, tripped over her fear, and caught herself against the wall. She left a bloody splash of red on the white paint.

Run, Christie, run.

The voice could have come from outside her head. The voice of a drill sergeant, a commander. The voice of authority that moved her with lightning speed. And suddenly, it seemed to her that everything was moving too fast. Like a record switched from 33 rpm's to 78. She flew to the front door and out into the blazing sunshine.

"Help me!" Her cry caught in her throat and whimpered into the afternoon.

Like a dream, she thought, like a dream where you can't scream. She tried again.

"Help me!" This time it rang out, carrying across the emerald lawns, the tended shrubs, reverberating against the sizzling asphalt. "Somebody call the police. Please, help me."

The street was totally quiet. A void of action in the blistering heat. She ran. Horror kept her from looking over her shoulder, but hysteria finally swiveled her head.

He hadn't followed.

Gulping at the taste of fear, she slowed, turning all the way around and backing away. She crossed the street, stopping by a tree.

The front door of her house gaped like an open sore. In the shadows nothing moved. Where was he?

She heard the whine of a siren in the distance. Relief made a very small sensation in the churning whirlpool of emotions swamping her.

She began to shake uncontrollably, her knees gave, and she sank to the soft grass. She needed a drink of water; she had to go to the bathroom. She wanted to let loose the anguished rage in her belly. Instead, she watched her front door.

The siren grew louder and a black-and-white—San Diego's Finest—pulled up to the curb. Christie stayed where she was.

The officer who bounded from the car had a gun and looked as if he knew how to use it. His badge glinted in the harsh sunlight as he crouched and approached the house. He turned every third step and checked his back. At the door, he paused. Ridiculously, or so it seemed to Christie, he rang the bell. "Police," he called into the house. His voice carried, clear and decisive.

A second police car skidded to a stop in front of her house. This policeman was bigger, but equally cautious. He maneuvered himself to the first man's side.

Christie didn't know if the officer received an answer to his call, but both men unsnapped their guns and swiveled inside.

Minutes—or maybe hours—ticked by, barely penetrating the husk of numbness that surrounded her. She really had to use the bathroom. The first officer came out of her house, holstering his gun on the way. He spotted Christie across the street, and, still checking his back, approached.

Crouching down in front of Christie, he eyed her torn blouse and blood-speckled body. "Are you hurt?"

She rubbed her bruised ankle and flexed her foot. "I don't think so."

"You're bleeding."

Silently she held up her hand. He looked at the raw fingertips that used to have nails and then back at her face.

"Your neighbor called the police. Said you were screaming."

Christie looked over his shoulder at the front door. "Did you get him?"

He stared at her for a minute. "The house is empty, ma'am. Officer Johnson is pursuing. Can you tell me what happened?"

Christie didn't answer. Her eyes fixed uneasily on the badge that glinted on his chest.

"Ma'am? An ambulance is on the way. Could you answer a few questions? It could help us find—"

Christie shook her head silently, tuning out his gentle voice. Instead she saw the attacker's eyes, heard again his voice.

Eyes, as cold as the Arctic ... a voice as haunting as the elusive snatches of an almost-remembered song. Both as indistinct as the shifting shapes in an obscurely shadowed alley.

She understood, at last, what she'd been waiting for all day. Unfortunately, with the understanding came the undeniable realization that she'd been waiting much longer than a day.

And the waiting had only just begun.

2

Sam focused on the blue Toyota in the driveway. This was the place.

Jumping from the Jeep, he marched up the brick walk that bisected the green lawn. He rang the bell and waited on the porch, rocking from toe to heel, slapping the newspaper against his thigh. To either side of him tailored yards and polished houses lined her street. Even the air smelled wealthy.

From inside the house he heard the excited yapping of her three dogs as they charged the front door, nails clicking against wood and tile.

Once, he'd been happy to say good-bye to those mutts. But then again, once, he'd been happy to say good-bye to Christie, too.

"Who is it?" she called from the other side of the white wooden door.

No peephole. He frowned, shaking his head. "It's Sam."

"Sam?"

She threw open the door, looking at him with surprised wonder.

Her eyes could be called brown, but not by Sam. They glittered with too many facets of amber and gold, green and mahogany, to be called anything but magnificent and jewellike. They made him forget why he'd stormed up the walk. Why he'd been angry with her.

8

But in the heartbeat it took to forget his reason for being there, she seemed to remember her reason for never wanting to see him again. The twinkle disappeared from her eyes and a dense layer of muddy brown masked their sparkle as quickly as storm clouds blot out the sun.

Sam felt the answering smile that had somehow invaded his lips dwindle to nothing.

"What are you doing here?" she demanded.

He thrust the newspaper out. As she reached for it, Snort dashed between her feet and straight up Sam's leg. Sam scooped the Pekingese into his arms and began scratching him behind the ear.

Christie shot the captured dog a look that said "traitor" and then turned her gaze to the newspaper. She scanned it once before zeroing in on the article.

La Jolla Woman Attacked . . .

She finished reading and handed the paper back. "So why are you here?" she asked.

Maybe it was her tone, probably it was Sam and the whole mess that had once been the best thing he'd ever known, but something triggered a switch and he blew.

"Why am I here?" he repeated incredulously. "I find out—by chance—that my wife has been attacked in some ritzy pad that she doesn't belong in, and you have to ask?"

"Who are you to tell me where I belong?"

"I'm your husband."

"Ex-husband."

"I'm not an ex yet. Who the hell is paying for this place?"

"That," she exclaimed angrily, "is none of your business."

"The hell it's not." He shoved open the door, stepping over Barney, the cocker spaniel, and charged straight inside.

Christie banged the door closed behind him. It echoed in the empty house.

Facing him with her hands on her hips, she shook back her short blond hair. He caught a glimpse of the diamond studs she'd kept long after she'd discarded him. His gaze bounced from the small, shell-shaped ears that had once been his to nibble, to the bare walls and vacant rooms that reflected cold solitude.

"You didn't answer my question," he said in a more controlled voice. "Whose house is this?"

"You're right. I didn't answer your question."

She spun on her heel and marched down the polished hallway to the kitchen. Three dogs followed. Cursing under his breath, Sam did, too.

"Are you living with someone, Christie?" He'd meant it to be a demand, but the question hit the taut silence between them like a plea.

"No, Sam, I'm not living with anyone. I leave that kind of thing to you."

"Well, then, why don't you have a peephole?"

Christie tilted her head. "A peephole?"

"Yes, dammit, a peephole. For your front door. I could have been anyone out there. Would you have opened the door if I'd said Federal Express? American Express? What if I was some other Sam? Son of Sam, for chrissake!"

She half smiled. "I saw your Jeep from upstairs, Sam."

"Liar. You were surprised to see me."

"Sam, don't you think I know your voice? I knew it was you, and, yes, I was surprised."

"You were glad to see me," he insisted. He sounded childish and he knew it. But he had to hear her admit it.

"Yes, for one brief second I was glad to see you. But since that moment has passed—"

"What about this?" Sam cut her off, waving the paper in front of her before she could ask him to leave.

"What about it? Someone broke in, I caught him, he ran away."

"That's not what the paper says. The pap—
assaulted you and you barely escaped alive."

"I surprised him, Sam. We fought; I got lucky.

"Jesus, Christie, this guy could've killed you." T.
very thought of it weakened his voice.

"But he didn't and now it's over."

She turned away from him and he noticed the dark
bruise on her neck. The sight of it gnawed at his in-
sides, amplifying his fear for her safety.

In the calmest voice possible, he asked, "What if he
comes back?"

"He's a thief. Why would he come back?"

Sam looked at the unfurnished family room behind
him. She had a point. "He must've been good. Did he
get everything?"

She tossed ice into two glasses and filled them with
soda. "No."

"No? What did he miss?"

"I never had anything for him to get," she said with
a dark scowl.

"Never ... You mean he didn't steal anything?"

"Not that I've discovered." She sat down on one of
the two stools that bellied up to the island counter in
the center of the bright kitchen.

"Then why the hell do the cops think he was a
robber?"

"Because they do. Why don't you sit down, Sam?"

"Why?"

"Because you look like you're ready to fall down."

"Not funny. Why do they think he's a robber?"

"Because he is."

"Give me a break. What moron detective would investigate a robbery when nothing is missing?"

"He wasn't a moron. After questioning me, robbery
was the only clear motive."

Sam took her advice and plopped down on a barstool.
"Christie, that doesn't make sense."

"It makes perfect sense, not that anyone asked you.

ink about it," she continued in a matter-of-fact tone.
'I just moved in. I live alone—''

Thank God.

"—and I keep a very tight schedule. He probably
thought he could break in and get away before I got
home. I surprised him by coming home early."

"But why would he want to break in here? You just
said you don't have anything."

"Well, obviously, he didn't know that."

"What? Was he blind?"

"No, Sam, he wasn't blind," she snapped. "Just stupid. The police agree with me."

"That doesn't mean you're right. Christie, the cops
are so busy with kid snatchers and drive-bys, they don't
have time for a case like this. They were probably
happy to jump at any plausible reason to close this
case. They'd have agreed if you'd told them the guy
was a lost ice-cream man."

"Don't be ridiculous."

"No, don't *you* be ridiculous."

"So what is it that you want from me, Sam? I could
be right; I could be wrong. Either way, what's it to
you?"

"That's a low blow. It's a lot to me."

"Let me ask you again, Sam. Why are you here?"

He looked over her shoulder, angry with her for putting him on the spot. Angry with himself for handling
things in the worst possible way. As usual.

"I came to check your locks."

"You came to see how I got this house."

"No," he shook his head. "That's the excuse I used.
But I came for the locks. I've got new ones in the
Jeep."

Christie's mouth fell open. "You're serious?"

He nodded.

"Then why did you barge in here like the aveng-
ing angel?"

"Because I was mad about you living here with who-ever you might be living with."

"Well, now you know. It's just me, Barney, Snort, and Bear. Satisfied?"

"How come you don't have furniture?"

"I'm saving for it."

"Where were the mutts when this guy broke in?"

"At the groomers, where they go every other Mon-day during flea season, as you should know. Which only goes to support my theory that I was watched."

"How long have you lived here?"

"Did you quit giving golf lessons and decide to take up criminal investigation since the last time I saw you? Excuse me if I'm not into this interrogation."

Sam suppressed a frustrated sigh and looked at the windows and sliding glass door. "You need some cur-tains, Christie."

"I know," she said. "I hung blankets last night."

With his toe, Sam absently stroked the smallest of the trio of dogs. Bear rolled over, trusting him with the tender underside of her belly.

"Chris, I'm sorry I barged in like I did ... It's just that ... Every day you hear about some new person who got it. I'm worried about you."

"You shouldn't be."

"But I am."

"Well I don't want you to worry, Sam. The guy was a robber. Nothing more. And now that he knows I don't have anything—"

"That's just it. Even an idiot would have the brains to look in a window. See nothing and move on."

She cleared her throat and looked away, avoiding his gaze completely. "But I don't have an alarm," she said, as if that were explanation in itself.

Sam frowned. "So what? That's not the only thing you don't have."

"Well, he probably thought it was worth a try to come in and check." Still avoiding eye contact with him, she gave a false-sounding laugh. "After all, next door they're wired like a bank."

She was lying. About what, he wasn't sure. Wanting to pursue, but knowing better than to push her, Sam reluctantly swallowed his argument.

"Speaking of next door," he said, "when did you start running with such a classy crowd?"

"A few weeks ago," she answered in a resentful voice.

He waited for her to elaborate, but she fell silent, apparently contemplating the black hole of the fireplace in the adjoining family room.

"So . . . did you win the lottery?" he probed.

Her smile was small and insincere. "No."

"Jackpot?"

"No."

"The Japanese buy your company?"

"No," she sighed. "If you have to know, my mother left it to me."

"Your mother?"

She forced an at-ease expression that didn't fool her dog Barney, let alone Sam. "Yes. She died."

Sam blinked, hard. "Christie, I'm sorry. I didn't know—"

"I didn't tell you."

"Why?"

She jumped up and dumped the last of her soda in the sink. Back turned to him, she answered, "I didn't see the point to it. If that satisfies your active curiosity, Sam, I have some things to do now." She closed the conversation with a resounding slam.

He wanted to ask how her mother had died, but her verbal slap in the face felt more like a punch in the gut and he didn't want another. Silently he cursed. What had he expected?

Sam finished his soda and stood up. "Will you let me fix your locks, Chris?"

"The police said my locks are just fine. The best,

actually. They aren't sure exactly how he entered, but it wasn't by forcing my locks."

"They don't have any idea how he got in?"

"Probably my bedroom window. There's a tree outside it and I must have left it unlocked by accident. The bedroom's the place I surprised him."

"Mind if I double-check? For my peace of mind?"

She sighed. "If you feel you have to."

Sam, trailed by Christie and the dogs, walked from room to room, checking the windows, checking doors. He tugged at the sliding glass door and tried to lift it from its tracks, discovering in the process the safety lock that prohibited him from doing so.

Barney dashed through the doggie door in the garage and waited, smiling and playful, for Sam to exit to the backyard.

"How's it going, boy?"

Barney chuffed, allowed with a lick that he was fine, and ran to fetch his ball. Sam played for a few minutes, watching the golden dog dash back and forth across the sweet, soft grass. Finally, admitting to himself that he was stalling, Sam went back inside.

"They're right," he told Christie. "The locks are all top of the line and in good shape."

"That's reassuring," she answered in a cool, professional voice.

"I'd be happy to add a few more to your doors, just to be safe."

"I really don't think that's necessary, Sam. But I appreciate your concern."

"Don't talk to me like I'm one of your clients, Christie."

"Well, forgive me for being polite."

"I don't like leaving you here alone one little bit."

"This is where I live, so you'll just have to force yourself to like it."

"Will you promise to call me at least? If you need

anything?'' He swallowed. ''If something happens? Don't make me read about it in the paper again.''

''Okay. If that will make you happy.''

''There you go again. I'm not booking a ticket to Atlanta, here. I'm serious. Will you call me?''

She nodded.

''Promise.''

''If anything else . . . occurs, I will call.'' She hesitated, avoiding his eyes. ''But you're worrying about something that's not going to happen.''

3

Throngs of people spilled from the bars on Avenue Revolucion in Tijuana as DC Porter made his way down the street. Rap music reverberated from the cavernous bars packed with half-naked girls and sweating, oversexed boys. It was barely nine o'clock at night, but most of the crowd looked ready to pass out or puke. Those who couldn't hang with the tough would soon be replaced by fresh reinforcements spilling over the border in a nonstop stream.

Young Mexican men standing in the open doorways of the clubs handed out flyers and called, ''Free margaritas. Lots of girls. Come this way. Best place in town.''

Winding his way through the adolescent drunks, DC kept his face in the shadows and his eyes averted. The underage drinkers screamed and laughed with drunken excitement, thankful to have a border to slip over when their parents weren't looking.

DC spotted the flashing sign to Bambi's Club and headed for it. Inside the dark bar young, copper-skinned women danced in G-strings and veils, shimmying down poles and doing the bump-and-grind to the fixed stares of the slack-faced sailors and civilians inside. Two teenage boys watched with saucer eyes as one of the dancers gave them a special show of her tricks.

Neither one of them would ever see a beer bottle again without thinking of her, DC thought with a black grin. He spotted Greg sitting in the very back. Slapping money on the bar, DC got a beer and joined him at the table.

"Buy you a beer?" he asked.

Greg looked up and frowned. "Get lost, man. I'm waiting for someone." With a wave of his hand, Greg dismissed DC and returned his attention to the dancers.

DC felt a dose of pleasure as pure as any drug he'd ever taken sing through his veins. He stood there, looking down on Greg. Waiting for recognition.

At last, Greg looked up again. "Did you hear me?" he demanded. "I said get—" He paused, his eyes widening as he stared into DC's face. "Holy shit," he exclaimed.

DC laughed and took a drink of his beer.

"What the hell'd you do to your face, man?"

"Beautiful, ain't it?" DC said.

"Beautiful, shit. It's a fucking miracle."

Greg took a swig of his beer, swallowing with an expression that looked close to pain. He couldn't seem to stop staring at DC's face. In shock, he lapsed into a silence that made DC impatient. He hadn't agreed to come to discuss his new face.

"So what's up?" DC asked at last.

Greg shifted in his seat, bouncing his gaze around the bar. "I've been thinking. . . ." he began slowly. "About what we talked about."

"Yeah?"

"I think it will work."

DC pinned him with a sharp look. "I told you that."

"I know, man. I had to make some calls first, though. Tie up the ends."

"And?"

Greg shrugged. "All the players are ready."

"You got a doctor?"

"Yeah. Took a little digging, but the world's full of desperate people. You know? Shake some coin in front of them and they start begging."

Greg grabbed a black duffel bag off the seat next to him and passed it across the table. DC unzipped it and looked at the jumble of manila folders inside. Each had a color-coded tab with a typed name on it.

DC gave a low whistle. "How'd you get these?"

"A little nurse who likes 'em big and black," Greg said with a nervous laugh. "They're old. You may have to hunt down some new addresses, but that shouldn't be too hard. Not for a smart man like you."

DC nodded. Keeping the bag concealed beside him, he flipped through the manila folders. "These are local," he said suddenly, looking up with narrowed eyes.

"Don't worry, man. If anyone can pull it off, it's you."

"It'll cost you more."

"Don't worry," he repeated. He began working the label off his beer bottle, peeling the damp edges back as he watched DC go through the files. "We want Jordan first. Call me when you've got her. I'll take care of the rest."

DC zipped the bag and looked up. "When do I get paid?"

"You worried I'll burn you?" Greg asked.

"Nah. You ain't that stupid. I'm just a little short on cash now."

"Keep digging in that bag. There's an advance. This time it's not much. As soon as we deliver, you'll get your cut. Don't worry, man. This is going to make us rich."

DC nodded, draining his beer. Greg scribbled a number on a napkin. "Call me here when you're ready, but watch what you say."

"I know that."

"Good. I'll talk to you then."

With that Greg stood, gave DC's face one last, in- credulous stare, then left without a backward glance. Smiling, DC leaned against the split vinyl booth, fingering the duffel bag. He felt like celebrating, but not here. Not now.

He glanced at his watch. He'd cross back over the border, and later he'd celebrate in style.

DC woke with a start, covered in sweat and the stink of his own fear. He'd dreamed about the dogs again. Always the same damn thing. Grandpa's dogs. Ripping him apart.

His legs were pushed up under his chin, pinned by the steering wheel, his swollen knee aching to the bone. Carefully, he eased both feet to the floor, wincing, as the blood raced to his toes. Needles of pain shot through every nerve. He endured it, as he always did after The Dream. The Dream turned him into a pretzel no matter where he was when he fell asleep.

Finally, he wiggled his toes without pain and stepped out of the seventy-six Ford Granada. He closed the door carefully behind him. The fresh air felt good. It chased away the residue of The Dream, if not the memories that had inspired it.

Under the cover of darkness, he relieved himself of some of the Mexican beer he'd drunk earlier, then pulled a rubber band from his pocket and looped it around three fingers. Stretching it, knotting it, loosening it, as he watched the back of her house from the street directly behind.

He shouldn't be here. He knew it was stupid. But he couldn't stay away, not when he knew she was there. Alone.

Not when he knew that she hadn't recognized him. The thought filled him with power as it consumed him with rage.

He swallowed around his anger. It didn't matter that he looked different. She should have *known* him. The fact that she didn't meant that she'd managed to forget him since he'd been gone.

Forget him.

That really pissed him off.

He stared at her darkened windows, simmering with anger. He figured he'd been asleep about an hour. That made it somewhere close to midnight. Now was as good a time as any for the little get-reacquainted party he planned. Favoring his sore leg, he cut through the neighbor's yard to hers.

A sliver of a silver moon gilded the dark night. Fog, white and transparent, hovered over the mats of grass that shivered against the elegant white porches. Silent and invisible, DC climbed up and over the top of her fence and made a soft, quiet landing in her backyard.

Shadowing the shadows to the back door of the garage, he tested the lock and found it secure. Bolted against the boogie man. DC dropped to his haunches. Back against the rough and cool bricks of the garage, he squatted next to the door.

Innocent in itself, the small flap of the doggie door still struck him hot with fear. Hands cold and clammy, DC tapped the rubber flap. It *swish-swished* softly against the metal rim. He knew the sound well.

He listened to the night. Listened to the crickets and wind talking in the dark. Listened for a signal that he'd been heard. No signal came.

Gently, he touched the flap again.

Swish-swish.

The sound amplified in his mind, and with it, the fragrance of terror. The perfume of his childhood.

Swish-swish.

But this door was plastic, not aged and dirty leather, and DC wasn't caged anymore. Still, three dogs waited for him on the other side.

A cold sweat dotted his upper lip as he reached out, lifting the door as carefully as a tourist's wallet. Looking into the dark cavern of the garage, DC could hear the echo of his own breathing and smell the damp concrete and oil mixture that permeated it.

Across the way he could see the twin to the door he

peeked through. Closing his eyes, he forced the rancid residue of The Dream from his mind, and, just as he'd done a hundred times before, to a thousand different doors, DC poked his head through the opening. He shimmied right and left, easing his shoulders through. Hips, legs, and feet. He was in the garage.

He moved to the second door, stooping to peer through into the kitchen. Like a snake in grass, he wiggled soundlessly into the house.

Inside the house.

Christie awoke to the hot-cold uncertainty that *he* was inside the house.

Hearing her wake, Barney's watchful gaze met hers from his spot on the floor. For a fraction of a second they stared at one another in the thick dark of midnight before some slight shift of sound sent Barney bounding to his feet. Teeth bared, fur standing fierce and on end, he charged the doorway and stairs like an enemy. His furious barks bounced from the high-ceilinged landing to the bare tiled floor.

Yanked from sleep by his barks, Snort and Bear jumped from the end of Christie's bed, slipping through her reaching fingers in their race to join Barney.

With the force and speed of a zooming bullet through a sawed-off rifle, fear shot Christie from the warm comfort of bed into the cold reality of her situation.

Why hadn't she listened to Sam? Because she hadn't wanted to believe what she knew was true, she answered herself. She'd hidden under the security of denial and now she'd pay for it.

In seconds she dressed, cramming her feet into her shoes as she yelled for the dogs to come back. Their answering snarls told her they were prepared to fight to the death.

She faltered only a second, knowing hesitation could cost her her life. The baseball bat propped in the corner mocked her. Had she really felt protected by its presence?

Quickly, she punched 911 and left the phone dangling on the cord, knowing they would come. She grabbed the bat and moved to the window that the police had so recently brought to her attention. She threw the lock and opened the window, glancing fearfully over her shoulder, feeling like a mother abandoning her children. She climbed out and stepped onto the ledge. Vertigo toyed with her as she balanced above the closest branch. She would have to step off and free-fall a few feet to catch it.

The fog twisted and played with the dark, rustling branches below, adding terrifying unseen monsters outside to the known monstrosity within. She tossed the bat to the ground and immediately wished it back, but she'd never make it down if she tried to hold on to it.

From the house, the war of dog and man escalated. With a fevered prayer, Christie stepped off the ledge.

The bark scratched and peeled the tender skin on the underside of her arm before she could halt the momentum of her fall. With a jerk the limb stopped her plunge, groaning under her weight. For a second she froze, suspended above the ground, below her window. She felt trapped, a bug in a web with a spider soon to be home.

She twisted, looking for the next foothold. A small twig jutted from the trunk offering her only hope. She tested it with her foot. It snapped.

Frustrated tears blurred her vision. She eased herself closer to the trunk, hand over hand. Rough bark lacerated her palms. Biting down on her pain and terror, she made it to the solid trunk of the tree and wrapped her arms and legs around it.

Carefully, slowly, she eased herself down. Six feet from the ground, she jumped.

She hit the ground with a thud that knocked her off-balance and sent her rolling to the street. Quickly she got to her feet and, for the second time in as many days, Christie ran screaming for help.

DC hit the floor at the first roaring bark and darted back to the doggie door. He was halfway through when the yellow dog rounded the corner, his paws skidding across the tile. Scrambling for footing, the dog sank its teeth into DC's calf. DC fought. Kicking the dog, he cursed himself for the instinctual lunge to the floor. Why hadn't he gone for a window? With incredible strength and determination, the dog pulled DC away from his small chance of escape and dragged him back onto the cold, hard tile.

Two smaller, but no less terrifying mutts appeared from nowhere and snapped at his face and fingers. DC struggled to his feet, feeling their teeth, their hot breath and spit, as they snarled and nipped at his legs and ankles.

The big dog got a hunk of DC's thigh and began chomping and gnawing, working his way up.

DC came unglued. Felt himself regress and revert as the dogs evolved into great gnashing beasts. His control tipped, came unhinged and ready to hurl away, when a lucky shot sent one of the little beasts winging across the floor. Its tiny skull whacked the wall and the dog lay stunned and still.

One down.

DC forced himself to breathe, expelling his breath like a lifeline in a storm. He caught the ugly, flat-faced one by the neck and hurled him across the room. The dog twisted and squirmed as it flew. Hitting the ground, it turned and charged again.

They were winning.

"No," he whimpered.

DC kicked at the yellow dog that continued to tear at him with fierce, strong teeth and steely resolve. The flat-faced dog closed in on the right. Snapping, growling, snarling. DC's frantic gaze cut from wall to window, where he could see his own reflection. Panic sizzled from his toes to his eyes.

He crouched, facing the biggest dog defensively. The yellow dog lunged, sailing through the air, all teeth and fur and fury. DC collided with it, bouncing the dog off his chest and following through with a chop to the throat.

Back on its feet, the dog charged again while the ugly one drew blood from DC's ankle.

They were winning.

"No!" DC hollered, throwing the full force of his weight at the yellow dog. He caught the dog from behind, gripping its throat with all his strength and jerking hard enough to snap its neck. The dog screamed, a chilling tortured wail, and then stilled. DC dropped it to the floor.

The tables turned. The ugly one backed off and cowered behind the island bar, suddenly not so fierce. From the distance, DC heard the rage of sirens.

He scrambled to open the sliding door but fumbled over the lock. Too frantic to leave the way he'd come, he grabbed a barstool and hammered the glass door until it shattered. Wicked shards tore at his clothes as he raced outside.

He paused as the protective cloak of night concealed him and looked back at the house. *His house. His woman.*

"You're mine, little Christie," he whispered. "There's no place I won't find you."

He smiled to himself.

DC Porter was back in town.

4

"**C**hristie?"

Sitting on the front porch, Christie hadn't realized how numb she felt until Sam's deep voice penetrated the haze and caressed her. She turned toward him, wanting to throw herself in his arms and cry away the fear and grief. The police lights spinning in the dark cast an eerie glow on his features as he studied her.

A light stubble shadowed his cheeks. Concern darkened his eyes. His shirt, buttoned wrong, hung loose and cockeyed over his worn blue jeans.

He knelt next to her, placing a warm hand on her knee.

"Christie, are you all right?"

"Barney's dead," she said, choking back a sob. Tears made a painless trail down her cheeks. Pain made a gaping wound in her heart.

"Aw, honey, I'm sorry."

He pulled her close, his fingers hard and callused against the softness of her nape. She felt stiff and awkward in his arms, but she needed his comfort more than she needed air. She willed herself to relax as tears trembled over her lashes.

He absorbed her. Arms holding tight, hands rubbing the sore spots in her shoulders, he shifted his weight and tucked her close to his side. Murmuring, he rocked her.

Inhaling Sam's fragrance, hot and salty, with a trace of yesterday's cologne, she shut out the stench of Barney's death that seeped through the very walls inside. She closed her mind to all the reasons why Sam's arms were the last place she should find comfort. She slammed the door on the attack. On the attacker.

At her feet, Bear and Snort lay in exhausted heaps. Whimpers and starts sent shivers through their bodies as they dozed. Swaying in the questionable security of Sam's embrace, she gave in to the sickening storm of fear and pain. Her face pressed to the arm hollow of his shoulder, she wept.

When her tears diminished to quiet sniffles, Sam touched her face, tilting her chin up. "Chris, what happened?"

"He came back," she whispered in a voice clogged by terror.

She looked into his eyes, seeing twin reflections of her own confused self. Nervously, she lowered her gaze, concentrating on his mismatched button job. She sensed his withdrawal a second before he pulled away. A wintry chill took the place of his warm solace.

"Will you be okay for a minute?" he asked softly.

Okay? Would she ever be okay again? Had she ever been okay before?

She nodded.

He hesitated before going inside, but finally he turned, leaving Christie on the porch in the darkest hours of the morning. Without his heat to hold it at bay, the night's cold invaded her bones, making her tremble and shiver. But still she stayed outside, on the step, alone with her dogs. She couldn't face the motionless form on the kitchen floor that had once been Barney.

A few seconds later, the policeman who'd arrived first on the scene stepped outside. "We'll be patrolling the area, ma'am, but that's about all we can do now."

He hitched a thumb at the house. "Your husband says he'll see you're safe for the night."

But what about tomorrow?

The question dangled between them. Unasked. Unanswered.

Watching the reflected police lights in the shine of his shoes, she returned his good-bye. He told her to contact them if she needed anything. He sounded like a clerk at a store promising prompt service. Satisfaction guaranteed. Thank you much, come again. His brake lights flashed once as he drove away.

"Chris?"

Sam's voice brushed against her nerves like the softest of suede. She looked over her shoulder to where he stood framed by the doorway, and fought the desire to throw herself into his strong arms and let them shelter her from her misery.

"Honey, do you have a box?"

"A box?" she repeated in a soft voice, knowing, but not wanting to know, why he wanted it.

He nodded grimly. "And a shovel. I'm going to bury Barney."

"No."

"Honey, the longer you wait, the harder it will be."

She felt as if she were swallowing sand, sun-baked hot and incredibly dry, as she forced the next word through her lips. "Where?"

"In the backyard?"

"No," she whispered, looking around her. "Not here. Not anywhere near this house."

"Where then?"

"The beach. Barney loved the beach."

She started to cry again when he brought Barney's box from the house and set it in the back of the Jeep. He rolled down all the windows before turning to her.

"Go get your things, Christie. You're going to stay with me for a while."

She sniffed back her tears and gave him a sad shake

of her head. "I don't think that's such a good idea, Sam. But thank you."

"I'm not asking. I'm telling," he said in a tight voice. "I shouldn't have left you here alone today. I'll be damned if I'll leave you alone tonight."

She could tell he expected an argument, and really, she should give one.

"Chris, for once, just listen to me," he continued, without giving her the chance to answer. "Go get your stuff. You can remind me how much you hate me tomorrow. Tonight, you need me, whether you want to admit it or not."

Too exhausted to do anything else, she nodded and went inside. The overpowering smell of the bleach he'd used on the kitchen didn't hide the darker, heavier scent of fear and death. She hurried upstairs and jerked a bag from her closet. In less than ten minutes, she was back on the porch.

Silently he held out a hand for her house keys and locked the front door. As the click of the bolt sliding home echoed against the black of night, their eyes met. They both knew that a locked door had no meaning anymore.

In one fluid movement, Sam scooped up Bear and flung the strap of Christie's bag over his shoulder. Silently, Christie and Snort followed him to the Jeep.

Christie sank back against the soft interior, remembering other trips she'd taken with Sam at the wheel. The Jeep rumbled through the night, lulling her into a painless trance of asphalt and moonlight.

"Tell me what happened, Christie," he asked once they'd reached the freeway.

She related the events of the night in a cool, emotionless voice.

"So are you going to tell me who this guy is?" Sam asked when she'd finished.

"What makes you think I know?"

"Do you?"

Christie stared, unseeing, out the window. "No."

"Why do you do that?" he demanded. "Why do you lie to me?"

"I'm not lying," she snapped back, still avoiding his searching gaze. "And why should I trust you, anyway? I mean, thank you for being here tonight, Sam. I needed you." She paused, collecting her thoughts and tamping down the feelings that cracked her voice and left a lump in her throat. "But don't expect me to suddenly forget all the other times that I needed you and you weren't around."

"Why not? I can't count all the things I've forced myself to forget. If I tried, I might be tempted just to say the hell with it."

"You did say to hell with it, Sam. Or don't you remember?"

He cursed softly under his breath.

"Could we drop this conversation?" she asked. "I'd rather not talk about it now."

"When then? When can we talk? I've been trying to talk to you since . . . Christie, we haven't even spoken since . . ." he paused, rubbing the point between his eyes wearily. "I feel like all I do is bang my head against that wall you've erected around yourself and you just keep fixing the cracks."

Christie refused to be swayed by the emotion in his voice. "*I* wasn't the one sleeping with my clients, Sam."

"*Client. One* client. *One* time."

"Is that supposed to make me feel better? Why should I believe you anyway?"

"You think I'm lying? Well back at you, babe. I'm not buying this little story you've concocted about your robber, either."

"Believe what you want, Sam."

"That's *your* specialty, isn't it?"

Her angry silence competed with the soft hum of the engine and the murmur of the road.

Sam made an exasperated sound. "Now you're going to clam up, is that it? Give me the silent treatment, like you usually do? Fine. But I tell you this, I was a fool to stand by and let you ruin our relationship, Christie. I'm not going to roll over and play dead again."

"Me? *I* ruined it?" she exclaimed. "That's a laugh."

"Is it? Strange, I can't find a damned thing funny about it. I'll drop it for now, but not forever. Things aren't over between us."

Palm trees stood dark and attentive on the sides of the freeway, their fronds brushing the stars and black velvet tapestry of night. Streetlights, softened by the fog, glowed like tapered candles along the side of the road, illuminating the cab of the Jeep.

Christie blinked back tears that his bitter words had summoned. She shouldn't have shown him any weakness. She should have known he'd pounce on it.

She armed herself with stony silence, her stare drifting in and out of focus as the shadowed landscape zipped by. She hadn't realized just how angry she still was until that moment. Her fingernails dug half-moons into her palms.

Sam's sigh managed to sound both hostile and sympathetic at once. "Why didn't you call me when your mom died, Chris?" he asked softly.

"What do you mean?"

"I mean, why didn't you call? I'm the only family you have left."

"I don't think of you as family, Sam."

He winced in the concealing shadows. "How do you think of me?"

"As little as possible, starting the day I interrupted your party with—"

"Jesus, back to that again."

She turned in her seat and gave him an incredulous look. "You say that like it's some trivial issue I've dredged up from nowhere."

"I say it like it's an issue that's best forgotten. Can't we just keep the past where it belongs for a while?"

"I'm sure *you* think it's best that way, but what about the next time it happens?"

"How many times do I have to tell you? It's not going to happen again." He took a deep breath. "Christie, I want to help you—"

"You want," she snapped. "It's always what you want. What *I* want, Sam, is for you to leave me alone. I don't need your help."

"Why? What makes you think that you don't need some help? I think you'd better wake up and look around, honey, because to my eyes, you need some serious help. And the news is, I'm the only guy in town."

He turned the Jeep and hit the brakes. Bright lights gleamed from tall posts, illuminating the swirling fog with a reflecting glow. Ahead she could see the ocean rolling toward them like a great black abyss. Whitecaps broke on the beach, their spray dancing high in the thick, misty air.

Christie jumped from the car. "If you're my only hope, Sam, I'd rather take my chances alone." She slammed the door.

Sam banged his fist against the steering wheel, staring at her retreating back as she walked away from him. Damn! Why did every conversation with her have to go this way? Snort and Bear sat shivering on her vacant seat, looking at him with big, wide eyes.

"What's she hiding?" he asked them.

The Pekingese made a disgusted sound and put his paws on the door to look at Christie. The reflection of the moon on the dark moving waters silhouetted her.

Holding the door for the dogs, Sam got out, then reached back for the box and shovel. He followed her, stepping over clumps of seaweed that lay scattered like corpses on the cold, damp sand.

"It's not the prettiest beach," he said softly as he

caught up with her, "but I'd get arrested if I started digging up La Jolla Shores. This is illegal as hell, you know."

She held herself stiffly, but gave him a small smile. "Thank you, Sam."

They walked in silence to a secluded area far up from the water. Clumps of grass struggled to grow in the sandy dirt. Snort and Bear sniffed solemnly at Barney's box.

"Is this okay?" Sam asked. "I don't think we should get any closer to the water. The tide gets pretty high sometimes."

Christie looked around the shadowed area he'd chosen, hidden from sight to anyone on the street. Only the ebony waters of the Pacific would witness the burial.

"It's fine," she said, her anger vanishing as overwhelming sorrow hunched her shoulders.

The earth made a soft, shifting noise as it sifted across the steel blade of Sam's shovel. When the hole was deep enough, Sam carefully lifted Barney's cardboard coffin and set it in.

Her eyes remained dry, but her heart cried tears of anguish and confusion. Tears for Barney. Tears for Christie.

Gently, Sam touched the back of her neck, pulling her closer. The ocean roared in her ears as it tossed the wind on shore to tease and tear at her clothes and hair. She turned into Sam's warmth.

Blocking their argument from her mind, she concentrated on his scent, taking comfort from its familiarity. His shoulder and chest muscles flexed as he pulled her closer to him. His hands rubbed her back, his fingers wearing down her tension. She felt herself melt and mold to his frame.

He stilled. And then his touch changed. Became searching. Questioning. Seeking answers to questions she hadn't even considered yet. His hands slid up her rib cage, possessively grazing the sides of her breasts on the way to the sensitive skin of her throat.

Her whispered "no" dissolved on her lips. She couldn't resist, not when his touch felt like a lifeline, securing her from the buffeting waves of reality.

As if he had every right, his fingers traced the line of her shoulder, her delicate collarbone. Cupping her chin in his hand, he tilted her face toward his.

She stared at him, at the intensity in his gaze. His eyes looked black in the night, his lashes thick and dark, framing the yearning that glittered in their depths. They demanded a response from her.

Unbelievably, her own hands crept from around his waist and burned a trail to his neck. Her fingers tangled in the silky brown hair at his nape and suddenly she was pulling him down as he lifted her up.

The stubble of his beard scratched her lips a second before his mouth, warm and firm, closed over hers. He tasted of toothpaste and salty night air and memories as seductive as the misted moon.

Rough and warm, his thumbs caressed the tender skin behind her ears. For Christie, breathing became an exercise of sheer will.

His legs pushed against hers as his tongue drew slow, soft circles on her lips. A parched flower in a sudden spring shower, she drank in his passion, blooming with color and perfume.

He dragged his mouth from hers, tasting the hollow under her brow, the smooth white skin of her throat. His face, silky sandpaper against her nerves.

She'd missed him so much.

He whispered to her, words she didn't understand, didn't want to understand, as he blazed back to her mouth. His hands roamed wildly over her body, stopping at the soft mounds of her breasts, moving on to the tantalizing valley of her stomach. Restlessly they traveled to her back, her shoulders, her face.

"I should've never let you go," he murmured. His breath plumed, mingling with the fog.

She clenched her eyes against his words, fighting the wave of memories that his kisses started and his words ended. The same touch that had felt safe only moments ago suddenly frayed, leaving her dangling over a precipice of confusion and fear.

What was she doing here in his arms? Anger and bitterness rushed at her with the roar of the tide.

Jerking away from him, she wiped his taste from her lips with an angry swipe. She shivered as the night air replaced the heat of his body.

"You didn't let me go, Sam," she said in a voice that cracked with pain. "I left you."

5

Sam closed the door behind them, dropped Christie's bag with a resounding thump, and banged his way to the kitchen. He returned a moment later with a bottle of Corona clenched in his hand. His suppressed anger hummed like an electrical current. It made her want to hover at the door, far away from its flow.

Squaring her shoulders, she stepped inside and eyed the living room, letting Sam stew in his own temperament. The place hadn't changed much since the first time she'd seen it. His furnishings were simple and comfortable. Earth tones. Plump cushions. Few knick-knacks to clutter the lines. Very Sam.

She stared at the healthy green plants hanging from hooks in the ceiling, their limbs swaying in the drafts. On the windowsill, cactus flowers dozed, semiclosed in the bright moonlight. A baby palm stood at attention against the wall between the dining and living rooms. Plants didn't like Christie much. In fact, the ones she'd attempted to grow had withered and died, just like her marriage.

Her gaze flitted to Sam, noting the brooding expression in his eyes. He'd always been this way. Sam was both the most gentle and the most ruthless man she'd ever met. He would never hurt her physically, but, when sparked, his temper ignited like a fire. Sometimes it flickered and died. Sometimes it roared, charring everything in its path to ashes.

Invariably, though, it sparked her own.

"Are you just going to stand there?" he demanded.

"No, Sam," she said, yanking her bag off the floor. "I'm not going to stand here. I'm getting out."

"The hell you are."

He slammed his beer bottle onto the table and crossed the room. She flinched back from the suddenness of his move. A frosty gleam entered his eyes.

"Don't start those mind games with me, Christie. I've never hurt you."

"Not physically anyway."

"You left your share of scars, too."

She shook her head, giving him a disgusted look. "Why is it you're mad, Sam? Because I didn't get swept away with the moment and the moonlight and forget everything else? Because I came to my senses?"

An angry flush darkened his cheeks and tightened his jaw. He stared at her without answering.

"It's going to take a lot more than a few kisses to change my mind about you, Sam McCoy. Let's get that straight right now."

He glared at her a moment longer, then turned his back and grabbed his beer, draining it in one long swallow. He got a fresh one and opened it.

"You fight mean," he said, offering a second bottle to Christie.

"I learned from the best."

Her fingers touched his as she reached for the beer. She jerked her hand away as if shocked by a spark. In a sudden silence that pressed against her eardrums, Christie looked everywhere but at Sam. Stiff-legged, she moved to the opposite side of the room.

"Don't worry," he snarled. "I won't touch you again. You can sit down."

She wasn't worried about that. What worried her was the knotted tension inside her that made her long to turn back the clock and do things over. She wished her temper would burn out the ashes of her dead feelings for Sam, but each time she looked into his dark eyes, the embers smoldered as if fanned by a hot breath.

"I'd rather stand," she mumbled.

A breeze clattered against the blinds and billowed them inward. Christie stood in its path, grateful for its cooling touch. She breathed deeply, hoping for a lungful of sanity with the fresh night air. She'd made a grave mistake in coming here. She should have listened to her instincts when they'd warned her not to.

"Look—" Sam began, interrupting her thoughts. "I'm sorry. You just make me so damned mad."

She spun to face him. "That's not so hard to do, Sam."

He smiled ruefully, the flame of anger flickering out as suddenly as it had kindled. He caught her off guard, his lopsided grin unraveling a few more seams in her threadbare coat of composure.

"You're right. I don't have any reason to be mad at you. It's just that seeing you again made me start missing you more than usual and—"

"Please don't talk like that, Sam. We're through. How much clearer do I have to make it?"

He gave a short, humorless laugh. "I don't know how you could make it any clearer."

"Then why won't you listen to me?"

"Because I know you still love me," he said, approaching her.

"Loved, Sam. As in past tense. As in not anymore."

"I don't buy it."

He stepped close to her and his clean, musky scent distracted her from what he said. She fought the urge to step back and forced herself to concentrate on his words instead of the way his full lips formed them.

"I know I still get to you," he said in a low, husky voice.

"Oh, you get to me all right, Sam," she answered with false bravado. "You make me sick."

He moved closer still, his body nearly touching hers.

One deep breath and her breasts would brush against the hard muscles of his chest.

"I make you sick? That's not how it feels to me."

The heat of his body burned through the ineffectual barrier of her clothes. She stared him down, refusing to remember how his hands had felt on her body. She concentrated on her anger. *Focused* on it.

"I can't believe how conceited you are. The only thing I feel for you is disgust."

He shook his head. "I don't think so."

"Who cares?"

Angrily she pushed away from him, not caring if he considered it a retreat. She needed space. She needed to think.

"Go ahead," she said. "Bully me because you didn't get your way. Because I didn't fall into your arms and beg you to stay with me. Grow up."

He watched her through narrowed eyes, the assured smirk vanishing from his lips. "Grow up? Coming from you, that's a good one."

"What do you mean by that?"

"I think I've finally figured you out, Chris. It's taken a damn long time, but I finally got your number. You pretend better than anyone I know. If you don't like the way something goes, no problem. You just sweep it under the rug. Pretend it doesn't exist."

"You're crazy."

"So you keep telling me. But if I'm so crazy, then maybe you could explain why your *burglar* would come back to a house he knew was empty?"

He caught her off guard again with this backward twist in conversation. She searched for a retort, then settled for evasion.

"How should I know? Besides, I don't owe you any explanations. I don't owe you a thing. In case I haven't made myself clear, I don't want you involved. No, let me rephrase. *I* don't want to be involved with *you*. I wouldn't have even called you tonight except the police insisted when I told them I'd go to a hotel—''

''*A hotel?* You weren't even going to call me?'' he exploded.

''It's not a federal offense,'' she said.

''Yes, it is. For *my* wife it is, dammit!''

''I'm not your wife anymore, Sam.''

''I don't remember signing any divorce papers.''

''Technicality.''

''Gotta snappy answer for everything, don't you?''

''No, Sam. Quick comebacks are your line. I'm just trying to keep up.''

Another weighted silence captured them, making them both realize they'd been shouting. Sam paced away from her, his aggravation reflected in his tense steps. He turned and they glared at each other from opposite sides of the room. Opposite sides of a chasm of hurt and lies.

''You hate me, don't you, Christie? Haven't you ever heard of forgive and goddamn forget?''

She could feel the blood rush to her face as her anger finally overcame her awareness of his lean body and rugged features. ''Did you expect me to forgive you, Sam?'' she demanded. ''Did you?''

Jabbing a finger in his direction, she insisted, ''Is that what you expected? Is it?''

His silence answered for him.

''It is,'' she mocked. ''Well, let me tell you a little story, Sam. Maybe you can figure out why I'm not interested in '*forgive and goddamn forget.*' Do you want to know why I didn't tell you when my mother died? Do you?''

''If that's where you want to start.''

''I think it's appropriate, since that's where it all ended.''

He frowned his confusion at her.

''She died four months ago, Sam. More specifically,

she died on the same day you chose to destroy our future together.''

She watched with satisfaction as he paled under his glowing tan.

"That's right," she said coldly. "I was at work when I got the call. At first, I couldn't figure out what they were talking about. She'd been in a car accident.''

Sam drained his beer and got another one.

"Trying to get drunk, Sam?"

He popped the cap and took a long drink. "Maybe."

"They wanted me to identify her," Christie said, keeping her voice low and controlled, so it wouldn't crack with the emotions tearing her apart inside. "I tried calling you first. At your office. When no one answered, I thought you must be giving a lesson. So I called the pro shop and asked them to check the range, but they couldn't find you."

Her voice sounded flat, unconnected to the pain her words caused both of them. "I wanted you to go with me. We'd just had that fight, but I still wanted you with me. Finally, I gave up and went alone."

Sam sank to the couch. His hands dangled between his knees, absently passing the Corona back and forth. She couldn't see his face anymore. Whether it was a blessing or a curse, she didn't know.

Taking a deep breath, she continued. "She'd been badly burned." Hot tears stung her eyes and she blinked them back. "They told me she'd driven into a telephone pole. Wrapped the car *around* it. The gas tank exploded on impact. When I got back home, I tried calling you again. This time the line was busy."

She stared at his bowed head. Slowly he shook it, as if denial could make the past disappear.

"I called the operator to break in. She told me your phone was off the hook. I wasn't surprised. After all, I'd seen your office. Half the time you're lucky to *find* your phone. It didn't seem strange to me that you'd knocked it off the hook and not known it—''

"Christie, don't."

"Don't what? I thought you wanted to hear this story."

"I figured out how it ends. You don't need to tell me."

"You know the ending? You know how it felt for me to walk in on you? To come looking for a shoulder to cry on? Strong arms to hold me? Only to find they were already taken?"

"Stop it, Christie. If I could do it over, believe me, I would. I'd be there for you. How many times do I have to tell you? I'm sorry. I screwed up and I paid for it. I'm sorry."

The agony of telling her story doused the vengeance that had sparked the flame. Now she felt empty and very alone.

"No, Sam. I'm the one who's sorry. Sorry that your apology means nothing to me."

She looked away, setting down her untouched beer.

"I didn't tell you to make you feel like scum, Sam. You wanted to know, there it is. I've dealt with it. But if you think I can forgive it, think again. As for forgetting—believe me I've tried."

"Have you, Christie?" he asked, looking up with a twisted smile and cynical gleam in his eyes. "I think you're fooling yourself. I don't think you ever even considered trying to forget. I think a part of you was glad I fucked up."

"You're crazy."

"I don't think so. Marriage scared you shitless. Having to share with someone else was something you couldn't deal with."

"You think I should have been willing to share my husband?"

"You're hell with the one-liners, babe. But it's the one-on-one you've got problems with."

Her lips moved silently over her retort, but her voice abandoned her. Confusion kept her rooted to the floor when she wanted to leave. To run away from him and his accusations.

"You know I'm right," he said softly. "I never meant to hurt you, Christie. I only wanted to love you. But you wouldn't let me."

He drained his beer and set the empty bottle on the coffee table with concentrated care. When he looked up, his eyes gleamed with darkness and his smile held no humor.

"Who knows? Maybe you couldn't love me back. Maybe it's not in you."

"I don't know what you're talking about."

She'd meant to sound cold and flippant, but her voice quivered across the room, full of ache and bewilderment.

"I know you don't, Christie. You've never understood me any more than I have you. I'm tired. I think I'll go to bed."

With that, he began unfolding the couch and making the sleeper into a bed. Suddenly, she found herself on the other side of a table she hadn't even realized he'd turned. She stared at him, trying to put a conclusion to this ending.

"Go upstairs and go to sleep, Christie. You'll think of something to say in the morning."

More uncertain than ever, Christie followed his orders.

6

Melanie Blackwell had been standing at the front counter when DC Porter first walked through the door of the Palm Valley Christian Preschool. He was of average height, lean and hard, with blond hair brushing his brow in a windblown fashion. He flashed a smile that nearly stopped her heart.

He had a way about him. A way of making a moment stand still. Making a space of time so vivid that it could be recalled in an instant, complete with scent and sound.

At least that's how it had been for her. The rest of that day Melanie replayed in her mind that first sight of him. She remembered how his cologne had drifted across the counter with the hot breeze and tantalized her with thoughts of warm skin, seasoned with a peculiar musk. She remembered how the sunshine had dappled his hair with glowing golden tints and how he moved with an animal grace even his slight limp couldn't disguise. He'd seemed both lovely and terrifying as he approached her while the sweet sounds of children's voices raised in song drifted down the hushed hallway.

She'd remember it all, just like it was happening again. It was the most distinct memory she'd ever have.

Later that night, it would also become the last memory she'd ever have.

As the front door closed behind DC Porter on the final morning of Melanie Blackwell's short life, she'd seen his sparkling gaze dance to the multicolored, finger-painted blobs that decorated every inch of the lobby. He'd looked both paternal and sexy at the same time and Melanie felt quivery and sick, like a bowl of hot jelly, as she watched him. She had to remind herself that he was probably married.

DC had tilted his head, giving Melanie that riveting smile again. He put his elbows on the counter and looked right into her eyes.

It took every ounce of control that she possessed to ask, "May I help you?" without stuttering, gasping, or drooling.

"Why, yes, ma'am."

His hand reached across the counter to shake. Placing her palm against his, chills shot down her spine. His grin seemed knowing.

"My name is DC Johnson and I would like to inquire about enrolling my son Tommy in your school," he said.

Married. Just as she'd thought.

"I'd be happy to help you with that, Mr. Johnson. How old is Tommy?"

"He's three, ma'am."

"That's just fine." Glad to have something to do with her hands, she jotted Tommy's name and age down on a notepad. "Please, come into my office."

She walked around the counter and led him through a door that opened off the reception area. She paused just inside, allowing him to go first. He seemed to study the room with intent interest as he entered.

Large white cinder blocks showcased a vast assortment of crayon drawings, cutout pumpkins, crooked Santas, and unidentifiable splotches of color. Melanie called it her wall of fame and she took great pride in her display. Each year she cleared the wall for fresh works, but at home, in a scrapbook, she kept her dearest prints pressed between the pages.

On one side of the room, plastic shelves held neatly stacked toys. Tot-sized chairs huddled around a bookshelf crammed full of giant picture and coloring books, fairy tales, and nursery rhymes. Windows on two walls caught the scarce afternoon breeze and chased it across the green indoor-outdoor carpet to the far corner, where her "office" squatted as if in apology. A relic of a desk, cleared of all but a black lamp and beige telephone with a rotary dial, faced off two green vinyl straight-backed chairs. Giant decal flowers sprouted from the front and sides of both the desk and an ancient metal filing cabinet that stood guard nearby.

The relic between them, they both sat.

Suddenly nervous to be alone with him, Melanie started talking right away. "I assume Tommy is potty trained?"

DC gave her a broad smile and wink. "Trained him myself."

"Yourself?"

"My wife passed when he was born. I've raised the little guy as best I could."

A widower.

"That's quite an accomplishment," she said, trying not to smile.

"You aren't a-kidding."

His chuckle gave way to an awkward silence that held a few moments hostage. Wishing for something witty to say, she stared at her hands clasped on the desk. She felt his gaze touch her face like the softest of feathers. How did he do that?

Flushing, she cleared her throat and launched into her standard monologue.

"What can I tell you about Palm Valley? It's a loving and safe environment for your son. Our classes have a maximum of eight children, which is below the twelve allowed by the State of California. All of our employees are licensed, except the kitchen staff, of course. We provide a hot lunch after prayer and two healthy snacks a day. The children are offered a variety of stimulating activities including music time, game time, and, of course, story time. Where is your son now, Mr. Johnson?''

He leaned forward, resting his wrists on his knees. His tanned hands dangled between, fingertips lightly touching. She found herself staring at them, as if mesmerized by their rhythmic action.

"Tommy's with his grandma in South Carolina. I'll be moving him out West next month. I wish it were sooner, though. I miss him a fair bit.''

"It's hard to be away from them.''

"You got kids?''

"I have lots of kids,'' she said.

"I mean, of your own.''

She shook her head. "Not yet.''

"How come?''

She shifted in her seat. "Well, for starters, I'm not married.''

"*You aren't married?* Why, ma'am, are the boys blind out here or are you just picky?''

It was blatant flattery, but looking into those crystal clear eyes, she felt a pleased smile spread across her face. He hadn't even seemed to notice her flat chest. She took another deep breath and another shot at composure.

"Would you like a tour before we get to the paperwork?''

He gave her an unexpectedly excited smile.

"Why, yes ma'am, I would.''

She held the door for him and beamed back his infectious grin. Guiding him down the hallway, she showed him the classrooms, the lunchroom, the fire escapes. Leaning over her shoulder, he peered intently through the square windows centered in each door. His heat burned through her clothes and touched her skin. He had a strange odor under the mask of his cologne. Different, but not offensive.

By the time he followed her back to her office, all of her senses were tuned just to him.

Taking her seat again, she asked, "So, Mr. Johnson, what do you think?"

"I think you've got a fine little establishment, ma'am."

"Good. I'm sure Tommy will be very happy here. Let's get to that paperwork so we can get him enrolled. It just so happens we'll have an opening next month," she said. "But it won't last long. We stay full here."

When he didn't answer right away she looked up from her search for a pen to catch his gaze traveling slowly over the gunmetal gray cabinet on her right. A questioning frown wrinkled his forehead.

Pausing, she followed his fixed look over her shoulder and back again. As if caught in an embarrassing blunder, his gaze snapped to her face and the frown vanished like a fleeting wisp of smoke. He coughed softly into his palm.

"Is something wrong, Mr. Johnson?"

"No, ma'am. Quite the contrary. I was just admiring the way you cheered up your cabinet with them flowers. What were you saying?"

"I was just explaining that I'll need emergency information and a deposit to hold Tommy's place for next month."

"Well, to tell the truth, Melanie—may I call you Melanie? I'm not anywhere near settled yet. Fact is, I'm still living in a hotel, eating food I have to unwrap first." His hand muffled another cough. "I'd be happy to put down a deposit, though, if cash's all right. I haven't got my bank picked out yet. I'll fill out your papers when I bring Tommy in."

"Of course. That'll be just fine, Mr. John—"

"Please, call me DC."

He grinned another blush out of her. Breaking free of his mesmerizing gaze, she bent to her bottom desk drawer and removed a small receipt book. "I'll need fifty dollars and cash is fine. I'll give you a receipt. Should I make this to DC Johnson or is DC a nickname?''

''No ma'am. That's my name,'' he answered, passing his money across the desk to her.

''Really? But what does DC stand for?''

''Why, for Devoted Christian. 'Course there's some that say the Devil's Choirboy is closer to the truth.'' He winked. ''But I don't pay them any attention.''

''That's quite a range of opinion,'' she said, casting a flirtatious look his way and intercepting another stare at the cabinet. Piqued, she tried harder. ''Which description best suits you, I wonder?''

''I imagine you'll have to make up your own mind about that, ma'am.''

A slow heat rose from the tips of her toes, traveling with dizzying speed to her face. On sensory overload, she tried to keep focused on the conversation at hand.

''Do you have any questions about the school, DC?''

Casually, he crossed his legs. ''I assume the children are never left alone?''

''That's right. Never. You won't have to worry about Tommy's safety here, DC. Safety is our number one rule.''

Cough. ''How about when they're napping?''

''The children are monitored at all times.''

''That's good. Can't be too safe these days.'' *Cough.*

''Were you transferred to San Diego, DC?''

''That's right. My company transfer—'' *Cough, cough.* ''Do you think I could have a glass of water, ma'am?''

''Of course,'' she said, jumping to her feet. ''I'll be right back.''

DC stayed where he was until the door clicked shut behind her. As her heels tapped the hallway floor, DC bounded out of his chair and raced to the filing cabinet. His heart banging against his ribs, he grabbed the handle of the top drawer and pulled it open. The metal

squealed in protest, freezing him to the floor. He shot
a look over his shoulder, half expecting her to crash
through the door and demand to know what he was
doing, but she didn't.

Adrenaline pulsing through his system, he went back
to work.

The filing system was as simplistic as Melanie Blackwell. In seconds his fingers flipped to JORDAN, JES-
SICA. He yanked out the file and flipped to the
emergency information sheet. An old address was
marked through and a new one inked in. Bingo.

Jerking his shirttail out of his pants, he shoved the
file into his waistband, flush with his back. Turning, he
snatched her receipt tablet off her desk, ripped out the
carbon and the next few pages and closed the booklet.

Just as her shadow hovered outside the door he skidded to his chair. The papers crinkled against his back
when he sat.

"Here you go, DC," she said, handing him a Dixie
cup with Big Bird on the side.

He took the water and drank. "Thank you, ma'am."

A film of sweat covered his upper lip and he looked
pale under his tan. He wiped his face, avoiding her
gaze.

"Are you feeling all right, DC?" she asked, concerned.

He waved her off with his hand. "Fine, fine.
Allergies."

She nodded sympathetically and gave him a moment
to recover. Moving back behind her desk, she bumped
a partially opened file drawer closed with her hip. When
she looked up again, the sexy southern gentleman
charm had returned.

"Melanie, pardon me if I sound forward, but you
mentioned that you weren't married. I wonder if that
might mean you are unattached?"

Could he see her heart leap in her chest? "That's
right."

"Is that right? Well these California boys must be

crazy to let you run around free. Must be the sun. They raise us smarter in the South. Melanie, I'd like to buy you dinner if I may?''

She hesitated, not wanting to seem too anxious. DC leaned forward.

"Come on, have some pity on a new guy in town. Say yes.''

She had no intention of saying anything else.

"Come on. Say yes. I'm tired of eating alone.''

"Okay, DC. Yes.''

"All right, then. What time is good for you?''

"Most of the time I'm closed up by six-thirty.''

"Six-thirty? I'll be a bit tied up then. What do you say to a late dinner?'' He waited for her nod before continuing. "Eight o'clock okay with you?''

"That sounds fine.''

"Good. Should I pick you up?''

Melanie chewed the corner of her lip, hesitating for one quick second. "That would all right,'' she said and scribbled her address on a piece of paper. "I'm just a couple of blocks from here. Do you want directions?''

"Naw,'' he said, taking her address with a grin and a wink. "I'm getting to where I can find my way around just fine. I'll see you later tonight, then.''

"That sounds great, DC.''

She stood and walked him to the door. "Oh, DC?''

"Yes, ma'am?''

"What *does* DC stand for?''

He leaned so close that she could see the large pores in his skin and feel his breath fan her face. He danced his eyebrows up and down and leered.

"Why it stands for Dangerous Criminal, ma'am. What else?''

Melanie giggled. "You're not going to tell me, are you?''

He smiled. "Maybe I will tonight.''

7

Christie woke exhausted. She stretched, alone in a bed she had once shared with Sam. During their brief, turbulent marriage, they had slept, loved, and fought in this very room. Yet this was the first time she'd ever slept here alone. She turned her head and stared at the empty pillow beside her.

The sun, glaring through the heavy drapes, toasted the room uncomfortably. Was it late? She hoped so. It would be easier to face the day if it were already over. She lifted her groggy head and looked at the face of Sam's ancient alarm.

Noon. Sighing, she dragged herself from bed. As she stumbled to the bathroom, where the faint scent of his soap and cologne lingered, she wondered if Sam was even home. The house seemed too quiet. She'd lived by herself for a while now. She knew what it sounded like.

The steam from her shower wrapped his scent around her. She made the spray cool and the shower brief. Feeling as pale and drawn as she looked, she dressed in shorts and a blouse and went downstairs for a cup of coffee. The day stretched endlessly before her.

A scrawled note, stuck to the refrigerator with a golf ball–shaped magnet, read, *Christie, I have a couple of lessons this morning. Don't leave. Sam.*

She stared at it, sipping her coffee, listening to the clock tick. Outside, the dogs reexplored Sam's backyard with wagging tails. Looking around her, she felt depression creep from the shadowed corners. Too much Sam in every room. She'd go crazy waiting here with only remembrance for company.

Making a snap decision, she pushed away from the counter and grabbed the phone. Whether Sam liked it or not, she needed to take care of things. She couldn't stay here forever and she certainly couldn't continue living at her house. She needed to move the rest of her things out and find a new place to live.

First, she called a taxi and then the police to find out if, by chance, they'd learned anything since last night. She knew it was probably a waste of time, but she had plenty of it to waste.

The phone at the police station rang twenty-six times before a gruff voice barked, "What?"

Christie explained who she was and why she was calling. Twice while she talked, she heard his hand muffle the mouthpiece and his voice bellow into the background din.

"Is there a point to this, ma'am?" he demanded, cutting her off in mid-sentence.

"Yes. I'm calling to find out if anyone's been arrested, so I know whether or not it's safe to go home."

Without a word he put her on hold and let her simmer in the juices of bureaucracy for interminable minutes. Finally, he returned.

"No one's been booked on that case."

"Will I be contacted if someone is?"

"Listen, Mrs—"

"McCoy. Christie McCoy."

"Mrs. McCoy, I'll level with you. Another kid's been kidnapped. We're busting our asses trying to find the guy who took her. We'll do our best to get someone working on your case, but the kidnappings have priority. Why don't you hire someone to keep this guy away from you? Just until we wrap things up."

The harried sympathy in his voice was annoying and

certainly held no reassurance. "Maybe I'll do that," she said. "Thank you for your time."

His receiver clicked in her ear. In shock, she stared at the phone before hanging up. So she'd get no protection from the police. All the more reason to get moving. She grabbed Sam's note and flipped it over to write one of her own. Pen poised, she hesitated. What should she say? *Dear Sam, on the run, see you later?* She glanced at a snapshot propped on the windowsill of the two of them on their honeymoon in Hawaii. She shook her head. How about, *Dear Sam, had to get out or lose my mind?*

She settled for, *Be back soon, C.,* and waited for her cab on the front porch with the rental section of the paper. She'd go to her house, load up her car, and find an apartment.

For once she was thankful that she didn't have much in the house. Deep down, she must have known it would never be home.

And that's what she needed now. A home. A real home. Not just a pretense. Not just an empty shell she lived in and slept in while mourning the emptiness inside her.

Telling Sam about the moments leading up to her discovery of his affair had brought her heartache bubbling to the surface, sent her emotions swirling in a boiling vat of hurt. She had to get away.

Away from danger.

Away from Sam.

She couldn't believe how susceptible she still was to Sam's charm. Five minutes alone under a fat moon and she'd fallen into his arms. Even now, after all that had passed. And living in Sam's house was seduction in itself. It would only be a matter of time before he'd have her smiling, laughing . . . forgiving him.

What future was there in that?

He'd destroyed a piece of her four months ago. *"It didn't mean anything, Chris. I don't even know her. I was mad. I was drunk. I was stupid.''* He'd confessed this to Christie, as if it would make everything better. What it did was tell Christie how easily he'd tossed away his marriage and commitment. She couldn't forgive it.

Her mother had been the kind of woman to look the other way or to believe mealymouthed excuses. But not Christie.

She sighed, watching the woman across the street try not to watch Christie. Nosy lady. Christie opened her paper and hid behind it. Columns of rentals blurred before her eyes. Determined, she focused and circled a few.

She'd feel better in a new home, but she knew she wouldn't feel safe.

Safe. When was the last time she'd felt that?

She shivered, remembering back to the months before her mother's death. She hadn't felt safe then, either. Then there had been another man, a different man she'd had to fear. A man so terrifying to her that to even think of him sent cold chills down her spine and furtive glances over her shoulder.

A man who somehow reminded her of last night's attacker . . .

She stopped the thought short. That was crazy. The man from the past looked nothing like the one who stalked her now.

But in her mind she could hear both men's voices, one an eerie echo of the other . . .

And the man from the past *had* promised he'd be back for her.

Four months had passed since he'd made that chilling vow. Four months and a lifetime in which she'd pretended she had nothing to fear.

And she was still pretending.

The taxi pulled to the curb unnoticed and honked, jerking her back to the present. Back to reality.

Settled in the backseat, she closed the door on the

past, concentrating on the paper until they stopped in her driveway. Paying the driver, she got out and stared up at her house.

A house, not a home. Even before the attacks had ripped all sense of security away, she'd never called it home. The only homey things that had ever existed in it were the dogs, and now one of them was gone forever. She went inside, feeling the empty rooms mock her.

She shivered, imagining again *his* icy glare traveling up her body. He wouldn't return to this house today. Somehow she knew it. But she hadn't seen the last of him either.

Her tennis shoes squeaked against the tile as she walked to the kitchen. Someone had been out to repair the sliding door that morning, but broken glass still littered the floor. The sight of it brought a fresh wave of fear.

Don't get too comfy, Christie. No place is safe for you now that I'm back.

The intrusive thought, its edges as sharp as the jagged pieces of glass clinging to the kitchen floor, bombarded her mind.

Stop it, Christie!

The man who'd broken into her house twice now couldn't be the same man who— The similarities were a coincidence, one of those twisted quirks of fate. She refused to allow herself to think any differently. She had enough to worry about today without torturing herself with fears from yesterday.

The silent kitchen still smelled of bleach and violence. She went outside to the backyard and gulped at the fresh, fragrant afternoon air. In the distance, a lawn mower whined. Stuffing her hands into her pockets, she circled around to the side yard. Even though she didn't want to see them, something compelled her to look for the footprints the police had told her were left when *he'd* jumped the fence.

Like a scar, the ground still bore the mark of his

passage. She followed the prints to the garage door and stared at the plastic flap.

No one had thought of the doggy door after the first attack. All the locks in the world didn't matter if *he* could pass *through* the door.

Curious, she got on her hands and knees and shimmied through the opening with incredible ease. Sitting on the cold concrete garage floor, she drew her knees under her chin and rocked. The dimness felt cool against her burning eyes.

In the corner beside her, Christie saw Barney's old tennis ball. She picked it up and bounced it against the wall. The *whock-whock* sound it made soothed her. Her last shot ricocheted off a wooden beam and the ball shot into the opposite corner.

Slowly she stood, shaking the stiffness from her legs. Crossing to the kitchen door, she checked the second dog's entrance to make sure it was still sealed off from the inside.

She turned to leave when a glimmer beside the door caught her eye. It sparkled in the thin, dust-filled sunlight, gleaming from the dirty pile of lint that clung to the floor. Looking closer, she saw a small key and picked it up.

Suddenly the garage seemed dark and ominous and the atmosphere inside, tainted and thin. She opened the door and hurried outside. A hot, teasing breeze billowed her blouse.

In the glaring sunshine, she examined the tiny key, noticing an inscription on the top. *Musclemen #5.* Musclemen Gym? A locker key? Going back into the house, she gripped it in her hand. It could have been lost by any number of people. The people who'd lived in this house before. One of the officers searching the scene of the crime.

Or last night's attacker, she thought, remembering his wiry muscles.

In the kitchen, Christie dialed information and got

the gym's phone number. A friendly male voice answered on the third ring.

"Musclemen."

"Yes, hello, ah—Could you tell me where you're located?"

"Imperial Beach," he said with obvious hesitation.

"What are your hours?"

"Five A.M. to eleven P.M.—but this is a men's gym, ma'am."

"What?"

"Men only—sorry."

"Oh." She paused a split second. "I'm calling . . . for my husband. He wanted me to contact you about his locker key. He lost it and I think I just found it," she lied. "If I give you the number can you look it up and tell me the name—"

"Can't do it, ma'am. Sorry."

Why not? she wanted to demand, but afraid she'd give her deception away, she backed off and politely tried again.

"Okay. How about I come down and try it? If it fits, then obviously it's the key, right?"

"Sorry, ma'am," the voice said pleasantly but firmly. "Men's gym means men's gym. No women allowed in the locker rooms."

"Isn't that a little strict?" she said, barely disguising her exasperation. "I'd only be a minute."

"The guys here pay for strict. They're serious bodybuilders."

Christie chewed her lip. "I see. Could I come there and give you the key and—"

"Sorry again. I don't touch the lockers. Policy."

"How about if I send my brother?" She sounded huffy and she knew it. Wasn't there a discrimination law or something about this kind of thing?

"As long as he has a key, there's no problem."

"Okay. Well, thank you for your help"

"Sure thing."

8

A gritty breeze, armed by the scorching-hot afternoon sun, gusted through the open windows of DC's car. This far inland, even the shade tree he'd parked under offered little sanctuary from the heat. He shifted uncomfortably, pulling his soaking shirt away from his sweaty chest. A glaze of salt and grit coated his face.

With an unobstructed view of the preschool, DC sat cleaning his nails with the tip of a neatly curved hunting knife. The action required concentration and it calmed him. He needed calm. He needed focus.

He needed to get his mind off Christie McCoy.

But he couldn't help himself. Every woman that crossed his line of vision reminded him of her. Since the first time he'd laid eyes on Christie, he'd been consumed with thoughts of her beneath him, above him, wrapped around him.

He nicked his thumb with the knife and cursed softly. Forget Christie, he told himself. It was her mother he needed to find. He'd be much better once he caught up with Mary Jane. She had the same scent as her daughter, Christie, and when he closed his eyes, it was easy for DC to imagine that he was holding the younger version. So far, though, he hadn't been able to find Mary Jane and it worried him. She was the only person who ever gave a shit about him.

He shifted in his seat. What if she'd left town? When

he'd gone to the house that they'd shared in La Mesa, her things had all been gone. At first he'd assumed she'd moved to the new house. The house in La Jolla. But there he'd only found Christie, and with Christie, trouble.

DC leaned his head against the seat. He wasn't going to think of Christie again. It was her fault he'd had to leave San Diego. Her fault that her mother had quit looking at him with love and started staring with disgust.

Now both of them hated him and he couldn't leave either one of them alone.

But where was Mary Jane?

Across the street at Palm Valley, parents began to arrive. In ones and sometimes twos, kids left hand in hand with their mommies and daddies.

Sheathing his knife in its leather sleeve, DC turned his attention to the preschool. He watched the girls who came out, playing a little guessing game to keep his mind occupied while killing time.

Which one was Jessica? He measured the name to each pony tailed youngster who trotted out the door.

That one? Maybe.

Defiant of the blistering sun, insane little children romped on the playground to his right. Wild monkeys, swinging on the jungle gym and screaming down the slides. On the air, the children's laughter whirled through his open window, the sound alien to him. He hadn't laughed much when he was a kid. Hadn't had much to laugh about.

Snapping a fat blue rubber band off the rearview mirror, he wove it through his fingers, and settled down to wait.

"Jesus, I'm a jerk," Sam mumbled to himself as he gave his watch a surreptitious glance. How could he have been so stupid as to come to work today?

"What did you say?" his student asked, pulling her

gaze from the yardage markers on the Padre Trails Country Club's driving range.

"I said, go ahead and hit it."

Sam had found Christie's note at lunchtime, when he'd gone home. Be back soon, which really meant, see you later. Kiss off, Sam. It was then that he realized what a critical error he'd made in leaving her alone in the first place. If he'd stayed home, she wouldn't be gone.

The message she'd left with the starter a couple of hours ago said she was okay and would be in touch with him later. He'd been watching for her ever since, but there was no sign of her yet. At least she'd called. He'd been surprised by it.

The last time she'd disappeared while he was at work, she'd gone for good. No note. Just empty drawers and closets to lead him to the inevitable conclusion. Not that he'd been surprised by her desertion. She'd caught him pants down with another woman and nothing he could do or say could change that.

All he could hope for was to convince her that *he'd* changed.

He sighed, staring at the rolling greens stretching from the edge of the blue-domed sky to the shore of the whitecapped ocean. To his left, ducks quacked as a golf cart nosed them off the trail that snaked through the heart of the course.

What had Christie been doing all day? he wondered. What was she up to? She was probably out right now, hunting for a new place to live in until it was safe to return to her house.

He glanced at his watch. Two minutes had passed since the last time he'd looked. He should have stayed home.

He cursed himself again, this time silently. Why had escaping to work seemed like such a good idea this morning? And why had it taken him until noon to figure out it wasn't?

"You have to keep your eyes on the ball, Jennifer," he said as if he'd been watching her instead of his ticking watch.

Nodding, Jennifer gripped the club and swung. Her drive sliced through the air with a whoosh, digging up a chunk of earth and sailing it gracefully over the ball.

Sam rubbed the back of his neck, squinting at the glare from the afternoon. He hadn't escaped his problem in coming here. He'd brought it with him and left the solution at home, sleeping in his bed.

He looked down at Jennifer's ball, still perched on the tee. "Why don't we call it a day?"

"I didn't even hit it," she said.

"I know, Jen, but it looks like you're having an off day. Let's wrap it up. I'll give you an extra lesson some other time. No charge."

She shook her head. "What good is another lesson going to do me? I can't even hit the ball."

"But you're hell on grass," he teased, bending to scoop up the hunks of sod around her club and gently tap them back in place with his shoe.

"I won't even get off the first tee tomorrow," she said accusingly.

"Sure you will. I've seen you hit the ball. You've seen you hit it. You're just having a bad day. You'll do fine tomorrow."

"I don't think so."

He gripped her shoulders lightly between his palms, trying to appear as he usually did, like he really cared. "Jennifer, trust me on this. The best thing you can do is pack up your clubs and have a beer. I know, I've been there plenty of times."

Now that was a lesson if he'd ever heard one. Maybe he should listen to it. Maybe instead of making things worse with Christie, instead of swinging wild shots into the soft turf, he should pack up *his* clubs and hit the bar. Christie sure as hell didn't want him anymore.

He looked off into the distance at the ball-speckled

driving range. She might not want him, but she sure as hell needed him. Besides, she was his wife, dammit, and he wanted her back.

"Earth to Sam."

Jennifer's voice beamed him back.

"I get the feeling you're not into this today," she said. "Look, if you show me one more time, I'll go. I just don't want to look like a clown tomorrow."

He quirked a smile at her. "Okay, Bozo, but you've got to concentrate. You're turning your club when you pull it over your shoulder." He mimed the action. "See?"

She shook her head. Sam moved to stand behind her and wrapped his hands over hers on the club. Slowly he drew the club back, correcting her when she would have rotated it. The club swung down and connected with a solid whack. He teed her three more and she packed up her clubs, waving a smiling good-bye.

Sam watched her sway away in shorts too tight and too short. He didn't see Christie until her voice startled him from behind.

"Sam?"

He jumped and turned to face her. Set against the rolling green lawns of the country club, she stood framed by the golden beams of sunshine. She wore khaki shorts and a soft, clinging shirt of peach that made him think of the curves beneath. Christie didn't need to wear revealing clothes to be sexy. Her taste simply added to her allure. The sight of her cleared his cluttered brain and gave him focus. What was he talking about, giving up? He couldn't give up on Christie. He owed her. He owed himself.

"Christie. I thought you were going to wait at home for me."

"For how long?" she asked, noting Jennifer's retreating back with a haughty lift to her brow.

"What's that supposed to mean?"

Her gaze snapped back to Sam's face. "Some things

never change, I guess. I saw that touching lesson you just gave. You're so dedicated.''

"You sound jealous.''

Her look was ice-cold. "Disappointed is a better word.''

"Why is that? I didn't think I meant anything to you. Why should you care who I give lessons to?''

"You're right. I don't. Do you have a minute? I need to talk.''

Frustrated, he stared at her. "Sure, I've got a minute,'' he said, leading her to the snack bar by the pro shop. "Want a soda or anything?''

"No. I just want to talk to you.'' She took a seat at a small, round patio table.

"Well, I want to talk to you, too, Christie. About last night—''

She shook her head. "Please, Sam, let's not get into that.''

Contemplating her request, Sam leaned forward and chose his words carefully. "Okay. I don't want to talk about last night either. I want to talk about today. Tomorrow. I'm not giving up on us, Christie. If I die trying, I mean to win you back.''

He waited for a reaction that never came. She just sat there, wearing that closed expression he hated so much. Just the sight of the chilly set of her features used to be enough to set his anger off. But not anymore, he warned himself. He was through with losing his temper. It never got him anywhere but alone.

Christie might not make the going easy for him, but he wasn't a quitter. It'd take a lot more than the ice maiden act to cool his feelings for her.

He cleared his throat and tried again. "I know I blew it, Christie, but dammit, give me a chance to make it up. I won't let you down again. Never again. I should have been there for you when your mom died. I know that I haven't been very dependable but that's going to change.''

Finally, his words seemed to register with her. Open-mouthed, she stared at him. Sam's heart banged at his chest and his palms felt cold and clammy. He hadn't realized how nervous he was, how important it was that she believed him . . . believe *in* him.

He exhaled his disappointment when she dropped her gaze. Pulling a napkin out of the holder centered on the table, she began shredding it into tiny pieces. He hoped that she was considering his words while she debated whatever inner issue furrowed her brow in a frown. Sam waited for the outcome.

"Have you slept with her?" she whispered softly.

"What?"

"Your lesson. Are you sleeping with her?"

He cocked his head, hoping to catch her eye again, but the napkin captivated her.

"Would you care if I was?" he asked.

"Yes."

"Why?"

She brushed the shreds of paper into the ashtray and started on another napkin. Her hands trembled over their task. So, she wasn't as composed as she pretended to be.

"I found a key today," she said, avoiding his question. Stilling her fingers, she looked up, over Sam's shoulder. "A key to a gym locker."

"That's not an answer. I wouldn't be the stud you know and love if I let you get away with that." He teased a grin out of her.

"You can always make me smile."

"Which still isn't an answer."

"I'm sorry, I can't answer your question. I can't."

He bit back his frustration and told himself not to push. Who knew what she was thinking? Maybe he was winning and just didn't know yet.

Deciding he'd better sit down, Sam hooked a chair around and straddled it, crossing his arms over the back. He forced himself to unclench his jaw.

"What did you want to talk to me about?"

She shot him a relieved glance. "I called the police this morning. Another little girl's been kidnapped. No one's interested in my case."

"What do you mean, no one's interested?"

"Unless I'm under twelve and kidnapped, they don't have time for me."

"Well that's just great."

"I know. I still can't believe it myself. I just assumed they would handle everything."

She shrugged and fell silent. She seemed to be searching for her next words.

Finally, she said, "I stopped by the house this morning."

"What house? Not your house? What the hell were you doing there? Christie, there's a lunatic—"

"I had to get away from your place, Sam. I couldn't stand being there." She paused and rubbed her temples. "I couldn't concentrate. I needed to pick up some more of my things anyway. I'm all right and I found the key, so don't start yelling at me."

"Okay, okay. What key?"

She pulled it from her pocket and handed it to him. "It's a key to a locker. I know it could be anybody's key. It could be yours."

"Never seen it before."

"It could be *his*."

"So?"

"So, this morning I called the gym," she said, looking at Sam expectantly.

Sam shrugged. "Do you want me to guess what they told you?"

"They told me I couldn't go in," she said. "The gym is exclusively for men—no women past the lobby. I want you to go with me and get what's in the locker."

"You want me to steal what's in the locker," he rephrased.

Blushing, she nodded.

"In that case, I have my own condition." He half expected her to get up and leave, like a child refusing to play by any rules but her own, but she didn't.

"I'll go with you," he continued, "but I want you to stay at my place until we get this guy—"

"No, Sam—"

"Let me finish," he said. "Just stay at my house. If you want, I'll sleep in the backyard. I'll pitch a tent, cook over a fire. Shower with the hose. I won't even come in to use the bathroom."

She fought a losing battle with a smile.

"You can just throw me some dinner scraps every once in a while—"

She laughed. "I get the picture, Sam."

"I'll keep my hands to myself. I promise. But I'll lose my mind if I have to spend every night worrying about you. Worrying that the next time ... the next time, you won't be so lucky."

"You think I'm lucky, Sam?"

He sighed. "I don't know what I think anymore, Christie. Where is this gym?"

"Imperial Beach." She stood, brushing the last crumbs of torn napkin into the ashtray. "I've got the address. Can we go now?"

"Do you promise you'll stay with me if I go with you?"

"Okay. I promise."

"Great." He jammed his hands into his pockets. "That was my last lesson. Give me a minute to lock up and then I'm done. I was just getting ready to go home, anyway."

They stood awkwardly together, avoiding each other's eyes.

"Christie . . ."

He touched her shoulder. Startled, her gaze met his. Gold, flecked with green. He found himself staring, unable to look away.

"I'm not sleeping with her. There hasn't been any-one else."

She stared back at him with an unreadable expression glimmering in her eye. He'd quit expecting a response from her, but he was still disappointed when he didn't get one.

He locked his office and they walked in silence to the parking lot. Sam automatically went to his Jeep. Christie's hesitant glance skipped to her battered Toyota parked in the next row. For a minute he thought she'd insist on taking her own car, but, with another shrug, she climbed into the passenger seat of the Jeep.

On the road, Christie studied Sam's profile. The tension between them had shifted, becoming dangerous and much too intimate. Christie searched for a way to shatter the feeling, but the air-conditioned Jeep co-cooned her, binding her in the sticky threads of her own emotions.

She didn't want to think about what he'd just said to her, didn't want to even consider trusting him again. So why could she still hear his voice rubbing against her feelings with the warmth of sincerity?

The quiet between them pressed in on her, forcing her thoughts into the narrow avenue of recall. Frantic to escape, she began to speak.

"I appreciate your doing this for me, Sam. I just know there's something in that locker." She paused. "I also wanted to thank you for all you did last night. I don't know how I would have dealt with things with-out you. I didn't do a very good job of saying that last—*this morning*—and I'm sorry."

He gave her a surprised look.

"I mean it."

"I'll bet that hurt to say."

She smiled, chuckling. "You're right, it did."

The traffic light turned red and Sam stopped the Jeep. Turning sideways in his seat, he said, "You're wel-come, Chris."

They stared across the narrow console between the bucket seats. Still locked by the flickering spark that had once made them lovers, they searched for the common ground that could make them friends again. Christie looked down at her hands, linked together in a tight ball of frustration.

"Was I really so bad, Sam?" she whispered, licking the dryness from her lips. "Like you said last night?"

Sam shook his head, his gaze fixed on her mouth. Her lips softened and parted, speaking a language of action and reaction that had nothing to do with the words they exchanged. He leaned close to her, as if to press his mouth to hers.

"I promised I wouldn't do that," he said, stopping before his lips touched hers. "Didn't I?"

As he spoke, his lips whispered above hers in a feathery caress. She ached to bridge the tiny gap that separated them as the seductive scent of him took hold of her senses, gripping her with inertia.

A driver behind them honked, the sound a jarring invasion of their intimacy. Slowly, Sam leaned back into his own seat, casting Christie a look so full of meaning that she caught herself answering with a nod.

Angry with herself for her weakness, Christie broke away and looked out the window, trying to ignore him and the thrills pulsing through her body. Although he had moved away, her awareness of him stayed just under her skin.

She thought of the golf lesson she'd witnessed him giving that evening, hoping the remembered jealousy she'd felt in seeing his arms wrapped around that woman would douse the insidious desire weaving its way through her. But the memories that surfaced were of her own body pressed against Sam's. Feeling Sam's chest, warm and hard, his heart beating in time with hers. Feeling the heat of his flat belly and lean hips, making her want to arch and rub against him.

As if he'd read her thoughts, Sam turned up the air conditioner. "Okay?" he asked.

She nodded.

But a jittery excitement took hold of her, blowing through the vents, fanning the white-hot sparks smoldering between them. Uncertain and afraid of her own emotions, she made the rest of the ride in silence.

9

Kathy Jordan tapped her fingernails against the steering wheel, glaring at the traffic as she fought the digital clock on her dash for every minute. Five-fifty-nine. She had one minute and five blocks.

The day had gone wrong from the beginning, when Jessica spilled her cereal all over the front of her dress and had to be changed before they could leave. Already late with an important meeting scheduled that morning, Kathy's patience had snapped and she'd yelled at Jessica. When she'd dropped her off that morning, her daughter's eyes had been red rimmed and teary.

Now she was late to pick her up.

"Way to go, Supermom," the voice of guilt sneered in her head. She hated that voice, but it followed her everywhere, dogging her steps, harping on her mistakes.

The next two red lights trapped her in traffic and the clock silently switched to 6:08. Damn!

She could see the school on the corner ahead, but she was already late. Melanie Blackwell had put Kathy on probation just last week, with an apologetic warning that had left Kathy feeling small and irresponsible.

Kathy parked her car, half-afraid she'd see Jessica sitting alone and bewildered on the doorstep. But the lights inside were still on and her daughter's bright little face glowed like a candle in one of the windows.

Kathy crossed her fingers as she walked to the door,

sighing when it opened, the lights within silhouetting Melanie Blackwell.

"Hello, Melanie. Sorry I'm late. I had a meeting—"

Melanie folded her arms under her flat chest and gave her an embarrassed little smile. "I'm sure you have a perfectly good explanation, Kathy, but you know that six o'clock pickup is not flexible."

"I know that but—"

"Honestly, I understand," she said in a kind voice, "but we do have lives of our own and after we run a twelve-hour day here, it's hard to have a personal life. I don't like to harp on it, but I must insist that you be more punctual."

Kathy shuffled her feet, feeling like a bad little girl with an hour of corner-standing in her future.

"You're already on probation. I don't want to ask you to withdraw Jessica, but if this continues, you'll leave me no choice."

Kathy nodded, squelching the irrational urge she had to cry. "Where *is* Jessica?" she asked calmly.

"She's in the other room. I asked her to wait there, so she wouldn't have to listen to our conversation."

"Thank you."

While Melanie went to get Jessica, Kathy stood at the door.

Too much. The entire day—lately, her entire life—had all been just too much.

How could she afford child care if she couldn't stay late at work occasionally? With a boss who worked eighteen-hour days, she rarely had a choice but to put in the extra time.

She sighed, putting on a happy face for Jessica. Somewhere, somehow, sometime, something had to give. But it wouldn't be here and it wouldn't be in front of her daughter. She'd save her breakdown for later, when she could enjoy it in the soothing comfort of her bathtub, with a glass of wine. She felt better just for thinking about it.

Kathy heard the sound of Jessica's laughter mingling with Melanie's a moment before they rounded the corner. As always, the sight of her daughter hit Kathy like a warm hurt. She ached when she looked into Jessica's innocent blue eyes. Eyes that sparkled with the same hues as her father's had. Dan had been dead for three years now, but he lived and breathed in his daughter.

Jessica's smile revealed small white teeth. "Hi, Mommy."

"Hiya, Jess. Sorry I'm late."

Jessica shot a worried look at Melanie. "It's okay."

Melanie kindly kept her thoughts concealed as she popped open her purse and removed a cracked compact and a tube of lipstick. She circled her lips in a cherry red that did nothing for her pale, blotchy complexion and fluffed the ends of her hair.

Kathy had never known her to wear any sort of makeup or be at all concerned with her appearance. She wondered what the occasion was. With a shrug, Kathy shuffled Jess out the front door and into the car.

"What were you guys laughing about?" Kathy asked when they left the parking lot.

"I can't tell. It's a secret."

Kathy scolded herself for feeling left out. Good grief, she really had the blues bad this time.

"A secret, huh? Can I have a hint?"

Jessica looked up, smiling Dan's smile. "We were just talking about the Daddy Fairy."

"The what?"

"The Daddy Fairy. I told her I wished I had a daddy and she said to ask the Daddy Fairy to give me one."

"Sweetie, there is no Daddy Fairy."

"I know. But it's fun to pretend."

"Pretending's fine, Jess. Just as long as you know it's only make-believe."

"But I might get a daddy."

Kathy shot her a serious look. "Only if Mommy marries again. You know that."

"But you might."

"Yes, I might. If I meet the right man. But that hasn't happened since I met your real daddy."

Jessica was not to be dissuaded. "But it could happen again."

Actually, Kathy didn't think so. How could she explain to her daughter just how unreliable men were? She'd lost Dan and Dan, while he lived, had lost everything of worth they'd ever had. He'd left Kathy and Jessica dangling over the wicked edge of homelessness. That experience had convinced Kathy that marriage was a very risky business.

And even if she were willing to take a chance on a new man, where would she meet him? She had no social life, no friends. Her world revolved around Jessica and work. The possibility of finding Mr. Right was too slim to consider.

But she couldn't tell Jessica that.

"You're right, honey. I *could* meet someone else, but don't get your hopes up. Tell me what you did in school today."

Jessica launched into an animated account of stories read and songs sung. She proudly showed Kathy a finger that had survived the removal of a splinter and told of her victory in musical chairs. Kathy listened, happy to hear the tales of her daughter's day, but before long, Jessica went back to her original topic like a bird to its nest.

"Emmie's mommy is getting married."

"What?"

"Emmie. Her real daddy died, too. Her mommy's going to get married again. Then she'll have a new daddy."

"That's nice for Emmie," Kathy answered noncommittally.

They stopped for a Happy Meal and a Big Mac on the way home. Kathy watched as Jessica frolicked on the McDonald Land playground until it was time to go.

When they finally pulled into the driveway that led to their small house, Jessica was still chattering about all the children she knew who had been blessed with new daddies.

Feeling more exhausted than she ever remembered feeling, Kathy stared sadly at the chipped blue-and-white paint peeling off the wooden slats, the fried brown grass and the stiff dead flowers in the front yard. Another wave of melancholy swamped her as she thought of the house she and Dan had shared. She'd had no idea how bad their financial circumstances were until after the funeral, when even the house had to be auctioned.

Dan had been a dreamer. When they'd married, he had big plans. She shook her head sadly. She'd learned after his death that Dan had no business, no pots on the fire, no deals in the making. Just a lot of ideas, boxed and stored in some overcrowded garage in his brain. And a lot of debts.

She cut the engine and opened her door. "Let's not talk about daddies," Kathy said. "Aren't we happy just you and me?"

"I guess."

"You guess? I thought we were friends."

"We are. But daddies build playhouses and let you pull their finger when they fart."

"*What?* Jessica, we don't talk like that," Kathy said, trying not to laugh as they entered the house.

"That's what Jeff says his daddy does."

"Jeff's a lucky guy, I guess. Go change your clothes and we'll see what's on TV."

"Mommy, do you still miss Daddy?"

Kathy sighed, looking at the dingy carpet, worn to gray threads in heavy traffic areas. Did she still miss Dan?

"Yes, honey. Your daddy was a good man."

Jessica smiled, apparently satisfied with Kathy's answer, and turned to skip down the hall. Kathy followed, staunchly ignoring the ugly wallpaper she couldn't afford to replace.

She entered the master bedroom, which was little more than a glorified closet with a toilet and shower the size of a phone booth. She'd sold most of her furniture and replaced it with secondhand artifacts that fit better into the tiny house than her Ethan Allan ensembles would have.

She pulled her silky white blouse from her skirt and began unbuttoning it.

"Mommy?" Jessica's voice called her from across the hall. "I'm done. Can I have a cookie? Please?"

"Okay. Just one, and don't make a mess in the kitchen."

Jessica skipped down the hall, dressed in a *101 Dalmatians* T-shirt and red shorts. Kathy smiled, wishing she could freeze her and keep her small like this forever.

Listening to the sounds Jess made in the kitchen, Kathy kicked off her shoes and peeled off her stockings, but as she reached for her skirt's fastening, she froze. An icy chill shivered down her spine and rooted her to the floor.

What was it? What had she heard?

A second of silence lapsed and then Jessica's scream, childish and terrified, bounced off the walls and echoed through the house.

Jessica!

Without thought, Kathy bounded down the hall, her heart beating against her chest like a caged bird bent on escape. She rounded the corner of the kitchen, skidding to a stop as her incredulous eyes focused on her daughter. There, pinned to the floor by a strange man, was Jessica. She thrashed against the man's grip.

"*Mommy!*" Her cries pierced the momentary inertia that made Kathy wooden legged and immobile. Enraged beyond terror, Kathy charged the man, pouncing like a tiger. She sank her teeth deep into his arm, gagging on his blood. Her nails clawed his hands, which gripped her daughter.

The sound of Jessica's fear bounced off her eardrums and pulsed through her body. He had Jessica. Jessica, her baby.

Her jaws ached from the effort of latching onto the iron muscle of his forearm but he didn't even whimper. Pulling one hand from the golden skin of Jessica's neck, he backhanded Kathy across the cheek with a force that knocked her into the wall.

Kathy's face exploded with pain and black stars sprinkled her vision, but didn't block out the terrible sounds of him struggling with Jessica. Compelled by an instinct stronger than survival, she attacked again, going for his eyes, with her nails pointed like daggers.

Releasing Jessica at the last possible moment, the man jerked Kathy's wrists up and away from his face, wrenching her arms backward and yanking them high up her back. Her shoulder joints bulged under her skin and she swooned from the pain. He pushed his face close to hers and his rancid breath covered her face, seeping into her pores like poison.

She kicked and flailed, jerking her panicked gaze to meet the horrified wide eyes of her daughter huddled on the floor.

Run, she managed to mouth.

She spoke with her eyes. Gesturing wildly for Jess to break free and *run, run, run, run.*

Jessica caught the message. She scooted backward and out of the room. Too late, he groped for her, but small and spry, she escaped.

With his attentions divided between them, Kathy freed one hand and clawed three rivers of blood into his face. She managed to kick at his shins, bucking her body away from his, but the advantage was his and he used it, slamming her to the floor and flattening her with his superior strength and wicked rage.

He grabbed the hem of her skirt and yanked it up.

Running his clammy hands over her bare legs, he ripped her underwear off her hips. His nails were jagged and they scratched her in horrifying places.

"What do you want?" she cried. "What are you doing?"

But she knew what he wanted. She knew what he was doing. She tried to blank it from her mind as she felt him against her bare flesh.

At least Jessica had run, but to where? Terror and revulsion fought for control of Kathy's mind. Was her daughter still in the house? Kathy's tears streaked down her cheeks, pooling in her ears.

Run, Jessica. Run.

Jessica pounded down the hall and darted into her mother's room. She grabbed the phone off the nightstand and dialed. From the living room, her mother's scream raced down the hall.

A woman answered.

"Help," Jessica cried. "Help. There's a man and he's got my mommy."

"Where is he?"

"He's in the living room."

"Are you in the house?"

"Yes."

"Get out of the house. Can you do that?"

"No. He's by the door. He's hurting my mommy."

"All right, honey. Someone's on the way. Can you tell me your name?"

"Jessica," she cried.

"Very good, Jessica. The police are on their way. Do you know who the man is?"

"No," she moaned. "He was in our house," she sobbed. "He's got my mommy."

"Hang in there, Jessica. Do you hear the sirens yet? Jessica? Can you hear the sirens?"

Jessica held her breath, cocking her head.

"No. No sirens. Mommy's screaming. Please hurry."

"Jessica, can you tell me what the man looks like?"
Jessica clutched the phone to her ear. "Yes."

"What does he look like?"

Jessica swiveled around, looking fearfully at the hall-way beyond the bedroom door. As she stood there, her mother's screams stopped, and then there was silence.

She dropped the phone. It clattered to the nightstand and bounced. She raced to the doorway in time to see him stand over the still body of her mother. Bright red splashes of blood soaked the silk blouse that only this morning had been white.

Jessica took two steps forward, thinking only of run-ning to her mommy's arms, which had always meant safety. But the man turned then and spotted her hov-ering in the darkened hall.

Blood dripped from his face. He smiled at her, mo-tioning her closer with his hand.

"Come on, Jessica. I'm not going to hurt you. Come to Papa."

Jessica cried out. Turning, she charged back inside the bedroom and slammed the door. She pushed the lock on the knob and backed away.

Hurrying, she hid under the bed.

He hit the door from the other side. Peeking from the lacy dust ruffle, she watched the door bulge on its hinges.

Was Mommy dead?

He hit it again.

And again.

The door wobbled. *Whack!* It flew open, bouncing off the wall behind and leaving a dent in the plaster.

He looked huge from her spot on the floor. He ad-vanced on the room, eyeing it, circling it. Grabbing the phone, he yanked it from the wall. He threw open the door to the closet and rifled through her mommy's dresses then swiped at the pretty perfume bottles and her mommy's jewelry box, knocking them off the dresser top.

Jessica screamed silently into her clenched fist, watching as he checked the bathroom. She saw his feet turn, move closer. Stop.

He was looking at the bed.

Christie breathed a sigh of relief when Sam pulled the Jeep to the curb in front of the gym. Joining him on the sidewalk, she faced the ocean and filled her lungs with salty, fresh air.

Sandwiched between a pool hall and a yogurt shop, the gym squatted on the cracked sidewalk. A battered sign, proclaiming it an establishment for *The Man Serious About His Body,* hung from rusted chains above the door. The picture on the front window showed a prime male specimen, inflated like Popeye after a dose of spinach.

Sam opened the chipped green door for Christie and they both stepped inside. The "lobby," barely large enough to hold the brown metal desk, was painted a beige that had withered to a mildewed gray. A naked light bulb hung from the ceiling, adding its flickering illumination to the sunlight filtered through the dirty window.

"No wonder it's exclusively men," Christie whispered. "No woman would even think of joining."

The smell of sweat—old, oily, and trapped—permeated the very walls. Not the scent of good, hard work, but the odor of hours of tortured strain, pushing muscles to do what they were not intended to do on their own. Like a closed room full of cigarette smoke, no breath was free of its pervasive reek.

A man whose shoulder span rivaled his height lumbered from the dingy hallway. His massive biceps bulged out of his skimpy body tank, forcing his arms to hang at strangely deformed angles.

He had an open, friendly face though, and a splatter of Howdy Doody freckles.

"Lady with the locker," he said.

Christie returned his smile. "That's right. I brought my brother."

"Great. Wait here." To Sam, he said, "Follow me."

Christie shuffled impatiently as the two men, Sam, tall and slim beside the shorter bulk of the other, disappeared down the hall. Faintly, from behind the walls, she could hear the clanking of weights and an occasional grunt from some unseen muscle man. The front door opened behind her and an enormous man stepped through. He gave Christie a curious look as he disappeared down the hall.

It seemed like hours that she waited in the airless lobby, but really only a few minutes passed before Sam reappeared. In his hands, he held a duffel bag. Quickly, he guided her from the sweat-shop and took a deep breath of fresh air as soon as the door closed behind them.

"Whew," he said.

Christie felt another smile curl her lips. "That bad?"

"Worse. Smelled like a bear cave back there. I've been in locker rooms that were bad before, but . . . The mildew was alive. Does the guy who's after you look like the Hulk in there?" he asked, cocking a thumb over his shoulder. "I've been picturing him a lot smaller."

"No, no. He is smaller. He's wiry. Scrappy. Like an alley cat."

"I was trying not to act suspicious by asking a lot of questions, but when we got to the locker, Hulk told me it had a hold on it. He checked the records and said that your husband should have paid dues when he came by last night. I had to pay before I could open the locker."

Sam handed her the receipt for the dues paid. Feeling an aversion she couldn't face or name, she glanced at the pink slip of paper.

The name scrawled on the top was DC Porter.

"Christie? Are you okay?"

Sam's voice sounded as if it came through a tunnel, intensified by the roar of the ocean. The waves crashing against the beach rivaled the tidal sensations swamping her.

DC Porter. She stopped walking.

Worse than any nightmare. More horrifying than any fictional monster.

DC Porter. Oh, God! How could it be him?

Of course it's him, her subconscious jeered. *Only a fool would have denied it.*

But he looked so different, she silently defended herself. His nose ... his cheekbones ... Even his teeth were different.

But the eyes, the jeering voice insisted. *The voice. Those never changed.*

She felt Sam's arm circle her, supporting her as he led her toward the beach. He stopped at a vacant picnic table.

"Christie? Talk to me! Are you all right?"

She shook her head, her voice coming in halting disbelief. "I just didn't think it could really be him. I mean ..." her words trailed off.

"You know him?" Sam exclaimed. "I knew it!" He glanced down at the pink receipt. "Who is he? Who is he, Chris?" His voice was soft, his words hard. A feather pillow with a hunk of steel hidden in its fluffy center. "Why have you been lying about knowing him? Are you protecting him or—"

"No! No, Sam, I ..." She took a deep, cleansing breath before continuing. "I really didn't know it was him. I swear."

"How could you not know it was someone you knew?" he demanded.

"He doesn't look the same anymore and . . . and he wasn't—*isn't*—someone I *knew,* exactly. He knew my mother."

"Your mother? How did he know her? Was he a friend or something?"

She nodded, avoiding his eyes.

"Why the hell would a friend of your mother's be attacking you?"

"I don't know," she said, her voice small and sounding unconvinced even to herself. "He was always . . . strange. He left just before my mother died. I didn't know he was back."

"Why didn't you say anything about him looking familiar before?"

"I thought I was crazy. I really did."

"So you didn't mention that he might have known your mother to the cops?"

"I didn't see the point in dragging her name into it."

"Didn't see the point? Jesus, Christie—"

"I don't expect you to understand, Sam."

"Damn right, I don't understand! Make sense, Christie! First you claimed you'd been robbed when nothing was missing, then you ignore your own instincts and withhold information that could help them find the guy who attacked you!"

Christie crossed her arms and stared out at the ocean.

"Okay, okay. I'm yelling. I'm sorry." He took a deep breath and asked more calmly, "What was his relationship with your mother?"

"He worked with her."

"At the clinic? Doing what?"

"He did custodial stuff. Handyman jobs. Ran errands."

"That's it?"

She sighed, feeling like a butterfly trapped in a jar. "DC and my mother . . . They were involved."

"Involved? How involved? Did he sweep her floors or—"

"They were involved romantically. I hate to disappoint your overactive curiosity, but I don't know any more than that."

"Wait a minute. You're telling me that your mother and this DC were *lovers?* He was her *boyfriend?*"

She nodded, frowning. "Everyone thought he was a nice guy."

"A nice guy? Obviously, he wasn't attacking people when your mom dated him, huh?"

She didn't answer. Her silence weighed heavy on the light breeze. Sam watched her intently.

Finally, with apparent care for his wording, he repeated, "Everyone thought he was a nice guy. Okay. How about you, Chris? What did you think of him?"

"I only met him a couple of times," she hedged.

"And?"

She looked down at her clasped hands. "And I thought he seemed like the kind of guy who'd go around attacking people."

"Did your mom know how you felt about him?"

"I couldn't tell her. She seemed so happy. So bubbly all the time. She seemed ten years younger when they were together. Then he just disappeared one day. I don't know why or where he went, so don't bother to ask."

"Okay, how about this, then: Why's he back now? Did she leave you any money with that house?"

"Not much. And, there's no way he could know about it."

"Maybe he thought she was loaded. Figured you got it all when she died."

"Sam. Read my lips. It wasn't much. We're talking about a few thousand dollars after all her debts were paid. She never had a lot of money. I didn't even know she had the house until she died."

"You didn't even know? You mean she never lived there?"

"No. None of her things had been moved from her house in La Mesa."

"Don't you think that's strange?"

"Of course I think it's strange. But no stranger than anything else that's been going on."

He nodded. "I wonder how this guy got a job at the

clinic? You'd think they'd do background checks there, wouldn't you? I'll bet this guy has a record.''

"Like I said, everyone else thought he was wonderful. And Mom . . . I mean, after he came into her life . . .''

"What?''

"Nothing. She just changed.''

"Changed how?''

"I can't put my finger on it. It's just a feeling I had. Things were different.''

"That's so enlightening, Christie,'' he said, throwing his hands in the air in obvious frustration. "With that kind of vivid recall, we'll track him down by the end of the day.''

"You can cut the sarcasm, Sam. If you're going to lose your temper, then I don't want your help.''

"I'm real sorry, Christie, but like it or not, there's a lunatic out there who, for whatever reason, is after you. I can't help it if that upsets me just a little.''

"And you think I like it? Is that what you're saying?''

"No! No, that's not what I'm saying, for chrissake. I'm saying there's got to be a reason for this guy to be after you and I want you to quit being so secretive about everything.''

She took a deep breath. "All right, all right. What do you want to know?''

"Back to the house,'' Sam said, leaning forward.

"What about it?''

"Is there something in it—''

"You're getting carried away, Columbo. You've been inside. There's nothing.''

"Maybe it's hidden.''

"Maybe it's not.''

His angry look smoldered. "There you go again. Why are you so unwilling to cooperate?''

"I'm not. I just don't appreciate the way you're grilling me. Making accusations about my mother—''

"What accusations?''

" 'Didn't they do a background check?' My mother would not have been with him if she'd thought he was a criminal."

"I wasn't implying she would have. I'm just trying to help you, Christie." He stared at her closed expression, then sighed. "Okay. Enough about your mother. Is there anything else you can think of that I should know about this guy?"

"No!" she answered too quickly.

His skeptical look said more than any words.

"Yes," she admitted at last. "Yes, there's more. But don't ask me to talk about it now. I need to think. I need to get myself together first."

He looked like he would press her, then managed a grudging nod. He reached for the duffel bag on the table. "Let's see what's here," he said, pulling out a stack of manila folders. Each folder had a colored, typed, last-name-first label. They both took one and opened it.

A business card fluttered across the table. Christie picked it up, recognizing the familiar logo of the soaring ball and 18th hole flag. Shock penetrated the numbing husk surrounding her.

"Sam, this is your card."

"What?"

She handed it to him, feeling as powerless as one of the red-and-white buoys buffeted by the waves.

A black cloud of anger darkened Sam's features. "Where the hell'd he get this? And what's it doing in that locker?"

"I don't know. What are these files?"

"They look like medical records," he said, frowning. "They're somebody's medical records. This DC guy isn't a doctor, is he?"

"No way. I told you, he was working as a custodian at my mother's clinic."

They stared at the files as if expecting them to speak.

"Should we put them back?" Christie asked.

Sam shook his head. "Hell, no. He's been making the rules until now. I don't know why he's got these files, but it's a good bet they're not his. Let's jerk *his* chain for a change and make *him* wonder what the hell's going on. Besides, he doesn't even have a key anymore."

Christie nodded, rubbing her temples.

DC Porter. He was like a nightmare that refused to fade, even after the sun came up. From the first time Christie had looked into his gritty blue eyes, she'd instinctively known that he was trouble. Not that she could convince her mother of it. Her mom had been on his short leash and sang his praises every time he gave a yank. Ten years her mother's junior, he had swept her right off her feet. She'd worshiped him.

Near the end, though, Christie thought she had glimpsed something different in her mother's eyes. A flicker of fear, a hope for rescue. Yet she steadfastly refused any lifeline Christie threw her. Until that day . . .

Sam began jamming the files back into the bag. "God, I hate this guy. Describe him again."

Christie stood, suddenly stiff as a board. "He's average height. He's blond and he wears his hair short now. He has this look about him. I can't explain it. He turned my blood cold the first time I met him. But he can be charming. I've seen him in action and he's good."

"At least he doesn't sound like any of my students. He's begging for a lesson, though. I can't wait to give it to him."

They walked back to the Jeep, the intimate mood gone, the humming currents banked. Although she tried not to admit it, she felt saddened by the loss.

10

DC parked outside his mother's house and waited in his car for her to come home. He didn't go to the door because he had no reason to believe he'd be invited inside. He figured if he hadn't been asked yet, he probably never would.

Perched on a hill, her house sat in the middle of an acre of real estate. A blanket of green grass stretched from the base of the house to a shrub border. A white stuccoed wall shielded the house from the street but, long ago, DC had found this spot on the hill to park. He'd spent many nights here, watching her cocktail parties, glittering with champagne and laughter. He'd seen his stepbrother, James, introduced like young royalty to his mother's smiling court.

Her car rounded the corner and zoomed up the drive. Stepping from his car, DC walked down the hill, scaling the wall with a groan of sore muscles. He'd fought three women in the past few days and each had left her mark.

Landing on the macadam drive, he hunched and shuffled to the concealing foliage along the base of the wall. His fingers brushed her shiny new car as he passed it in the horseshoe driveway.

DC had never had the nerve to come so close to her domain, to actually sully the ground with his passage, and now he felt a sick nervous tension grip him. He knew she wouldn't welcome him.

He slipped into the backyard, where patio tables and chairs clustered around a pool that glittered like a gem centered in a red tile setting. Last July, they'd celebrated James's thirteenth birthday out here. Their mother had carried a cake out and everyone sang, their voices drifting up the hill to DC's secluded hideaway.

Now, rap music blasted from an upstairs window as DC crept to the back door and peered through the screen into the kitchen. His mother stood just inside, the phone cupped between her shoulder and chin. A frown marred her face. Barefoot, she paced.

"I thought you'd be home," she said into the phone. She sounded pissed, her pause weighted, her response tight.

"I know you're busy, but so am I." Another tension-filled pause. "I don't *know* what he's doing. That's my *point*. Unless one of us is here, there's no way to know what he's been up to."

She was talking to her husband, probably about James. DC's stepbrother was a punk who didn't know how good he had it. James wouldn't have survived DC's childhood. The two sons shared a mother, but their lives couldn't have been more different.

DC's mother coiled the phone cord around a finger, listening to the voice on the other end.

"Just call me next time. I'll come home early. It's just not safe to leave him alone. Okay?"

She apparently received her answer and hung up without saying good-bye. DC stayed where he was, listening to her fuss in the kitchen. Except for James upstairs playing his music, she seemed to be the only one home, but he wanted to be sure.

Inside the kitchen, she replaced the phone and stared at it. Lately every conversation she had with her husband was centered in a conflict that revolved around James. Stopping a sigh before it reached her lips and tipped her over the edge of melancholy into depression, she looked up to find James watching her with cold, hostile eyes.

"Was that Dad?" he asked.

"Yes, it was."

"Why didn't he pick me up from school?"

"There was a problem with one of his patients—"

James made a sound of disgust. "Figures."

"Have you had dinner yet?" she asked, pretending to smile.

"Cut the shit, Mom. I can feed myself."

"I don't doubt that, James. I simply asked because I'm going to make myself a tuna sandwich. Would you like one?"

"A good home-cooked meal? No thanks, I'll just do drugs like I usually do."

"James!"

"Don't worry, I won't tell Dad or any of your friends."

"That's not what—"

"Save it, Mom. I don't do drugs. I don't need to. I'm fucked up enough as it is."

Staring at her son, she felt swamped with the hopelessness of her situation. No matter how badly she wanted to, she just couldn't communicate with either her husband or her son. She knew James was trying to get a rise out of her, so she tamped down the surge of frustration that made her want to scream.

"James, I wanted to apologize for yelling at you this evening when I got home," she said, trying to sound reasonable, even though his freezing glare told her it was no use. "It wasn't your fault that your father was unable to pick you up—"

"Like you care. It's too late, Mom."

He grabbed a soda and left before she could think of anything to say. Sighing, she put her head in her hands, her appetite nearly gone.

Feeling older than she should, she took a can of tuna from the cupboard anyway. Setting it on the counter, she turned around to find DC sitting in her kitchen with his feet propped on the table.

DC.

NO! she wanted to scream.

He looked like an alien imposter peering at her through DC's eyes. But she knew that smile no matter how she wished she didn't. And the scratches on his cheek were a glaring indication that he hadn't changed inside.

He watched her reactions with smug satisfaction. Surprise attacks were his MO and he took pride in his unpredictability. He always had.

"What happened to your face?" she asked.

"Looks good, huh?"

"Not to me. I'd hoped to have seen the last of you," she said, opening the tuna as if it didn't bother her in the least to have him there.

"I knew you'd be thrilled."

"What do you want?"

"What are you having?"

She glared at him. "Tuna fish."

"That'll be fine."

"I wasn't offering."

"Of course not. I heard you and James. Has the little prince upset the palace?"

DC stood and sauntered to the refrigerator. He opened it and grabbed a Heineken from the bottom shelf. Water condensed on the bottle, dribbling down the sides and moistening his fingers. When he pushed the door shut, he left a bright red print on the shiny white surface of her no-smudge refrigerator. It looked out of place in the sparkling relief of the glittering kitchen. Feeling sick, she grabbed a paper towel.

"Yours?" she asked, pointing at the blood.

"I doubt it."

"Whose?"

A light blond stubble shadowed his cheeks, glinting in the muted light. It made his smile look wicked and wild, the scratches mean and ominous. He shook his head and laughed into his beer bottle, watching her. With a shiver she wiped the bloody print away.

"Some pad you got, Mommy."

"Don't call me that. I'm not your mommy."

He laughed again, enjoying himself. "Hurry up that sandwich. I'm hungry."

Her vicious glare only made him laugh harder. Deliberately, he sat and propped his feet back up. How could she get rid of him before her husband got home?

Standing indecisively before him, she watched as he looked around the bright kitchen, craning his neck to peer at the rooms beyond. His casual glance felt like an armed invasion.

"Real nice place," he said. "Not like the old days, huh?"

"I've worked hard for what I've got."

"I know, Mommy. No one has sacrificed as much as you."

His sarcasm earned him another glare. Inside, she shook with anger. How dare he come back?

"I know *I* didn't sacrifice that much," he mocked. "No sir, living with Grandma and Grandpa was just fine with me."

He tilted his head back and downed his beer. His throat muscles convulsed and droplets leaked out of the corners of his mouth. He glugged the last swallow and wiped his mouth with a sleeve that was black with dried blood.

"Oh, my God."

"Just fine with me," he continued. "I thought Grandpa was a damned good screw, even if I was ten."

"Shut up!"

He chuckled again. "Get me another beer."

"You can't stay. My husband is going to be home soon."

"Sounds like you got a problem. I'm hungry."

"If I give you something to eat, will you leave?"

"Maybe. Maybe I'm looking forward to meeting your husband after all this time. Maybe I want to talk to my *brother*, too."

"He's not your brother, you animal."

Her vicious words only brought a smile to his face. On shaking legs, she turned and began pulling things from the refrigerator. What time would her husband be home? What if James came back downstairs?

DC ate everything she put before him and drank three more beers before leaning back and patting his stomach.

"Now will you tell me why you're here?" she asked.

"Business, Mommy. I'm here on business."

She felt her heart straining against the paralyzing terror that his words evoked.

"We don't have any business," she said in a voice suddenly hoarse. She cleared her throat. "We never will again."

"Oh, you're wrong. Dead wrong. We've got a lot of business. Shit, we just opened up shop."

He laughed without humor, his eyes glacial.

She could see herself, framed in the glass door by the darkness pressing against it from the other side. She looked defeated even in reflection. DC appeared commanding and in control.

Outside, a mockingbird twittered to the moon and a dog barked in response. She winced at the sound and noticed DC doing the same. He'd inherited her fear of dogs, it seemed. She tilted her head back, looking at the etched globes glowing beneath the antique ceiling fan. Taking a deep breath, she caught the scent of the honeysuckle growing around the patio, perfuming the night with a scent as light as mist. The stench inside had no odor, only the texture of futility.

"Whose blood are you wearing, DC?"

He opened his shirt and showed her a gash on his ribs. Worried, she eyed the chair he sat on and the carpet underneath him for traces of red, but his shirt was stiff and the wound had long since dried. She felt shaky with relief. How would she have explained blood to her husband?

"Your concern's touching," DC said. "I figured you'd want to doctor me up."

Without a word she went to the bathroom off the kitchen and grabbed the first aid kit from the cupboard. Back in the kitchen, she dropped to her knees and eased DC's shirt up over the gash in his side. His skin felt hot and it puckered around the wound. She didn't want to touch him, and he knew it.

"It's not too bad," she said.

She wet a towel with cold water and roughly wiped the blood away from the cut, her nostrils filling with the sourness of blood mixed with sweat. While she cleaned and bandaged, her mind seemed to disassociate itself from the action of her hands. Sweat trickled down the side of her face to pool in the hollow of her throat. She stuck a last bandage to his skin.

"I'm done."

DC nodded.

She took his shirt and the bloody towel to the laundry room, returning seconds later with a clean button-down clutched in her hand.

"You can have this and I'll give you one hundred dollars. But you'll have to leave."

"A hundred bucks isn't going to do. You should know better than that. We've got business. I've got a cargo."

"I'm not in the cargo business," she said with false bravado. Inside, she felt sick and weak. This couldn't be happening. This chapter was supposed to be over.

"Oh, I think you are. I think you still got a lot to do with cargo. Don't think you can jerk me around, either." He glared her down, licking his lips. "Those sure are ugly uniforms they make them wear at James's school. Must be private."

She spun on her heel, staring at him openmouthed. "You keep away from my son."

"Such loyalty. I'm impressed." He gave her a mea-suring look. "Where's Mary Jane?"

"She's dead."

He paled. "Don't bullshit me."

"It's true."

DC shook his head from side to side, shock shadow-ing his features. She thought she glimpsed tears in his eyes but didn't believe for a moment that they were genuine. DC cared for no one but himself.

"When?" he asked, the word sounding small and strained.

"Right after you left. I guess she couldn't deal with it."

"She knew I'd be back."

"That's what I meant."

His face hardened and the trace of remorse vanished. His expression became unreadable.

"How did she die?" he asked.

"Suicide. No note," she lied.

Again he looked away from her, shielding his feel-ings behind a blanked mask. "And the house?" he asked in a husky voice.

"How would I know?" she said, taking satisfaction from his shock. The bastard. "What do you want, DC?"

"I need a place to stay. Me and my cargo."

"I told you. I'm not in that business anymore."

"Well I suggest you get in the business. Or else I might decide to get in the business of talking. I bet your husband would be interested in what I have to say. Your *son,* too."

She knew exactly what DC's threat was about. She knew exactly what he would do. If her husband ever found out ... If her son ever learned the truth ...

"How much money do you want?" she asked desperately.

DC blinked his blue eyes. "Why, a lot." He laughed. "A whole hell of a lot."

She sank down into the chair by the door, her gaze darting around the room, as if looking for escape. "How much, DC?"

DC smiled. "You tell me."

"Ten thousand dollars. I'll have it in the morning."

DC stared at her while the distance between her returning husband and home lessened with each passing moment. Her anxiety rose to fever pitch. Her nerves stretched to the breaking point.

Finally, DC answered.

11

Sam and Christie went to dinner, as a couple, for the first time in half a year. Without asking, Sam drove to the same place they'd dined on their first date.

He liked the place because it sat on a low hill, right next to the foamy wash of the ocean and because it reminded him of happier times with Christie. The boardwalk passed its front door and beachgoers mingled with diners. The aroma of cinnamon rolls, cooked fresh and served hot by a beach vendor, teased their appetites as they climbed the outdoor staircase to the glass front doors.

Inside, the lounge coupled the breathtaking view with subdued intimacy. Deep, barrel-shaped chairs nuzzled plump love seats and tiny smoked-glass cocktail tables. The muted lights illuminated only the important, letting the dazzling vista of waves crashing against the coast dominate the room.

A waitress wearing a Spandex bodysuit and black wraparound skirt took their drink orders, informing them that a table would be ready in thirty minutes.

"I didn't expect it to be so crowded," Sam said.

"That's okay. I could use a drink before dinner."

Finding a table pushed in a corner, they settled back to sip their drinks, cloaking themselves in the muted roar of the surf.

"Do you remember the first time I brought you here?" Sam asked after a few minutes.

"Was that you?"

"Smart ass."

She peered at him through lowered lashes. "Yeah, I remember."

"I was going to bring you back for our first anniversary, but . . . What happened to us, Chris?"

"I don't know. I guess we changed."

He nodded, as if to let the conversation drop. But for the first time since they'd split, Christie wanted to know the truth.

"Sam . . . If we're going to be honest, then tell me, what did you mean last night when you said you didn't understand me?"

"I was just mad, Christie. I didn't mean anything."

"Yes, you did. Tell me. Tell me the truth."

He flagged the waitress and made a circling motion with his finger. Another round arrived before he answered Christie's question.

"I always felt like you were hiding things from me, Christie. Not that you were doing anything wrong. It's hard to explain. I just wanted to know everything about you and you had so many secrets. I guess I wanted to know them all. Pretty selfish, huh? You're entitled to have your own thoughts."

"I never knew you cared so much about what I was thinking." She looked out the window, battling the walls within as the tide beat the shore. "When we were married, Sam, I was very worried about . . . about losing my identity. You're a dynamic person. People like you. They want to be around you. I was jealous of that. Jealous, and a little intimidated. You're always so decisive. You want something, you go for it. I didn't know what hit me with you."

"I know, I know. I rushed you into things—"

"But I wanted to be rushed. It's just that after, I got scared." She shrugged, giving him a sad smile. "I'd seen my mother do the same thing so many times. Hook up with Mr. Wonderful only to have him ruin her life.

Not just *her* life, either. Usually mine too. Every time *she* got dumped, *my* life was disrupted. Usually we moved. It didn't matter if it was in the middle of the school year, or if I was in a play or on the speech team. She'd tell me to pack my room, and we'd move. I went to fifteen different schools before I graduated from high school.''

"Wow."

"After each time, she'd swear off men for a month or so. And then it would happen all over again. I always swore that I'd be in control if I got involved with someone. But you didn't give me a chance. Or maybe I didn't give me a chance. I'm so confused, I don't know what's right anymore.''

"But we could try again, Chris. Now that I know how you feel—''

"Wait. There's more, Sam. I'm ready to tell you about DC.''

He sighed, looking as reluctant to hear as she was to tell. "Okay,'' he said, "shoot.''

With a shaky hand, Christie lifted her glass and drank the rest of her wine. Reaching for her second glass, she took a deep breath and plunged into her story.

"DC ... I mean, the attacks this week ... They weren't the first. He attacked me two other times. Both happened a few weeks before ... before my mother died.''

It was obvious by the way he blanched, his eyes becoming round and luminous in the ashen pallor of his skin, that her declaration was completely unanticipated. His jaw worked convulsively before he managed to force out a sound.

"He *what?* When we were still married? Why the hell didn't you tell me? I would have killed him for you.''

"It wouldn't have been for me. It would have been for you. And that's exactly why I couldn't tell you. You've never been very good at controlling your tem-

per. You would have put him in the hospital at the
very least.''

"Are you saying that's wrong?''

"He was my mother's boyfriend, Sam. She loved
him.''

"So you protected him?'' He gulped at his drink,
glaring at her over the rim of his glass. "That's crazy.''

"I thought I could handle things myself. And besides, you were as much a stranger to me as I was to
you. All you ever did was work and watch sports. By
then, we didn't even talk.''

"But—''

"I wanted to speak with my mother first, anyway.
But then things happened so fast . . .''

"What things? What did your mother say?''

"DC had come to my work. It was a really slow
time of year, and I was there alone. He had me cornered
before I knew what was happening. Fortunately a cus-
tomer came in and I guess DC panicked . . . he ran out
the back door before he could be seen.''

"And you didn't call the cops?''

"He didn't get the chance to actually *do* anything,
Sam. Even I know he wouldn't go to jail for that, not
these days. I didn't know *what* to do. I felt filthy. When
I got home you were still at work and I . . . I decided
I'd tell my mother and take it from there. I went to the
clinic the next day. . . .''

She stared at the candle on the table as it faded into
her memory of that day. Christie had stepped onto the
slate gray carpet of the Beth McClain Clinic and walked
through the lobby. Dramatic, beautiful charcoal
sketches of mother and child decorated the walls with
warmth and emotion that seemed to mock her. Peach
chairs fringing a whitewashed circular table made the
waiting area seem calm and peaceful, but nothing short
of a tranquilizer could have settled the knotted tension
inside Christie.

The office on the left belonged to Beth, the owner. Christie popped her head into the office on the right.

Her mother jumped and squeaked when Christie said "hi."

"Mom, sorry. I didn't mean to scare you."

Her mother made a shaky sound and masqueraded it as mirth. "It's okay, I just didn't hear you."

"I came to take you to lunch."

Distress lines waved across her forehead. "Lunch? Today? I'm sorry, honey, but I can't."

"Why not?"

"Because she's having lunch with me," DC said from behind Christie.

Christie's stomach clenched with fear and disgust as she faced him. How could he act so cool? She glared daggers as he crossed the room to stand by her mom.

"I'm having a private conversation with my mother, DC. So get the hell out—"

"Christie!" Her mother jumped to her feet. "Christie, I will not—"

"You don't know him, Mom!"

"What are you talking about? Of course I know him. Why are you acting this way?" The clock on the wall ticked off the tense seconds of silence that gripped them. Finally, her mom broke free and looked at the large-numbered face. Frowning, she double-checked her watch.

"Christie, honey. I don't have time to get into this now. DC and I have a business lunch to go to."

"You and DC?" Christie stabbed a finger at DC. "He's the janitor, Mom. You don't have to lie to me."

"I'm not lying. DC is helping me place an infant with a couple. A couple who are very anxious. I don't want to keep them waiting, honey."

"How is *he* helping?"

"He knows the young lady who wishes to give her child up."

"I'll bet he does."

"Christie . . ."

Christie sighed. "Mom, I really need to talk to you."

Her mother rubbed her temples, glancing back at her watch. "Okay. Let me make a quick call first. Then we'll have a cup of coffee. I'll be right back."

"No—Mom—"

But she'd rushed out of the room, the door closing behind her before Christie could stop her.

Nervously, Christie glanced at DC. Leaning against the desk with assumed nonchalance, he watched her like a hawk.

"Tell my mother I'm waiting in the lobby," she sneered at him, turning to leave.

Nostrils flaring, he shoved himself away from the desk and lunged across the room. She darted for the door but he hooked her waist with his arm and slammed her into the corner. He covered her mouth with his hand and shoved his hand up, under her dress.

"You thinking of telling on me, baby sister?"

He ground her lips against her teeth with his palm. "You want her to know about us? I thought we'd keep it a secret, but if you want her to know, let's just show her."

Christie struggled, trying to squirm out of his arms or get a breath of air so she could scream. When would her mother be back? How far was the coffee machine?

DC whispered into her ear, his foul breath fanning her cheek. "She should be back soon, eh? Won't she be surprised."

As if in response, Christie heard her mother gasp from the doorway.

"DC!" she shouted. Two cups of steaming hot coffee dropped from her hands and splashed over the floor.

DC immediately stepped back and Christie shoved his arms away from her. "Get the hell away from me," Christie yelled, slapping his face. She crossed the room, wiping viciously at her mouth.

"Get out," Christie's mother whispered, her face pale, her eyes wide and shocked.

For a fleeting moment, Christie thought her mother spoke to her. Tension shivered in a triangle among the three of them. Finally, DC shrugged.

"I'll see you later, baby sister. Bet on that," he said as he sauntered out, without apology or explanation.

Left alone with her mother, Christie searched for something to say.

"Is that the first time?" her mother asked in a low voice.

Christie stared at the floor, shaking her head. "No."

"That's what you wanted to talk about, isn't it?"

"Yes. It happened yesterday. He came to my work."

Her mother looked at the ceiling, blinking her eyes. "I'm sorry," she said, emotion cracking her words in two. "I'm so sorry."

"It's not your fault. He's sick, Mom. He conned you."

When Christie looked into her mother's eyes, she could see that something inside had died. Christie felt overwhelmed with sadness. Why did this always have to happen to her mom? Why couldn't her mother, just once, find a decent man who wouldn't use or abuse her? She wanted to shake her mom and scream, *"Don't be this way. Not over a loser like DC."*

Instead, she said. "I'm sorry, too, Mom. I know you thought he was a nice guy."

Her mother looked away, out the window. "He'll be leaving soon, anyway. Leaving forever."

"Forever? Where's he going?"

"Away. Another state. I don't know and I don't care."

Christie stared at her mother's profile. "You mean he was already planning to go away before . . . ?"

"Yes."

Her mother wiped her face with a tissue and then

blew her nose. "I really do have to get going, Christie."

"You're not still going to a meeting with him, are you?"

"Honey, I have to go. Other people depend on me."

"Mom, he's dangerous—"

"Don't worry. He won't hurt me. Not any more than he already has."

Christie said, "But, Mom—"

"If he was going to hurt me, he'd have done it already."

"Listen to me—"

"Christie, I have to go. Don't worry, I'll be careful. I'll call you when I'm through . . ."

On the table, the candle flickered and Christie's eyes refocused on the flame. The sound of her mother's voice faded into the roar of the lounge. Outside, the ocean gleamed like a rolling black monster. She met Sam's gaze and gave him a sad smile.

"After that, DC did leave. I hoped for forever, but I should have known better. When my mother died . . . I felt responsible. I've always wondered if she killed herself on purpose."

Sam stared at her with an unreadable expression in his eyes. Finally, he dropped his face to his hands and rubbed. When he looked up, a sad smile gleamed from his face.

"When you keep something to yourself, you really do a number."

So different from any of the responses she'd expected, Sam's statement struck her as funny. She chuckled.

"Is there more?"

She shook her head and then began to laugh.

"Thank God," Sam said, beginning to laugh, too.

Their laughter felt clean. Cathartic. The sick feeling of DC's control slipped away. Until that moment, she hadn't truly realized how much he'd dominated her life.

When Sam and Christie finally stopped laughing, Sam reached across the table and took her hand in his.

"We're going to get this guy, Christie. And he's going to pay for everything he's done. I promise you that."

12

The engine of DC's car roared to life, growling for the open roads. He pulled away from the bushes, leaving behind the sweet smell of his mother's neighborhood for the toxic fumes of the freeway. Merging with eastbound traffic, he tried to block out his mother's words, but they haunted him, replaying over and over in his mind.

"Mary Jane's dead . . . Suicide. No note. Maybe she just couldn't take it. . . ."

His mother had enjoyed telling him. He'd seen it in her eyes. Alone, he felt grief rise up on him. Mary Jane dead? How could that be? He missed her. He needed her.

He turned the radio down, coasting onto a cul-de-sac of small, postwar bungalows. Darkened windows reflected his headlights and shot them back as he passed. DC slouched behind the wheel, scanning the street. Empty cars. Silent driveways. Dry gutters marking the borders of each of the stone-faced structures. Not a single light glowed behind the drawn curtains.

"Suicide. No note . . ."

Glancing at his directions, he willed his mind silent. He counted five drives down from the stop sign and turned. His tires brushed the curb and the hood cleared the thick border of an overgrown hedge as a blinding searchlight pinned him to the street. Gasping, he instinctively ducked behind the wheel, listening to the bright stillness. Cautiously he peered over the dash.

Motion detector light.

He let out a shaky breath and stepped on the emergency brake before slipping from the car. His jittery glance scanned the "For Rent" sign leaning against the trunk of an ancient pepper tree. Dozens of seedlings sprouted through its roots like a mutant forest. DC opened the garage and hurried back to the car.

The garage echoed with the sound of his engine as he pulled inside. He turned off the car and the silence seemed equally loud. The drop of the door, thunderous.

He left it dark as he popped open the trunk. The interior light reflected off the pale, tear-streaked oval of Jessica Jordan's face. Her eyes seemed to have swallowed her, the blue irises encircling giant pupils. She squinted in the dim light.

"Out," DC said, reaching for her arm.

She cowered back against the spare tire and whimpered. DC grabbed her by the arms and yanked her out. He set her roughly on her feet and shoved her to the door that led inside the house.

She stumbled, moving as if her legs had turned to rubber. After four hours in the trunk, maybe they had. It had been hot in the car. The trunk must have been an oven. Her hair stuck to her scalp, wet with sweat that dampened her shirt and streaked her face. DC followed her inside.

The house smelled of fresh paint and pesticides, sealed up for a long time. The girl hovered in the center of the living room, framed by the white shadow of the streetlight filtering through dirty sheers, as he made a silent inspection. DC yanked the curtains shut, plunging the room into darkness. Going back to the car, he grabbed a grocery bag and a hot pizza box from the front seat. When he returned, she was still in the same place.

He went to the kitchen and emptied the bag on the

counter. Plastic cups, toilet paper, a six-pack of beer, and a fifth of bourbon. Grabbing a beer for himself, he filled a cup with tap water.

"Jessica? Come here."

She shuffled in, her skinny arms wrapped around her torso in a protective hug. Her gaze silently tracked his movements.

"You did real good today, Jessie," he said, holding the cup above her reach. "I didn't hear a peep out of you, and I was listening. I guess you took my advice. Just keep on doing that and we'll get along just fine."

She nodded, standing mutely on the linoleum floor, and waited patiently for the water he finally handed to her. She gulped it down and held the cup out for more.

"Later. Let that hit your stomach first."

Tears welled up in her eyes as she stared at him, still holding her cup out. Shrugging, he took it and filled it again.

"You're going to barf," he said, giving it back to her. "Drink it slow or you'll be woofing."

She nodded and sipped, her gaze scanning the kitchen. It landed on the pizza and shot back to DC, as if she'd been caught looking at dirty pictures and feared punishment.

"Scared?" he asked.

She nodded, shivering.

"Good. You wondering about your mom?"

The girl's eyes filled with tears again. Another nod.

"Don't. She's gone."

"Gone where?" she whispered.

"It doesn't matter. She's gone."

"Did you kill her?"

He smiled. "Of course not. I don't look like a killer, do I?"

"I saw you."

"Saw me what?"

"Hurting her. She was screaming."

"No, you didn't."

He stared at her, daring her to argue. She didn't.

"You're pretty smart, girl. Sit down."

She remained as she was, staring at him with those terrified eyes.

"I said, sit down."

"What are you going to do to me?"

"No telling. Sit down."

She looked around as if expecting a chair to pop out of one of the walls. She sniffled and sat on the floor.

"Okay, Jessie. This is the way it's going to be. I'm God. I'm God and I own you and your mommy isn't coming back."

"I don't believe you," she said.

"Yeah? Well, you'd better start believing."

Slowly the girl scooted backward on the floor, gaze fixed intently on him. She tucked herself into a shadow in the corner. DC took another swig of his beer. The kid gave him the creeps.

"She will too come back," she said.

"Uh-uh."

"You're mean."

He chuckled. "I'm mean's big brother, little Jessie."

"That's not my name."

He ignored her, opening the box of pizza and grabbing a piece. He slapped it on a napkin for the girl. She scooted out of her shadow just far enough to reach it, then scurried back. Like a mouse. After a while, she peeped out again for another piece and more water. When she finished, he heard her yawn.

"Come with me," he said.

He pushed her toward the hallway. At the bathroom door, he stopped, swinging it open. A toilet, bathtub, sink, and cabinet took up all of the floor space, leaving only a small patch for the door to arc through.

He grabbed a blanket he'd brought in from the car and tossed it to her. Closing the door on her, he sank to the floor in the hall.

Suddenly he felt very tired. He blinked as the booze

and exhaustion fought for control of his mind. The kid was bawling. He could hear her scared sobs through the door, lulling him into a fitful sleep, where the sound of crying was his own. Outside, a dog began to bark. The floor of DC's mind shivered and cracked open over a terrifying darkness.

He was crying. DC was five years old again and he was crying.

His mother had a hold on his arm and she was marching down the dirt road. The air smelled wild and clean, full of honeysuckle and lilac. A bird called from the branches of a giant tree and, from over the hill, he could hear dogs barking.

"Keep up, DC," his mother said, yanking him along.

"But I don't wanna go to Grandpa's," he cried. "He's mean."

"Stop whining, Dwight Calvin. You're lucky he'll even let a bad boy like you under his roof."

"I don't want to be under his roof. I wanna go with you."

"I've told you, you can't go. I don't have enough money for that, but when I can come get you, I will. Now quit your crying. He'll change his mind if he think's you're a crybaby."

They crested the hill and looked down at the tiny brown house and matching shed centered in a dirty yard below. In the shadow of the house, two old cars sat on brick tires, looking like scary metal monsters to DC. A broken fence encircled an empty corral. Beside it, a giant chicken wire cage held three pacing dogs. One of them lifted its head and tested the air, as if smelling humans even at this distance. It began to bark.

"Let me see your face," his mother said, spinning him to face her.

He stared at her pretty red dress as she spit on her handkerchief and wiped his face. He wanted to wrap his arms around her legs and beg her not to leave him, but his mother didn't like him to touch her and he knew she wouldn't listen anyway.

"There you go," she said. "Listen to me, DC. This won't be so bad if you behave yourself. Your grandpa won't take none of your lip, so you best keep your trap shut. Just stay out of his way as much as you can."

DC nodded and sniffled. His mother picked up his small duffel bag. Suddenly, he was gripped with panic.

The dogs started circling their cage, barking fiercely as DC and his mom got closer. The air took on the thick smell of dog poop. DC wrinkled his nose. From inside the house a woman hollered, "Lou, would you shut them animals up?"

His mother's grip on DC's arm tightened and she shot him a warning glance. He blinked back more tears, stumbling along at her side.

She stepped onto the bottom step of the porch and then hesitated. She looked down at him, and something in her eye scared him.

"Wait here, DC, and don't you move. Hear? You sit right down on the steps and stay put."

He nodded, releasing her hand with reluctance. She wiped her palm on her hip before stepping up to the screen door and knocking.

"Mama?" she called. "Mama, it's me."

"Come on in," DC's grandma answered from the back of the house. His mother disappeared behind a slamming screen door, leaving DC in the hot sun with the caged dogs. They growled at him, sitting in a row and watching him through black eyes. Quickly he looked at his shuffling feet, making some patterns in the dust with the toe of his shoe. Finally, he looked up and stuck out his tongue at them.

"Like my dogs, boy?"

DC jumped and spun to see his grandpa standing behind him. He wore a dirty undershirt, and hair poked from the armholes and two jagged rips on the chest. He had scrawny white arms, the skin around them flabby and wrinkled. On the right one, a snake tattoo slithered from shoulder to elbow, its wicked tongue flicking from a scaled green head. His trousers were worn, and they stopped short of his ankles, revealing black boots without shoelaces.

"I asked you a question, boy. You stupid?"

DC shook his head.

"Is you a dummy?"

"No, sir."

"Then answer me when I talk to you, boy. I seen you looking at my dogs. Like 'em?"

"No, sir. They look mean."

Grandpa threw back his head and laughed. He whooped for a while, slapping his leg and wiping his face. DC didn't know what was so funny, but he smiled anyway.

"Mean they is, boy. Mean they is."

As if in response, the dogs' growling and pacing increased. DC flashed them a glance from the corner of his eye.

"Come on, boy. Let's go take a look at 'em."

DC shook his head.

"Aw, come on, boy. They's caged. You afraid they gonna eat right through and gobble you up like a rat?"

As he spoke he moved closer to DC and grabbed him, tickling his ribs hard enough to hurt. DC squirmed away and ended up closer to the cage. The dogs barked louder, the sound cracking through the clear air. A flock of birds gave up singing and took flight.

DC backed away, but Grandpa stood right behind him, pushing him forward. DC stumbled and fell in the dirt at the foot of the cage. His grandpa reached down and yanked him to his feet.

"You're acting like a goddamn sissy, boy. Is that what you is? A sissy?"

"No. I just don't like dogs."

"All boys like dogs. Except maybe sissies."

Bravely DC faced the cage, remaining as far away

as he thought he could without Grandpa pushing him closer.

"What kind of dogs you got in there, anyway?" DC asked. "Wolves?"

Grandpa belly laughed again, swatting DC on the back of the head. It hurt, but DC tried not to let it show.

"Them's pit bulls, boy. Best dogs in the world. See that one?" he asked, pointing to a mean-looking one with a tan body and white feet.

The dog's stubby ears swiveled at the familiar sound of his voice and it turned its huge head their way, grinning. Its thick neck bulged and its body tensed as it waited for a command.

"That one's Chopper. I seen him rip the head off a big ol' hound once. I ain't a-kidding, either. Clean off."

Grandpa tee-heed. DC felt sick.

"Want to pet him?"

DC shook his head violently.

Grandpa grabbed DC's shoulder roughly and pulled him toward the cage. "Come on, pet him. He wants you to. See? Look at his eyes."

DC *was* looking at his eyes and they looked mad as a swarm of bees. A streamer of slobber hung from Chopper's jagged rubber lips. He growled and the other two dogs, sensing that something exciting was about to happen, stopped their circling to watch.

"I don't want to pet him," DC cried as his grandpa pushed him closer. "I don't want to pet him. I don't want to. I don't—"

His grandpa snatched DC's hand from his side and thrust it through the chain link. Chopper looked at the small white fingers as if they were chicken wings. The muscles in his thick body coiled and Chopper flew across the small distance that separated him from DC just as DC's scream pierced the dusty yard.

With a mighty twist, DC wrenched his body from his grandpa's iron grip. He yanked his hand back through the fence as Chopper's teeth grazed the meaty flesh beneath his pinky finger. The pain seared up his arm as he collapsed to the ground.

"Dwight Calvin!" his mother yelled from the porch. "What are you doing? Bothering those dogs?" She stomped over to where he lay on the ground.

DC glared at his grandpa, who smiled serenely back. "What happened here?" she demanded.

"Just like you seen," Grandpa said before DC could squeak a sound out. "He was pestering my dogs. Lucky for him I was here to pull him back, else Chopper might'a eat him alive." He glared at DC. "Them dogs is in a cage for a reason, you damned fool boy."

"Oh, Pa, I'm so sorry," DC's mother said.

He shook his head. "Looks like he got bit, too."

His mother turned on DC, hands propped on her hips and anger glinting in her eyes. "Let me see that hand."

He held it up for her, feeling swamped with injustice and pain. She pulled her handkerchief from her purse and spit on it again, roughly wiping at the drying blood. "It's just a scratch," she announced. "You're darn lucky, young man, that your grandpa was here to help you. Now you stay away from them dogs. Come on, now. I want to talk to you."

She helped him off the ground and brushed the dust off him. They walked back, the way they had come, stopping at the foot of the hill.

"I didn't go near them dogs, Mama, Grandpa—"

"DC, I don't want to talk about the dogs and don't you start lying on top of it, anyway. I want you to say good-bye to me, now. I need to be leaving."

"When're you gonna be back?"

"I told you, I don't know for sure just yet. As soon as I can."

"But Mama, Grandpa made me put my hand in the cage. I didn't want to—"

"DC, what did I tell you about lying?"

"I'm not—"

She stared at him with exasperation. "Now why

would Grandpa go and do a thing like that? DC, I know you want to come with me, but you can't. I'll be back, though."

"When?"

"Soon. Just as soon as I can."

DC jerked himself awake. Outside, the dog had quit barking and behind the bathroom door, all was quiet. Easing his sore muscles from the hard floor, he went to the kitchen and grabbed the bottle of bourbon. He took a swig, chasing it with a warm beer. When his vision began to blur and the leftovers of his nightmare faded to a ghostly whisper, he staggered back to the hall and sat on the floor in front of the bathroom door.

Soon, his mother's voice still echoed in his mind. She'd said she'd be back soon.

But soon had turned out to be never, and DC was a big boy now.

13

Kathy Jordan awoke to the bleep of her own pulse dancing on a monitor to her left. She opened her eyes slowly, taking in the pulled curtains and shadowed silence of the white room. She understood immediately that she was in a hospital, but couldn't comprehend why. A feeling of panic nudged the back of her consciousness, demanding attention, teasing her with disjointed flashes of brutal memory.

And then it hit her.

Jessica.

Kathy jerked, bolting upright in bed.

Where was Jessica?

After three grueling hours of questioning and an unsuccessful attempt at hypnosis, the police finally left. Kathy sank back into her pillows as the early morning news droned on, scarcely varying tones with newscasters. Sports. Weather. Special Interest story. Kathy watched. Numbed by shock, sedated to the point of eye-tugging exhaustion, she forced herself awake for local news.

Jessica's kidnapping dominated the segment. While police scoured the scene for evidence, Jessica Jordan remained missing. Undeniable similarities existed between her abduction and other recent kidnappings. The police refused to comment on the differences.

A stone-faced reporter looked sympathetic as she broadcast to the whole world news of the brutal attack that Kathy had survived. She cringed as the screen flashed with the image of herself on a stretcher, wheeled by paramedics through a mass of blazing lights and blaring sirens.

Twelve hours later her condition had been downgraded from serious to stable and she would be released that afternoon. Her throat was purple and swollen and when she swallowed, it throbbed and burned. Teaching Jessica to call 911 in an emergency had probably saved Kathy's life.

Every inch of her body was bruised and battered, but her physical pain could not compare to the agony of the yawning emptiness inside when she thought of Jessica. It made her wish she had died. She brushed a stray tear from her cheek.

If this was stable condition, what was critical?

On the TV, the news reporter shoved her microphone under the nose of a big, blond man. Like a bear in street clothes, Mike Simens seemed out of sorts with the bright lights and attention. Kathy watched, surprise rooting her to the floor while recognition narrowed her gaze.

Mike Simens.

She hadn't thought about him since the last time she'd seen him—at Dan's funeral. The sight of his face now gave her hope in spite of the animosity that had always tainted their relationship. If anyone could find Jessica, Mike could. He was the best.

In response to the reporter's questions, Mike hemmed and hawed his way through excuses and explanations concerning the department's investigation into Jessica's kidnapping as well as the others as yet unsolved. Bottom line, they didn't know who the kidnapper was. Last word, all but a few bodies had been found.

All but a few . . .

Kathy blinked, her vision blurring as she stared at

her hospital room, barren but for the flowers sent from her office. It showed her just how alone she really was. Her tears raced down her cheeks in a flooding wave.

Where was Jessica? Where was her baby?

Thoughts too terrifying, too *horrifying* to think arched her back against the mattress and pulled her knees to her stomach.

"Where's my baby?" she whispered. "Where's my Jessica?

By noon, Kathy was easing her sore body from the backseat of the taxi. Standing on the curb, she stared at the yellow police tape that encircled her yard. It whipped in the hot breeze, making a snapping noise that jarred the tenuous grip she had on her composure. Two police cruisers were parked in her driveway, one Chevy on the curb in front. She felt as though she should have knocked as she opened her front door and met the startled looks of the workers inside.

She hesitated on the threshold, poised half-in, half-out. One of the men separated himself from the group and approached. He donned a sympathetic expression.

"Mrs. Jordan."

"Has there been any news of Jessica?" she asked.

"Ah, no."

"Have you discovered any clues? Do you have any leads?"

"Well, ma'am, we've recovered some *excellent* forensic evidence. That's what you want in court."

"I don't care about court. I care about Jessica and where the hell she is," Kathy said, her voice heavy with desperation. "Has he called for ransom?"

"Well, he wouldn't call us, ma'am."

"What about the other kidnappings? Did they have ransom demands?"

"No, ma'am."

"Just bodies when it was all over?"

He shifted his weight, flushing an angry red. "Yes,

ma'am, but we hooked your phone up with a tap just in case he calls."

"Thank you" seemed too ludicrous under the circumstances, so she settled for a nod. Looking at the busy crew, she felt in the way. Extraneous. She needed action. Results. Anything to keep her thoughts off Jessica and the gut-wrenching fear her daughter surely was feeling.

"Is there something I should be doing?" she asked.

"No, ma'am. We'll be here a few more hours, then we'll be out of your hair and you can get on with things."

Get on with things? Was he serious?

"Where is Detective Simens?"

The man faltered, clearing his throat as he avoided eye contact. "Detective Simens isn't on this case anymore."

"Why not?"

"Reassignment, ma'am."

She frowned, looking at the fine dark powder that dusted her counters and tabletops, while her brain teased her with flashes of terror and fear. A hand ripping her underwear ... Her screams pounding against the walls ... *Stop it.*

She felt nauseous and the floor beneath her suddenly felt soft. She excused herself and went to the bathroom, locking herself in and the cold voices of reality out. She sat on the lid of the toilet and hugged herself, gently rocking her empty arms.

She didn't know how long she'd been that way when a knock on the door woke her, as if from a trance.

"Mrs. Jordan? Are you all right?"

"Yes. Yes, I'm fine."

She stood and turned on the water faucets, filling the sink.

"Not a good start," she whispered to her reflection as she splashed water on her face and rinsed her mouth. "Not if you want your daughter back."

The sound of her own voice reassured her. She'd made it through Dan's death, and she would make it through this. But she would not sit and wait for tomorrow to happen. Never again would she leave something to chance.

She would go to see Mike. Ask why he'd abandoned Jessica's case. Convince him to return to it.

Mike had been Dan's best friend. Surely he wouldn't have left the investigation if he'd known that the kidnapped Jessica and Dan's only child were the same little girl. She could use that relationship to guarantee Mike's cooperation. Even though their dislike for each other was mutual, Kathy couldn't imagine him turning his back on her. She was, after all, Dan's widow and Jessica, Dan's daughter.

She ignored the workers' curious looks as she left the sanctuary of the bathroom. She searched out the man she'd spoken to before and asked, "Where can I find Detective Simens?"

"At the station. Least that's where he was when I left."

No one argued when she stepped out the front door. They all knew there'd be no phone call to wait for.

A uniformed woman at the front counter of the police station directed Kathy to Mike's desk. The sight of him, a big man sitting at a too-small desk, amplified her anxiety. Kathy couldn't help regretting their last encounter, when she'd accused him of being responsible for the biking accident that had killed her husband.

He looked up as she crossed the room, acting neither surprised nor concerned about her appearance. He let her hobble to his desk with barely a flicker of sympathy.

"Well, this is just what the day needed," he said in the deep, gravelly voice she remembered so well.

She lowered herself into the chair at the side of his desk. "It's good to see you, too, Mike."

"What are you doing here?"

"I saw you on TV. You were investigator in charge of Jessica's case. Now I'm told you're reassigned. Why?"

"Why?" he repeated, his bushy brows nearly disappearing under a thatch of hair that covered his forehead. "Well, I'll tell you, Kathy," he said sarcastically. "The captain thinks someone else would do a better job. You see, I'm not finding the bad guys fast enough, so they've decided to give someone else a shot at it."

"You can't be serious."

"Hell, they did me a favor," he continued, his angry tone belying his words. "The FBI's in on it now. I hate those guys."

"FBI?"

"Yeah, today one of the girls—not Jess, the other one—she was sighted in Seattle. Crossing state lines gets the FBI involved. I keep telling them that Jessica's still here, but they don't listen to lowly detectives."

"You think she's still here in San Diego? Alive?"

"I don't have anything to back it up with, but yeah, my gut tells me it's true."

"I can't believe you've been taken off her case. How can they even consider bringing in someone new? Someone who doesn't know what's going on? Someone who has to start all over? You're the best! Where's your superior? I want to talk to him."

Mike's thunderstruck expression quickly changed to one of displeasure. "Don't you start defending me. I've got enough problems without you on my side. Holy shit, I need a vacation."

He stared at her, finally acknowledging her bruises with a lingering look.

"How are you, anyway?"

"How do I look?"

"You look like hell."

"That's pretty close. Were you there last night?"

"At your house?" he asked, tapping his desk with

his pen. "Yeah, I was there. Then I got called on the second kidnapping and all hell broke loose."

He dropped his face into his hands and rubbed. A heavy blond stubble covered his cheeks. It looked like it had been days since he'd last shaved.

"Do you have any leads, Mike? Please tell me you have some clues."

"Clues? I got more clues than I know what to do with. Trouble is, I can't make any sense out of them. I'm still searching for a motive—I *was* searching that is. Have you remembered anything yet? About what Jessica's kidnapper looks like?"

"No. I can remember what happened, but he's just a shadow. No face. They even tried to hypnotize me while I was in the hospital, but it didn't work."

"That's pretty typical in trauma cases. Don't beat yourself up about it. It will come in time."

"I don't have time. *Jessica* doesn't have time. Someone has punched a hole through my chest and yanked out my reason for living, Mike, and I want some justice."

He lit a cigarette, watching her through the smoke. She blinked, her eyes watering as a stinging cloud drifted her way.

"What are you doing here, Kathy?" he asked at last.

She looked down at her jeans, smoothing the fabric with her finger, groping for an easy way to beg for his help. Being here went against the grain, but the sound of Jessica's terrified screams echoing in her mind gave her strength and determination to do whatever it took.

"I want you to help me find Jessica," she said.

He took a drag of his cigarette. "I told you. I'm off the case."

"I want you back on."

"Well, I hate to say this, but what you want doesn't have a lot of pull around here. I can't even get the inside on what's happening anymore."

"So investigate on your own."

"I could lose my job for it."

"So take a vacation. You said you needed one."

"Vacation, hell, that would be early retirement."

"I suppose it was naive of me to expect your cooperation. I thought you'd want to help me, if for no other reason than out of loyalty to an old friend."

"Oohh, that one hurt. And here I was afraid you'd turned nice on me. You hate my guts, Kathy. Why come to me?"

"Because you're the best damn cop on the force. I don't expect you to want to help me, but what about Dan's daughter? Don't you care about her?"

He ground his cigarette into an overflowing ashtray and glared at her through the haze. She stared back, refusing to be intimidated by his glowering expression. Refusing to back down when she had nowhere else to turn.

"Hell, what a goddamn day," he said suddenly, his gravelly voice so deep it vibrated. "Okay. Let's hear it."

Kathy paused, blinking her confusion.

"What happened?" he said. Then, with a deep sigh, "Tell me what happened last night."

"He was waiting in the house when we got home," she answered.

"What time?"

"About seven. Around there."

"Were any of your doors unlocked when you got home?"

"I don't know. I can't remember if I locked the back door when we left that morning. We were late and . . . and I don't know how he got in."

"So he was waiting? Did he go for you or Jessica first?"

"Jessica was in the kitchen and I was in my room when I heard her scream. I ran out and then he . . . we fought. He knocked me out. Jessica ran away, but she ran to my room. She didn't know any better. She thought she'd be safe there, I guess." Her voice cracked on the last words.

"How could you see where Jessica ran if you were unconscious?"

Kathy paused defensively, her chin jutting at an angle. "Jessica must have run first. It all happened so fast."

"How did he knock you out? Did he hit you with something?"

"You're enjoying this, aren't you?" she demanded.

He lowered his chin and gave her a look that made her squirm. Of course he wasn't enjoying it. She was just being defensive. Mike had always brought out that side of her.

"If you want my help, I have to know the facts," he said.

"Well, what does it matter how?"

"It matters a lot."

"If you want the facts, why don't you just read the report?"

"I have read the report. Look, Kathy, I know you're trying to forget last night instead of remember it, but you're an eyewitness. You know who took Jessica. Give me the facts and maybe I can figure out who it was, too. Then we'll catch us a kidnapper."

Mike lit another cigarette. With a pointed stare, Kathy moved her chair to the other side of his desk, out of the path of smoke.

"You know I can't remember everything that happened," she said at last, keeping her words low and controlled.

"You seemed to be doing all right to me."

She straightened her back and steadied her gaze. Slowly, in a detached voice, Kathy repeated what she remembered of that night including as many details as she could muster. ". . . and then he raped me. He was strangling me. Squeezing tighter and tighter until I couldn't breathe anymore . . . I blacked out."

"How tall is he?"

She paused, picturing his faceless form hovering above her. "About five-ten, I think."

"What color hair does he have?" Mike whispered.

She gave him a blank stare.

"Hair, Kathy. What color?"

"Blond."

"Eyes?"

She widened her own in amazement. "Blue."

"Can you picture his face? Try, think about his eyes, think about his face."

She shook her head, sighing. "No. No face."

"It's okay," he said. "It'll come. In the meantime, we'll check out the mug shots again. What happened next?"

"When I regained consciousness I was on my living room floor. The police were already there and so was an ambulance." She lowered her face so he couldn't see the tears in her eyes. "Jessica was gone."

"Okay," Mike said. "So let's get her back."

14

The next morning when Christie came down the stairs, Sam was waiting for her. He sat on a barstool at the counter, sipping coffee and reading the paper. He hadn't showered yet and his hair stuck up in a swirl from the side to the front. A light stubble shadowed his lean cheeks and his eyes glowed with the same sleepy brightness that they always had when he first woke up.

He smiled at her, letting his gaze touch her. When they were still happily married, Sam had told Christie that he loved her best in the morning. It hurt now to think of those happy times when she considered that such sentiments had been tossed out, without thought, like bright pennies into a fountain.

"Good morning," he said.

She answered his greeting, feeling suddenly shy and very aware of her crumbling defenses. She poured herself a cup of coffee and sat down next to him. His shoulder brushed hers as he handed her a section of the paper. The light scent of coffee and newspaper dragged her farther into the past.

"Christie?" he said.

She looked up to find him staring at her. He seemed to be choosing his words with care, as if each were of utmost importance. She held her breath, waiting expectantly for him to continue.

126

"I was thinking . . . Why don't we go see the lawyer who handled your mom's estate?"

She exhaled, wondering what she'd thought he was going to say that made her feel so disappointed now.

"Why do you want to see him?" she asked.

"He might know something about DC. Do you remember who it was?"

"Yeah, I remember his name. We corresponded forever, it seemed. But I've only actually spoken to him on the phone a few times and I never met him. What do you think he'll know about DC?"

"Maybe nothing, but it won't hurt to check."

"I guess."

The sophisticated letterhead that Leonard Pfeiffer used matched the elegance of his office. The elevator transported them to his floor with a swish of closing doors and the humming cadence of precision. The air had a lingering floral fragrance that managed to smell both synthetic and recycled.

Inside the box-shaped lobby, Southwestern paintings hung from the pristine walls, their peaceful scenes at odds with the sleek technology between them. The secretary ceased her rapid-fire assault on her keyboard long enough to look their way with a generic smile.

"Mrs. McCoy?" she said before Christie had the chance to introduce herself. "Mr. Pfeiffer will be right with you."

Christie and Sam took seats on the seafoam green sofa next to a whitewashed oak end table with a clay lamp in its center. After a few minutes Leonard Pfeiffer hurried through the door. Dressed in an expensive charcoal gray suit that hung awkwardly on his frame, as if it had been tailored for a man of a different build, he smiled and offered a cool and moist handshake. His palms felt silky smooth.

Christie shook his hand, trying not to stare at his ears, which stuck out like handlebars from a V-shaped face. The light bounced off his shiny forehead and disappeared in the edged valleys of his cheeks, giving him a weasely look that didn't quite match his regulation crew cut.

"Pleasure to meet you face-to-face," he said.

"Thank you for making time to see me on such short notice," Christie answered, introducing Sam. Pfeiffer motioned for them to follow him down the hall.

His office echoed the tasteful theme of the lobby, full of whitewashed wood, Native American pots and carved totems. His diploma hung on the wall, encased and matted, at obvious cost. Above it hung the certificate reputing excellence in the law by the Supreme Court of the State of California. Christie and Sam sat in the two chairs facing his oversized desk.

"Now what can I do for you, Christie?"

"I'm not really sure you can do anything," she began when Sam interrupted.

"How long were you Mary Jane's attorney?" he asked. "I mean, before she died?"

Pfeiffer blinked several times, bouncing a questioning look between the two of them. When he answered, he spoke to Christie.

"A couple of months, I believe."

Sam nodded. "How did she find you?"

"How did she . . . ? I imagine she used the phone book."

"She wasn't referred?"

Pfeiffer's expansive forehead furrowed in a frown. "No, I don't believe she came by referral. As I recall, she wanted to write a trust and I assisted her. I advertise as an estate lawyer in the yellow pages as do most of my colleagues. You said on the phone that there was a problem with the estate?" he prompted. "Some trouble?"

"We're trying to piece together some facts about Mary Jane's estate," Sam said. "Specifically, we want to know how she got the residence in La Jolla that is now Christie's.''

Pfeiffer stared at him hard, his eyes squinty and measuring. "Are you with the police, Mr. McCoy? Because I have the definite feeling I'm being questioned.''

"I'm sorry, Mr. Pfeiffer,'' Christie answered before Sam had the chance. "We don't mean to make you feel that way. It's just that things have been a little . . . *stressed* lately and it may have something to do with the house.''

"Well,'' the attorney said. "I assume your mother purchased the house. She had it in her possession when she came to me.''

"And when was that?'' Sam asked.

"A few weeks before she died.''

Sam leaned forward, his hands gripping the edge of Pfeiffer's desk. "I thought you said she'd been your client for months?''

"That was an approximation, Mr. McCoy, and since you are asking for privileged information. I'm afraid I won't be able to assist you further. I simply cannot violate client confidentiality laws.''

"But the client's dead,'' Sam insisted. "You can't keep a dead person's confidence.''

He leaned back in his executive chair and studied them over templed fingers. "Tell me, Mr. McCoy. Where did you get your law degree? Confidentiality goes to the grave. I will tell you this, as the trustee of her estate, I've transferred all the property. There is no more. As simple as that.''

Christie nodded. "We understand your position, Mr. Pfeiffer, but we are desperate for information. Could you tell us if she ever mentioned a DC Porter in your dealings with her?''

He blinked again, considering her request. Apparently making a decision, he pushed back, the wheels of his chair whirring over the plastic mat underneath as he reached for his phone. He punched a button, then spoke to his secretary, requesting Christie's mother's file. The secretary whisked into his office moments later and gave it to him. Pfeiffer scanned the contents.

"DC Porter, DC Porter," he mumbled to himself as he flipped through the pages. "Relative?" he asked Christie.

"No."

"I don't see his name."

"She asked if Mary Jane ever mentioned him. Does his name mean anything to you?"

The attorney leveled a cold look at Sam. "I am a very busy man, Mr. McCoy. I don't have time to familiarize myself with the personal lives of my clients."

"Of course not, Mr. Pfeiffer," Christie said, giving Sam a warning look. "We thought she might have discussed him, though."

"Not that I recall." He checked his watch. "If that answers your questions, I have another appointment now that I must prepare for."

"Well, thank you for your time," Christie said, rising.

Sam looked as if he would argue, but then thought better of it and followed Christie out of the building into the blinding sunshine.

When the door closed behind them, Christie looked at Sam and said, "You didn't have to bite his head off, Sam."

"The guy was lying."

"About what? He said he handled her estate and I know for a fact that he did."

"He was lying about DC."

"How do you know? It seems more likely that he was telling the truth. There's no reason for him to know anything about DC, Sam."

"You're telling me you think he's for real? Did you really buy that confidentiality crap?"

"It sounded legit to me. I think you're getting yourself worked up over nothing."

"Nothing? Don't tell me you didn't notice how he evaded my questions."

"Sam, you may not realize this, but you came on just a wee bit strong in there. He was probably waiting for you to whip out your automatic and blow him away. I wouldn't have cooperated with you either."

Sam seemed to consider what Christie said, then surprised her by grinning.

"I guess I did get a little excited and carried away," he said with an embarrassed smile.

Christie nodded, feeling an answering grin on her lips as she climbed into the Jeep. Suddenly, it occurred to her what she was doing. Smiling. He had her smiling. Wasn't that what she'd just warned herself about yesterday?

Smiling, laughing, forgiving him?

Already she was feeling happy to be with him and last night she'd begun to think that maybe he hadn't been so wrong ... But that wasn't true. He had been wrong. He'd betrayed her trust. No matter what the reason, Sam had betrayed her.

She gave herself a mental shake coupled with a warning. It would be easy to forget the past and move on, but Sam had ripped her in two when he'd cheated on her. She wasn't strong enough to survive that again, and she wasn't so naive as to think there wouldn't be another time. She'd seen her mother battle the same problem in too many relationships and she'd never emerged the winner. Sam had been breaching Christie's barriers at warp speed, but she wasn't ready to surrender the fort to him.

He jumped in on his side and started the Jeep, glancing her way as he did.

"Christie?"

She forced the smile back on her face, but it didn't fool either one of them. "I was just thinking of DC."

He nodded, accepting her answer without question. "The bastard. And that ... that *attorney* is in on it too.

I'll admit I jumped the gun a bit in there, but I still think he's lying.'' Sam checked his watch. ''Let's go see what they know at your mom's clinic. We should have gone there in the first place.''

As they pulled into the heavy traffic on La Mesa Boulevard, Christie stared at her surroundings, realizing for the first time just how close Pfeiffer's office was to the house her mother used to live in. Suddenly, Christie wanted to go there and see it.

''Let's drive by my mom's old place.''

''Why?'' Sam asked, glancing from the road.

''I don't know. Just to see. It's not far and it's on the way.''

They headed east, into the bright morning sun, fighting traffic that bunched in narrowed lanes. Angry drivers blared their horns at the construction crews that seemed to tear up roads just so they could repair them. The business district bordered tiny neighborhoods that degenerated as they made their way past the numerous apartment buildings. Christie leaned against the door, withdrawing into herself as Sam drove. Several times she knew he glanced her way, wordlessly questioning her sudden silence. Staunchly, she avoided his looks, afraid of what he might see in her eyes if she allowed him a glimpse.

Finally free of the jammed cars, Sam turned and parked in front of the small, pale green house. They sat for a minute, neither making a move to get out.

''Christie? Is something wrong?''

''No.''

''Then why are you so quiet all of a sudden?''

She shook her head. ''No reason.''

''You're sure? Because something about the way you're sitting over there—way over there, as in as far away from me as you can get in a car—that reminds me of something you used to do when you were mad at me.''

''I'm not mad, Sam,'' she said, scooting from the

car before he could question her further. She didn't
want to get into her private feelings with him. She'd
already said too much to him and now she felt vulnerable. She heard Sam's frustrated sigh as he followed her.
Ignoring the tight corners of his lips and the irritated
gleam in his eyes, she stepped onto the sidewalk and
faced the house.

It was just as she remembered, but now a brown
layer of neglect covered it, giving it a faded, run-down
look. The lush carpet of grass her mother had nurtured
was now withered to a dried sienna.

How fast things change.

Broken glass surrounded a front window that had
been "repaired" with a piece of cardboard. The screen
door hung cockeyed on its hinges. On the side of the
house, a haze of frenzied flies buzzed over a black-
green trash bag and nearby, a couple of wild-looking
cats lolled in the sunshine. Christie wrinkled her nose
at the pungent odor that drifted toward her, frowning
at the trash.

"Pfeiffer sold this house to settle the estate," she
said.

"The new owners don't take very good care of it,"
Sam said. "Your mom would cry if she saw this."

"I wonder if someone is living here? See that
trash?"

Sam nodded and shrugged.

"Don't you think that's strange?" she asked.

"That they have trash?" he said. "No."

"But it doesn't look like anyone's even living here."

"Do you want me to knock on the door?"

"Are you crazy?" Christie said. "What if *he's* in
there?"

"Then I'll kick the holy shit out of him."

"He's a killer, Sam."

He stared at her coldly. "He's a woman-beating
chicken shit and if anyone should be scared, it's him."

With that, Sam marched to the front door and

pounded, waited a few seconds and banged again. Christie watched in the anticlimactic silence as a prickle of sweat slipped down her back.

"Hello? Anyone home?" Sam called.

A stranger's voice answered from behind them. "He's not around."

They both jumped and spun to see the old man on the sidewalk at the end of the drive. He'd approached silently, even though his six-foot framed carried considerable bulk.

He wore camouflage pants and a flannel shirt buttoned to the neck in defiance of the blazing heat. His smile unearthed yellowed teeth that were staggered in the uneven turf of his gums like ancient ivory tombstones. Whiskers poked from his face like spines from a shriveled cactus. His flesh was the color of eggshells and it sagged on his bones.

"He's not around. Hasn't been since yesterday," the man said, nodding while he spoke, as if agreeing with himself.

Sam stepped off the porch and approached the man. "Him who?"

"DC. That's who you're looking for, aren't ya?"

"DC? You know DC?" Christie asked.

The man nodded, stepping closer. He smelled of Old Spice and motor oil. "I know him by sight. I know his comin's and goin's, you might say. Not that I spy. He's just the loudest sumbitch I've ever heard. He's got a car that sounds like a goddamn locomotive. That's the truth."

Christie shook her head in disbelief. "And he lives here?"

"Well he's only been back a few days. He took off just before the woman died. You related to her?"

"I'm her daughter."

"Thought so. It's the eyes."

"Did you know my mother?"

"Just to share a hello. I was sorry when she passed. She took good care of the place."

Christie shook her head in confusion. "I thought this house had been sold after my mother died?"

"Naw. It hasn't been for sale that I've seen, anyway."

Sam frowned, staring at Christie. This time he didn't even attempt to disguise his irritation with her. In fact, it seemed to have boiled to quite pissed off.

It was typical of him to get mad at her simply because he didn't understand her. Some things change too fast; others, not at all.

"Didn't you see the documentation on the sale, Christie?" he asked.

"I had a lot on my mind at the time, Sam. I thought I saw it, but I don't know."

"You would have had to sign it."

She looked away.

"Don't tell me you signed something that *Pfeiffer* gave you without reading it first?" he said, as if the very thought were too unthinkable to verbalize.

"I had a lot on my mind, Sam," she repeated through clenched teeth. "I don't even *remember* everything that I signed at the time."

"Do you have copies?"

"Yes, at home."

"I think it might be smart to take a look." Sam looked back at the man who watched them with interest. "What about DC? You say he's living here?"

"If you could call it that. He's in and out like a wild wind. Lights go on and off a hundred times a night, but he don't stay put longer than an hour or two."

Christie looked over her shoulder as if expecting DC to zoom into the driveway as they stood there talking about him. She couldn't suppress the shiver that shook her at the thought.

"When was the last time he was here?" Sam asked, following Christie's troubled gaze down the street.

"Like I said, I saw him yesterday, hanging around like a skunk with the runs."

"Huh?"

"Back and forth. In the house, out the house. Screen door must have slammed fifty times if it slammed once. Not that I was watching him, mind you. It was just too damn hot to sit in the house. I was on my porch."

"What time did he leave?" Christie asked.

"I'd say it was about three. I hope he's gone for good, but I know that that's too much to ask for. He'll be back, that shitty sumbitch."

Sam reached in his pocket and pulled out a business card. "Would you give me a call if he comes back, Mr. . . . ?"

"Ives. Delmont Ives. Folks call me Del."

Sam shook Del's hand, introducing himself and Christie.

"I'd be glad to give you a ring if I see him. Got a beef with DC, do you?"

Sam's grin held little amusement. "You might say that."

15

"What do you think?" Christie asked as they walked away.

"I think we need to go over the estate papers as soon as we get home."

"You think Pfeiffer lied?"

"I'd say that's a fair bet."

"You're upset, aren't you?"

"Another winner."

He turned to watch her. "I just don't get you, Christie. One minute I think we're connecting—the next, you're huddled against the door like I'm some kind of monster. I thought we had an understanding. I thought we were going to try to talk and be open with each other."

"We are," she said, not quite meeting his eyes. "I've told you everything."

"Everything about DC—maybe," he said softly. "About your mother—maybe. But not about you. When it comes to you, I'm always left waiting."

The sincerity in his tone made her feel lost and defensive. "What do you want from me, Sam?" she demanded more sharply than she'd intended. "We have one morning of shared coffee and suddenly everything else is changed? I don't think so."

"What about last night?"

"Oh, sorry. One night and one morning. You're pushing again, Sam."

"And you're running away again, Christie."

She stared at him hard. "I never stopped running."

He opened her side of the Jeep and slammed it after she got in. By the time he circled to his side, though, he closed the door with less force. He started the Jeep and asked in a tired voice, "Where to? The clinic?"

"If you still want to."

They drove in awkward silence, with a depressing gnaw of tension between them. Back to square one.

Christie sighed. "Pull over if you see a pay phone, please. I don't know what good it will do, but I want to leave a message with the police. Let them know DC's name and tell them what Del said."

Sam pulled into a Circle K and bought a couple of sodas and a bag of chips as he waited. He chomped a few Fritos, watching her make the call.

She was right. He was pushing. What was it about her that made him act that way? He shook his head, starting the engine as she hung up and walked back to the Jeep. The wind teased her hair, chasing it across her face. She brushed it back with a careless hand, the movement somehow graceful. Sam didn't need to ask himself what it was about her that he couldn't resist.

"Well?" he asked, handing her a soda once she'd closed the door and fastened her seat belt.

She shrugged. "At least this time the person I talked to had a sympathetic ear—he listened, not that it'll do me any good. Did you know that two little girls got kidnapped yesterday?"

"Two?"

She nodded. "The police don't know if they're related or separate crimes. I get the impression that they're afraid all the sickos are coming out of the woodwork and snatching those poor kids."

Sam passed her the chips, merging back into traffic as noon drivers attacked the roads. He dodged an illegal U-turner bent on reaching a drive-thru before anyone else and tried to concentrate on what the lunchtimers weren't—the road.

"This whole damn city is full of nuts," he said. "DC fits right in."

"You've got that right," Christie agreed, glad for the truce that seemed to have been struck while she was on the telephone.

"You know what though?" Sam said. "This DC, he's not just crazy. I've got this feeling . . . Maybe *I'm* the one who's nuts, but I think DC and Pfeiffer have something going. Maybe some scam . . . something to do with the houses. Who knows what Pfeiffer had you sign."

"You think I signed everything over to him or something?"

"That's exactly what I think. And then he hired DC to kill you."

"Let's not get carried away."

"It makes perfect sense."

"But it doesn't explain where the house in La Jolla came from in the first place, Sam."

"That's right. But we're going to go through those papers as soon as we get back. I'll bet somewhere we find the name of the original owner. If not, I've got a friend who'll help us out. I want to get copies of your papers to *my* lawyer too. At least she's honest."

Christie stared out the window, thinking about Sam's theory. Pfeiffer and DC. It didn't sound right, but then again . . .

"You know, Sam. I do remember something Pfeiffer said in a phone conversation. He told me he'd helped my mom make some shrewd investments—" Christie turned halfway in her seat. "He said he'd helped her acquire the house with the profits. I just remembered that. At the time, it made sense. At the time, he could have said it was a gift from the king and I'd have believed it. I wasn't thinking clearly. It sounded plausible anyway."

"But Pfeiffer just told us she had the house when she came to him."

"I know."

Sam parked the Jeep in the lot that the Beth McClain Clinic shared with Vons and Osco Drugs and stared for a moment. A concrete walkway flounced the sunset-stuccoed building on two floors. An outside stairway with a wrought-iron railing climbed the side and connected the top to the bottom. As they stepped from the air-conditioned comfort of the Jeep, the hot sun burned them.

"I'm so sick of this heat," Christie complained, unconsciously eyeing the parking lot for DC's menacing face.

Sam grinned. "What heat?"

He could be comfortable in a sauna.

In spite of her complaint, Christie shivered as she stared at the door to the clinic. Suite 103. The last time she'd been there replayed in her mind. She'd been so scared. It seemed now that she'd spent each day since in a state of waiting. Waiting for DC.

"Hey? Christie? You there?" Sam asked, pausing to look over his shoulder at her.

She nodded. "I guess I just realized how much I hate DC. All this time, all these months, I've been so busy being afraid of him. It never occurred to me how much I hate him. That he should be afraid of me, too. I wonder if he's smart enough to know that?"

"Not yet, but we'll educate him."

Sam opened the door to the clinic and they entered the hushed reception area. The air conditioner silently chilled the climate to an icy cool and the carpet muffled their steps. A small bell tinkled as the door swung closed behind them. The place was bittersweet with memories of Christie's mother. She missed her so much.

They stood just inside while their eyes adjusted to

the muted elegance of the dim lobby. In seconds, a woman appeared from around the corner.

"Christie?" she exclaimed. "Christie, is that you?"

Beth McClain crossed from her office to where they stood, opening her arms like a soft, worn quilt and wrapping Christie in a warm embrace. Pressing her face to Beth's sweet-smelling shoulder, Christie felt tears prick her eyes. This woman had done so much for her mother. Employed her. Shown her respect. Taught her respect. Given her the confidence at last to be a mother to Christie.

"Oh, it's so good to see you. I wanted to call you, and then I'd change my mind and decide to come see you and then . . . time just got away and I was embarrassed by it. I'm so sorry. I should have gotten in touch."

Christie pulled back, sniffling and nodding. "It's okay, Beth. I thought about calling too . . ."

"Well, you're here now. And who's this? Your husband?"

Sam leaned forward and shook Beth's outstretched hand. "Sam McCoy."

"I thought so. Your mother was so pleased when you two married." She winked at Christie. "She thought a lot of her son-in-law."

Christie felt a blush creep up her cheeks. Someone should invent a separation announcement to prevent scenes like this one.

"What am I doing, standing here gabbing? Come in. Let's have a cup of coffee or tea or something."

As she spoke, Beth led them down the hall. On the way, they passed the closed door that once opened into Christie's mother's office. A new nameplate was stuck on the door.

"You did get your mother's things, didn't you?" Beth asked, following Christie's gaze.

"Yes, thank you for sending them. I wasn't looking forward to coming down and packing them myself."

"I figured as much. I felt so bad about missing the services. I was out of town when I heard and I couldn't get my flight changed for anything."

"The flowers you sent were beautiful, Beth. She would have loved them."

They'd entered a cramped lunchroom, equipped with a Mr. Coffee, an honor snack bar, and a small refrigerator. A steel-legged table sat in the middle, surrounded by plastic chairs. The room was uncomfortably cold in both temperature and atmosphere, but Beth didn't seem to mind. She busied herself at the coffee machine.

Sam and Christie sat down.

"So what brings you to visit this old lady, Christie?"

Christie laughed. "You're not old, Beth. You'll never be old."

"Bless your heart."

Christie searched for the words to explain why they were there, but none came. Sam, for once, remained silent.

"We came," Christie began slowly, "because . . . Do you remember DC Porter? He used to work here?"

Beth faced them as the coffee began to drip into the pot. "You mean the custodian?"

"That's right."

"Of course I remember him. Why?"

"Well, he's been bothering me—actually, he's attacked me. Twice. I was hoping you might have some information that would help us find him?"

"*Attacked?* Christie, I can't believe this. Did you call the police? Of course you called them. What are they doing?"

"Not much. They're pretty wrapped up in the kidnappings."

"This is unbelievable. But why would he . . . I mean he and your mother . . ."

"Yeah, they had a thing going. And then he left town suddenly. Do you know why?"

"I certainly do. I fired him."

"Why?" Sam asked, leaning forward.

"Because he was lazy and a thief. And I caught him smoking marijuana right here in my clinic."

"Do you know where he went after that?"

"No. I don't, Christie. I paid him his final wages and told him to hit the road. That's the last I've seen of him."

Beth poured three cups of coffee without asking if they wanted any and set them on the table. Packets of cream and sugar appeared from a white cupboard. Finally she sat down.

"Did you fire him before or after he helped my mother with the adoption?" Christie asked.

Beth froze, her coffee cup suspended halfway to her lips. "What adoption?"

"I was here one day, before he left. I came to take my mother to lunch, but she was on her way to a consultation. DC was going with her."

"You must be mistaken, honey. DC was the custodian. He cleaned the toilets. He never assisted with adoptions."

Christie sipped her coffee, now grateful for the warmth. "My mother said it was a special situation. That DC knew the mother—"

Beth was shaking her head. "Impossible. I am familiar with all the proceedings that take place in this clinic. I certainly would have remembered a case that involved DC."

She paused, seeming to choose her words with care. "Christie, I hate to say this, but maybe your mother . . . She knew how much you disliked DC, and I must admit I shared your opinion of that man. Maybe she felt she had to lie to you."

Silently Sam watched the exchange. Christie met his gaze for a moment, then looked away. Beth could be right. When Christie thought about it, her mother would have lied to avoid a scene over DC.

"I loved your mother, Christie. She was one of the

dearest, kindest people I ever met. She was perfect for
this job. Her caring just reached out and touched people. The girls who came here for help took to Mary
Jane and she held their hands through every step. She'd
even take the time to follow up. Let the girls know their
babies were fine. Make sure the girls were doing okay.''

Christie felt tears well up in her eyes as a traitorous
thought popped into her mind. *Why couldn't my mother
have been there for me, as she had been for those
unknown girls?* Under the table, Sam covered her icy
hand with his, kneading warmth back into her fingers.

"Your mother was a saint, Christie. But she didn't
know a damn thing about choosing a man. Every time
she'd come in singing and giggling and talking about
her latest love, I'd wish he'd get run over by a car or
something quick and merciful, because I knew he'd end
up breaking your mother's heart. I couldn't help myself.
And I was never wrong. Not once.''

"I know," Christie said in a low voice. "I used to
think the same thing.''

"DC was the worst of them. I always felt responsible
because I hired him. And to tell you the truth, I was
just looking for a way to get rid of him when I caught
him smoking in the bathroom. I don't think your mother
ever forgave me for firing him.''

"I'm sure she did, Beth. Mom couldn't hold a
grudge. Especially not against you.''

"It seemed that she changed, though, after that. I
was prepared for her usual mourning period. A week
or two and she'd be back on the hunt. You know how
she was. But she never did snap out of it. She never
had the chance.''

Christie sniffed. "I know. But if DC had stayed
around, he might have hurt her worse. He might have
even killed her.''

Beth looked up, suddenly very still. "Do you think
he did?''

"Kill her?" Christie exclaimed. "No, I never considered that. He was gone—had been for weeks before . . . And it was an accident. Wasn't it?''

The women stared at one another across the table.

''Of course you're right,'' Beth said. ''I'm letting my imagination get carried away. He was long gone when her accident happened.''

Sam gave Christie's hand another squeeze and then asked, ''Do you still have your records on him? His last address?''

Beth hesitated for a moment. ''Well, let me see if I do.''

She pushed away from the table and left the room, high heels clicking against the stark tile before being silenced by the carpet in the hallway. After she left, Christie looked at Sam.

''Are you okay?'' he asked in a soft voice.

''I guess. It's just hard to talk about my mom in the past tense. I've barely said a word about her since she died, and now I've talked about her every day. It's bringing all the hurt to the surface.''

''It's good for you, Christie. You can't keep bottling up your emotions.''

She smiled. ''What is this, therapy?''

''No, that comes later.''

''Here we are,'' Beth said, entering without warning, holding a slim file in her hands. ''All I have is his application, and I'm afraid everything on it will be out-dated. DC wasn't the type to stay in one place very long.''

''Any chance we could have a copy of it?'' Sam asked.

She hesitated for another brief moment. ''I suppose it would be okay, as long as you keep it between us. I certainly don't want it to get around that I gave it to you.''

Beth disappeared again, returning with a copy of the application. Sam took the sheet of paper from her.

"Thank you, Beth. We appreciate this. One other question, though."

"Shoot."

"Do you know how she got the house in La Jolla?"

The question clearly startled Beth. She blinked her eyes several times before answering. "House?"

"She had a house in La Jolla. Didn't you know?" Christie asked, surprised.

"No. No, I didn't know. She never mentioned that she'd bought a new house. Did she sell the one in La Mesa?"

"No," Christie said. "That's what so strange about it. She never could have afforded the second house, even if she had sold the first."

Beth shrugged. "I'm sorry I can't help you with that." She glanced at the clock on the wall. "I wish I had more time to visit, but . . ."

"We should let you get back to work. You've been so nice to take the time to talk to us," Christie said, standing.

"Oh, honey, I'm glad we had the chance. I think about you all the time. We're going to have to quit thinking and start seeing. Maybe you two could come over for dinner one night?"

"That would be nice, Beth. I'll call you when things settle down a bit."

"Now you be careful, honey. That DC's a scoundrel. You let me know if you need anything," she said, walking them to the door.

Outside, the blazing heat seemed a welcome relief from the icy interior. As Christie's eyes adjusted to the bright sunlight, she caught herself eyeing the parking lot. How many times a day did she scan her world for DC? She couldn't count them.

As Sam climbed in on the driver's side he glanced at her face. "Christie? What happened?" His gaze followed hers. "Now what's got you upset?"

She shook her head, feeling her bottom lip turn traitorous and trembly. Too many emotions had bubbled to the surface in the past forty-eight hours. She felt tiny and defeated underneath them. She shook her head, but he pressed.

Her words came haltingly at first and then tumbled out in a rush of emotion she couldn't have suppressed if she'd tried. For once, she just let her feelings pour out without thought or censorship. It felt so good.

"I'm so scared, Sam. I keep trying to block it from my mind and pretend that I'm not. I haven't thought or talked about it . . . about what happened . . . since . . . since it happened. I thought he was going to kill me. Even when I wasn't sure who he was, a part of me just knew. A part of me always knew he'd come back. Come back. For me." She looked away. "He's not going to give up."

Sam pulled her against his chest, sitting halfway between the bucket seats without complaint. She buried her face in his hard chest and cried.

"Come on, Chris. So hate him back. I'm not going to give him the chance to hurt you again. If the police are too busy, I'll track his ass down myself and then I'm going to stomp all over it."

"But Sam—"

"No, buts, Christie. You can't wait this out and hope it gets better. Don't you get it? Right now, he owns you. That's no way to live. You've got to keep fighting him."

She wiped her eyes with her hand. "I know."

"I'm going to take you back to my place. I want you to take a cool shower and a nap."

"But we need to get those papers—"

"We'll get them later. In the meantime, I'm going to get in touch with a friend of mine and get him going on that title search."

He pressed his lips to her temple. "We'll get him, babe. I'm too selfish to share and how can you be mine if you're his?"

"But this is what I was afraid of in the first place."

"What?"

"That it'll come down to you and him. And he'll kill you."

He rocked her in his arms. "The only one who's killing me, sweetheart, is you."

cried herself to sleep to the soft lullaby of the whirling ceiling fan.

The knock on the door jerked her awake, her slumberous brain already in the grip of fear. DC? Had he come back? Even as adrenaline shot through her system, the voice of reason reminded her, knocking wasn't DC's style.

The dogs began to bark.

"A little late, guys," she whispered in a shaky voice as she tiptoed to the door and peered through the peephole.

A badge filled her vision as the man on the other side held it up. "Police," he said in a deep voice, knocking again.

Surprised, she opened the door. The man on the doorstep wore jeans and a blue button-down shirt. He handed her his badge to inspect.

"I'm Mike Simens," he said. "Detective Simens."

"Christie McCoy," she answered automatically. Handing back his badge, she gave him a curious stare. "I didn't expect a visit from the police. I was under the impression you guys were too busy for me."

He nodded and shrugged, whether in apology or acknowledgment, she didn't know.

"Do you have a few minutes to answer some questions?" he asked.

"Of course. Please come in." She opened the door wider and moved aside for him to enter. "Has something happened? Did you catch DC?"

"No," he said, managing to look both irritated and friendly at once.

"I didn't think I'd be so lucky. So have you been assigned to my case?" she asked.

"Not exactly, but I may be looking for the same guy who attacked you."

Christie blinked in surprise and waited for him to elaborate. But, having made this statement, he seemed in no hurry to further enlighten her.

He stepped into the cool house, pulling his sunglasses off and folding them into his pocket. He looked around, as if searching for a place to put himself.

"Would you like some iced tea?" she asked. "Come on into the kitchen and I'll make some."

Snort and Bear sniffed his shoes as he followed her to the kitchen and sat down at Sam's breakfast bar. He looked at the dogs as if they were some new breed of rodent.

"I've got some questions about Porter," he said at last.

"I didn't think anyone had time to worry about him with all the kidnappings going on."

"Yeah, well, Porter's on the suspect list for the kidnappings."

Christie caught her breath, exclaiming, "DC's a suspect?"

Mike nodded. "He's been identified from a mug shot along with three other possibles."

"I'm stunned. I mean, I knew DC was a sick individual, but I had no idea he'd go this far . . ."

Mike shrugged, patting his shirt pocket for his cigarettes. "Porter may be a false lead. The department's number one suspect is among the three our witness picked out."

"So you don't really think DC is involved?"

"It's too soon to say. Mind if I smoke?"

"Actually, I'd rather you didn't."

His surprised expression appeared comical on such a large man. He looked from Christie to his cigarettes for a moment, as if searching for a way to take back his polite question.

"Hell," he said, crunching the pack in his big fist. "I should just quit."

"You'll feel better."

"Better than what?" he asked, handing the crumpled pack over. Christie threw it away and gave him a glass of tea.

"What was I saying? Suspects—so far the department's found a lot of dead ends, but that's typical."

"I heard that two little girls were taken last night," she said.

"Yeah."

He told her about the sighting in Seattle and the subsequent transfer of authority to the FBI. Christie sensed he needed a sounding board for his theories and she was glad to hear him out.

"The hell of it is, the department's been claiming that one guy took both of them, if you can believe that. And now the FBI's involved and they're all for continuing the investigation on the same line."

"How do you know? Maybe they'll—"

"Believe me, I know how they operate. I've worked with them before."

"You speak about the department as if you weren't part of it."

"Yeah, well, lately I'm not. They refuse to pursue the two-perpetrator theory at this time and they told me to butt out."

"I can see their request made a big impact on you. Why aren't they 'pursuing'?"

"There's some *forensic* evidence that's got them convinced it's the same guy taking all the girls. Since that fits nice and tidy with what they want the public to believe, they're not going to rock the boat. They don't want our good citizens to think there's more than one bad guy out there and panic."

"So they won't even investigate DC?"

He shook his head with disgust. "If the media caught wind of that, this whole town would stink."

"But they could be right, about the one guy. You said there's evidence."

"Yeah, but evidence can be planted. If this Porter is involved, he's tried to make it look like the other kidnappings. He's copying. But he made mistakes."

Mike shifted on the stool, leaning forward as he spoke.

"See, until Monday, the department's guy never grabbed a kid away from her mother. Never. He always caught her alone, on the way home from school or out playing. But last night the guy gets into the house through a little crawl space." He paused, looking at Christie expectantly.

"Like a doggie door?"

"Exactly. The victim's mother didn't even know it was there. Then he *waits* for her to get home, brutally attacks her, and grabs the kid." Mike paused. "Bells are ringing all over with me about DC Porter. Mrs. Mc—"

"Christie."

"Christie, I read your statement. At the time, you thought he was a robber. Now you know who he is . . . Could you fill me in?"

She could feel the comforting cloak of her privacy, her self-preserving silence, being tugged away. But there was no way she could deny Mike Simens any answer he sought.

Taking a deep breath, Christie explained about the locker key and her confirmation of DC's identity before revealing, in detail, DC's relationship with her mother, ending with his attempted rape and ultimate disappearance.

"You never reported the assaults?"

"No. I didn't want to go public for a lot of reasons. Once he vanished, I didn't see the point."

"You say he worked with your mother? Does she know where he is? How can I get in touch with her?"

"My mother's dead, but I think DC's staying at her old place." Christie told him of their meeting with DC's neighbor, watching as he scribbled it down with the address. "I called the department with the information this afternoon, but I didn't expect to hear back."

"Is there anything else you can think of?"

"Well, I don't know if this has anything to do with anything, but in the locker Sam and I found that belonged to DC, there were some files. Medical records."

"Medical records?"

Christie grabbed them off Sam's dining room table and handed them to Mike. He flipped through the stack, a frown on his face.

"I don't know why DC had them." Christie said, hesitating, as she wondered if she should give him DC's application. "There's one other thing, Mike, but it has to stay between you and me where you got it."

"Okay."

She retrieved the application from her purse, double-checking that it was a standard form without the clinic's logo or name printed anywhere on it. Nervously, she handed it to Mike.

"The information is old, so I don't how much use it will be to you."

He took it, scanning the contents. "Thanks."

He asked a few more questions but Christie didn't think her answers told him anything he didn't already know. Giving her his number, with instructions to call if she thought of anything else, he left.

17

She had almost managed to convince herself that DC wasn't her son, but he persisted in showing up at unexpected times to remind her of his existence. Remind her of the pain and filth in which he'd been conceived. Remind her of his father—a man she desperately wanted to forget.

When her parents had finally agreed to take DC off her hands, she'd dumped her son without a second thought and never looked back. As if casting off chains, she'd looked forward to the future for the first time in her young life.

Never admitting, even to herself, that she'd seen her father offer DC's hand as an appetizer to his dogs, she simply blocked the episode out, as she did with DC's existence. Until he'd come back.

She met her own gaze in the rearview mirror. The first time DC had reappeared in her life, it hadn't been so bad. She'd needed him. He'd helped her out. Solved some problems. Took his share of the take and left again. The perfect arrangement. Except he refused to stay gone.

She understood now what she hadn't then. DC would always be back.

Turning onto the quiet street, she pulled her car into the drive of her rental house. Feeling conspicuous even though she had every right to be there, she hurried to the front door and let herself in with her key. Her footsteps echoed on the tile as she closed the door behind her.

"DC?" she called softly, looking around.

When he didn't answer she began a silent search of the bare rooms that had once contained the memorabilia of her life. Her *real* life. The life that included her *real* family. Now it was contaminated by the return of DC.

She ended her inspection at the closed bathroom door. A hinge and padlock had been installed, locking the door from the outside. She found the key on the kitchen counter and went back to open it.

The bathtub had been padded with a blanket and a girl sat inside it. On the lid of the toilet, a bowl of cornflakes drooped in milk. The girl looked at her with widened, hopeful eyes and then shrank back, as if sensing an enemy instead of a savior.

Glaring at the kid, she felt swamped by two emotions. Pity and rage. Indirectly, the child was the crux of her problems, the hinge on which the door of dilemmas swung. What should she do about DC? What should she do about Jessica? Back and forth, back and forth.

She could care less what happened to DC. She wished a bus would run him over. She wished she had the nerve to do away with him herself. He was a fool.

The kid was another matter entirely and her whole future depended on what DC would do with her. She watched Jessica as the child sat staring back at her.

"You better eat your breakfast, kid. Who knows when you'll eat again."

Jessica nodded.

Sighing, she glanced around the room again. Over the bathtub was a tiny window, but it had been accidentally painted shut years ago. Even if the kid could reach it, she wouldn't be able to force it up. Good. The bathroom was secure.

She stared at Jessica for a moment longer before locking the door behind her and leaving the house. She had to keep cool. Keep all her balls in the air. Stay sharp. Stay *very* sharp.

18

Mike saw Kathy sitting on his doorstep when he got home and cursed. She'd drive him crazy before this was over. She bounded down the walkway and was face-to-face with him before he even got out of the car.

"What happened?" she demanded. "Did you talk to her?"

"Yes," he said, automatically reaching for a cigarette, then remembering that he'd thrown them away. That had been a stupid impulse.

Kathy trotted beside him like a kid. "Well? Did she know anything?"

"I have a lead but don't get all worked up. It could be a dead end."

"But you don't think so?"

"No. I think it's your guy."

Kathy's agitation was palpable. "And?"

He stopped and faced her. "I have an address but he hasn't been there for a while. I'm on my way now to question the neighbors."

"I'm going with you."

Mike continued to the door. "No you're not."

"Yes, I am. Just try to stop me."

Mike unlocked the door and walked into his house. He went straight to the back door, where a giant german shepherd waited patiently to be let in. The dog stopped just inside the door and watched Kathy expectantly.

"Don't worry, he's harmless."

"He doesn't look harmless. He looks like a cross between a horse and a bear."

"Come here, Rookie," Mike commanded. Immediately the dog obeyed. "He used to be a police dog. Took a bullet that was intended for me. Now he's mine."

"I'm sure you feel safe at night," she murmured. Taking a deep breath, she opened her mouth to pick up the end of their argument.

Mike interrupted before she had the chance. "You're not coming with me, Kathy. That's final. It could be dangerous and I've got enough to think about without worrying about you."

Kathy paled. "Of all the nerve! I fought this guy single-handedly—"

"—and lost. Did you forget that part?"

"You bastard."

Mike spun around to face her, grabbing her shoulders between his hands. Rookie looked instantly alert.

"Listen, Kathy. I know you're tense. I know you're worried sick about Jessica. But you're not making it easy for me to want to help you."

"Easy? Is that what you want? Easy?"

"Yes. Is that too much to ask?"

"Damn right. Easy was how I let you drag my husband where he shouldn't have been. I'm not going to let the same thing happen to my daughter."

For a moment he was so stunned by her accusation that he could only stare. Her embarrassed expression did little to stop his rising anger.

"I'm sorry, Mike, I shouldn't have said—"

"I've really had it with you," he interrupted her apology without hearing it. "*You* pushed Dan. You were every bit as responsible for his death as I was. You drove him to it."

"That's a lie. We loved each other." She felt tears prick at the back of her eyes and wrenched herself from his hands. "You're just trying to hurt me. You've hated me since the first time you saw me."

They were glaring at each other, their faces only inches apart.

"That's not true," he whispered in a cold voice. "The *first* time I saw you, I thought you were beautiful. Breathtaking. But then you opened your mouth and the whole picture vanished. I'm going to find your daughter, Kathy. And then I never want to see you again."

"Perfect," she answered. "But I'm still going with you to see the neighbors."

"You just don't get it, do you? I don't want you there."

"It's *you* who doesn't get it. We're talking about my daughter. My baby. I'm going."

"Use that selfish brain of yours, Kathy. I'll work better without you."

"You'll work harder with me."

"You just don't give up, do you?"

"I can't afford to give up. My daughter's life is on the line."

Her eyes and her voice pleaded, begging him for help. Mike's sigh came from his gut. "Okay, but you get in my way, you wait in the car."

"Okay."

"I'm going to the can. Is it okay if I do that alone?"

He closed the door behind him leaving Kathy in the living room alone with Rookie. Waves of self-pity convulsed through her at his accusations. Slowly, she sank to the sofa. A great hiccuping sob caught in her chest. She'd never felt so lost or alone. Even when Dan had died.

A giant, crystalline tear rolled over the widened rim of her eye and careened down her cheek. She lowered her head to her knees, drawing herself into a tight, pain-filled ball. Rookie whined and put his big head in her lap. Unconsciously her fingers stroked behind his ears.

How could Mike be so cruel?

She wiped her tears and straightened her shoulders. His accusations about Dan had hurt, but Dan was dead. Jessica wasn't. She wouldn't even permit herself to think otherwise.

Jessica.

Like a bright light that still seemed to glow even after it had been extinguished, she could picture Jessica. Her smile. Her sparkling eyes.

"Wait for me Jess," she whispered. "Wait for me."

In the breeze through the window, she imagined a sighing response.

Hurry, Mommy . . .

"Ever heard of Dr. and Mrs. John McClowsky?" Sam asked as he walked through the front door.

Christie shook her head.

He unfolded a computer printout and spread it on the table. "Title on the house was transferred from them about a month before your mother died."

"DC was still around at that time."

"That's what I thought, but I wasn't sure. You're sure you never heard your mother mention the name McClowsky? Think hard."

"I am thinking hard, Sam. It doesn't ring any bells. You say the house was transferred? Not sold?"

"That's right. Frank has a friend who checked out some tax records—don't ask me how he got them because I don't know—but he told us that McClowsky used the house as a tax deduction. A donation."

"A donation? To my mother?"

"To the MJ Collins Agency."

"*Agency?*"

"I take it you knew nothing about your mother's plans to start her own business?"

"Sam, she would have told me if she'd been thinking about that. Even with the DC thing between us, she would have told me."

"Maybe that's what she was working on with DC that day you went to the clinic."

"What do you mean?"

"Well, Beth claims she knew nothing about DC having anything to do with an adoption, right?"

"Right, but she had a good point about my mom lying. I mean, it wouldn't be the first time she'd lied to me about a boyfriend."

"Okay, but maybe it wasn't a lie. Maybe she planned on opening her own adoption agency and was working under the table on the first transaction."

"Sam, she wasn't that underhanded. I mean, lying about a lunch date is one thing, but I can't believe she'd double-cross Beth."

"But DC would and you said yourself that he had a powerful hold over your mother. I know you don't want to believe it, but I think it would be worth the drive to give these McClowskys a surprise visit. It's almost dinnertime. We might be able to catch them at home if we leave now."

On the way to the McClowskys house in El Cajon, Christie told Sam about Mike Simens's visit. He listened, his expression becoming grim, the set of his jaw even more determined.

She finished talking as they exited the freeway and turned to the south side of El Cajon, where sprawling estates dotted the sloping hills like patchwork. Looking out her window, Christie was amazed at the difference a few miles could make in a city. They passed several kennels and fenced-in meadows with sleek horses grazing in the sun.

They drove through a nice neighborhood filled with the sounds of children laughing and playing. The different models of homes were unique duplications of one another. Here, someone had added an extra room. There it was RV parking. The community's upgrades sparkled with middle-class comfortableness. Enough, but never enough.

Following a road that snaked between the hillsides, twisting without obvious plan from one side to the other, they stopped at the foot of a driveway marked by a barn-shaped mailbox with McClowsky painted on the side. Feeling suddenly nervous, Christie gave Sam a glance.

"Are you sure this is a good idea? Don't you think we should have called first?"

"And give them time to make up a story?"

"Sam, you're talking as if these people committed a crime. At worst, all they did was make a donation to my mother."

"You don't really believe that, do you?"

In truth, she no longer knew what to believe, so she kept quiet, staring out her window as they climbed the steep drive to a flat surface that circled a man-made pond. Sam parked the Jeep next to a maroon Volvo and stepped out. Slowly, Christie followed.

The house was gray, dusky yet bright, with happy white trim. It was freshly painted and the yard was immaculately tailored. Bright splashes of flowers lined the walkway. In the distance, someone mowed a lawn and the fragrance of freshly cut grass mingled with the scent of sprinklers splashing hot concrete. Summer. It was the kind of neighborhood in which Sam had grown up. The kind in which Christie had dreamed of living.

"Let me do the talking," Sam said as they approached a door with stained glass insets and fancy woodwork.

"I don't have the slightest idea what to say anyway. You're not going to pull another act like you did at Pfeiffer's office, are you?"

"Pfeiffer deserved to have his lights knocked out. I think I showed considerable restraint under the circumstances."

Sam knocked on the door and they waited in the cool shadow of the doorway. They heard footsteps from within and assumed they were being watched through the peephole. After a moment a woman opened the door.

At first glance she looked very young, but as she stepped forward, the sun highlighted finely etched lines around her lips and laughter fanning from the corners of her eyes. Christie guessed her to be in her late forties. She wore a white cotton pant outfit with a quilted pattern on the front. Cigarette smoke hovered around her, swirling in sunbeams and shadows. She gave them a warm smile as her gaze darted cautiously between them.

"Mrs. McClowsky?" Sam asked.

"Yes."

"I'm Sam McCoy and this is my wife Christie. We're sorry to bother you but we're here about Mary Jane Collins—"

"Mary Jane? Of course. I'll bet you're here for a reference. You have that nervous look I remember having. Please, come in. I'd be happy to talk to you." She stood aside for them to enter, shushing them with a finger across her lips as they passed the stairs. "I just got the baby to go down."

Sam gave Christie a look that said "play along" as Mrs. McClowsky led them down the hallway. Reluctantly, Christie followed.

"Is your husband home?" Sam asked casually.

"No. He's in LA on business. I'm not sure when he'll be back. Soon, I hope."

They stopped in a glass-walled room that overlooked the picturesque valley through which they'd just driven. After they refused her polite offer of refreshment, she perched on a matching chair and gave them another smiling look.

"I can see how nervous you are," she said. "I understand. I was the exact same way. How long have you been trying?"

Their blank expressions made her giggle. "I mean, trying to adopt?"

"A while," Sam said.

She nodded sympathetically. "Well, don't worry. If you're working with Mary Jane, you're working with the best. The *very* best. She'll move mountains to get you a baby. She delivered little Karen to us, just as she promised. Of course you always have to worry about the mother. That's a given. But Mary Jane counsels them extensively before she even tells you about the baby. At least that's how it was for us. We'd worked with several private agencies and the mothers changed their minds. Twice. Twice that happened to us. I was at the point of giving up."

"That must have been hard," Sam murmured.

"Hard isn't the word. We'd even gone to Lamaze classes with one of the girls. She said she'd let us be coaches in the delivery room. Too good to be true. She had a little boy. My husband cut the cord, I gave him his first feeding. She took the baby right out of my arms and went back home to her parents. It was devastating. It nearly destroyed my marriage. Are you two feeling the stress?"

"We try and work through it," Sam said, giving Christie's shoulders a squeeze. She couldn't believe how natural he acted, while she felt as flexible as glass. Seemingly at home with the charade, he elaborated. "It's hard, but we try and keep each other's spirits up."

"That's the best approach," Mrs. McClowsky said. "It will rip you apart if you let it." A sad, dreamy look glazed her eyes for a moment. "We would have named him Timothy. After my father. He passed away two years ago."

She grew quiet for a few moments, gazing out the window. Then she blinked, beaming another smile their way. "But I wouldn't trade Karen for Timothy, now."

"Did you get to see Karen's birth?" Christie asked her first question.

"No. They didn't tell me about her until she was mine."

''They?''

''My husband and Mary Jane. After the *mother* changed her mind and kept Timothy, I had to be hospitalized. I wanted a baby so badly and knew I'd never have my own. My husband and I are double cursed. He's sterile and I had an emergency hysterectomy when I was a teenager. When we married we decided we'd adopt, but my husband's over sixty and I have some major health problems . . . We were so naive. I'm sure you've had quite an education by now on how difficult it is to get a baby. Unless you're willing to take on someone else's rejects, that is. You know, a crack baby or disabled or abused child. We wanted a healthy baby, not someone else's problem.''

She seemed not to know how callous her words sounded.

''I'm running at the mouth, aren't I? That's what my husband says I do. What else can I tell you, if I haven't already blabbed your ears off?''

''How did you choose Mary Jane?'' Sam asked.

''Well we started with Beth McClain. Don't work with her, if you can help it. The woman's got so many rules and regulations that you'll be grandparents before you're parents. And she's absolutely inflexible on payments. I don't like that woman at all. But when Mary Jane's assistant approached my husband—''

''Her assistant?''

''Yes . . . what was his name? He went by initials. I'm sorry I can't remember. Wonderful, caring man, though. Mary Jane was too ethical to talk to us independently of the McClain woman. She felt it was a conflict of interest. But her assistant said they could help us and once we terminated our business with McClain, Mary Jane agreed to assist us. Not to take credit away from her, but I don't think she'd considered opening her own agency until she dealt with us.''

Sam raised his brows in polite surprise, casually asking, ''Why is that?''

"Well, I didn't know this was going on at the time it all happened. Like I said, my husband kept it a secret until it was a fait accompli. He didn't want to see me go through the disappointment if it fell through. The way he explained it, though, is that there was a young woman who was expecting. She had several children already and couldn't support another and she didn't know what to do until Mary Jane's assistant—what was his name?—"

"DC Porter?" Sam offered.

She smiled. "Yes, that's it. DC Porter. He told her about us and talked her into giving the child up."

"You say Mary Jane was flexible on payments?"

"Oh yes. As a matter of fact she was very accommodating."

"Would it be too personal a question if I asked just how accommodating?"

She smiled with warm understanding, as if they were old friends. Christie felt small and cheap, sitting in her cheerful sun-room pretending to share a common problem.

"Mary Jane needed an office. We had a house that we'd been trying to sell forever because of my poor health. The house is in La Jolla—quite pricey, but the climate was just too damp for me. This far inland is so much better. We couldn't sell though. I mean, no one has that kind of money these days. I'll tell you, it was killing us. We were making payments on both houses . . . We'd used all our reserves on the previous adoption attempts." She shivered. "Bad times. Anyway, my husband worked out a deal and we donated the house to Mary Jane—took it as a deduction—and she took over the payments. It's perfect for a home-based business catering to a wealthier clientele. And it must be doing fine because here you are."

They both smiled and nodded. Yes, here they were. Christie could tell there were other questions Sam wanted to ask, but his tongue was tied by their charade.

"Do you want a boy or a girl?" Mrs. McClowsky asked.

"We're not picky," he answered glibly. "How about one of each?"

"Actually," Mrs. McClowsky began, leaning forward in a confiding manner. "I'm trying to talk my husband into giving it another go. I know he'd love a son . . . But who can afford to do it twice?"

Sam and Christie murmured their agreement and stood to leave.

"Thank you for talking to us, Mrs. McClowsky."

"Oh it was my pleasure. Good luck to you both and say hi to Mary Jane for me. Tell her not to be surprised if she hears from me again."

19

Christie stared out the window as she and Sam left the McClowsky residence behind, but what she saw in her mind shrouded her sight with the thick wool of introspection. She couldn't believe that her mother had planned to open her own agency and hadn't bothered to tell her. It hurt to think she'd keep something so important from her daughter.

"Hey? Christie, are you there?"

"What?"

"You're starting to give me a complex. I've been talking to you for the last five minutes."

"I'm sorry, Sam. I was looking out the window."

"I can see that. Does that mean you can't hear?"

She smiled. "Maybe."

"You and 'maybe.' One of these days you're going to have to choose yes or no."

"Maybe."

"Are you hungry? I'm hungry. Let's get something to eat and then swing by and pick up your copy of the will. Feel like Mexican?"

"How can you be hungry? My stomach's in knots after that. I hate to lie."

"You weren't doing any of the lying. I was. Besides, who's it going to hurt? She didn't suspect and it's not like we'll be running into her again."

"But what if she does look up my mother and finds

out she's dead? Or goes to the house and I answer the door? I just hate to lie, Sam.''

"Okay, okay. But at least we know how your mom got the house. Aren't you glad about that?''

"Yes, but it seems that every new thing I'm learning is just showing me how little I knew about my mother.''

"So? Christie, I couldn't fill an index card with what I know about my mom.'' He made a couple of turns and pulled into the parking lot of a taco stand shaped like a giant sombrero. Dropped in a desert blindfolded, Sam could find Mexican food.

In front of the hat's brim, three stone tables dotted the patio area. Christie sat down at one of them.

"What do you want?'' Sam asked.

She shook her head. "I'm not hungry.''

"You sure?''

She nodded. Sam went to the window and ordered, pacing as he waited for his food to appear. She caught herself watching him, her gaze taking in his broad shoulders and slim hips. The way his hair fell over his forehead, ruffled by the hot breeze. He saw her watching and winked with a sexy smile.

Returning to the table with two sodas and three white bags packed full of food, he began spreading paper-wrapped items on the table.

"I got you a carne asada burrito, just in case you change your mind.''

Her favorite and it smelled wonderful. Suddenly she was hungry. She reached for it and her stomach gurgled thankfully. Sam wolfed a taco, washing it down with a Diet Pepsi.

"Can I say something?'' he asked, reaching for a burrito.

"Why start asking now?''

"Because I know that however I word this it's probably going to come out wrong and I don't want to piss you off.''

She chewed, thinking about this for a moment. "Okay, what is it?" she said finally.

"I think you've got a big hang-up about your mom. It's like you're always making excuses for her faults."

"What faults? I don't—"

"She wasn't there when you felt she should have been. I saw your face when Beth was talking about her, Chris. I know what you were thinking."

She scowled at him. "What makes you think you know so much?"

"I listen. It's like somewhere along the line, you and your mother did a little role reversal. She quit taking care of you so you started playing mom."

"That's a pretty big leap you're making."

"No, it's not. Ever since we met you've been worrying about your mother. Even before DC. Even back when we were dating. Hell, you're still doing it. Sometimes I don't think you're even aware of it."

"I cared about her. That didn't stop just because she died."

He unwrapped a tostada and smothered it in hot sauce. "I think you confuse worrying and caring."

"Do tell, Dr. Sam, what is that supposed to mean?"

"Okay, let me ask you a question. If she'd been against you and me getting married—if for some insane reason, your mother hadn't liked me—would you have quit seeing me?"

"No."

"Even knowing how things would turn out with us?"

She lowered her face so he couldn't look in her eyes. "I certainly wouldn't have trusted my mother's judgment about a man."

"My point exactly. But you always expected her to take your advice on what men she saw—"

"That's different, Sam. You heard what Beth said, my mom had no sense—"

"It doesn't matter, Christie! It was her life. It wasn't

even any of your *business*. What's right for you wasn't necessarily right for her.''

Christie could feel her entire body go rigid with hurt and anger. "What are you saying? That I tried to change her?"

"I knew you were going to get mad."

She forced her shoulders down and tried to be less defensive, but it was hard to talk about her mom this way.

"I'm not accusing you of anything, Chris. I just want you to let go of the past and move on. You'll drive yourself crazy if you don't. Right or wrong, your mother made her own choices. You can't change that now any more than you could when she was alive. So give yourself a break."

Christie stared at him, suddenly captivated by his husky voice and dark eyes. His words touched off a thawing warmth from within that made her skin feel suddenly cold. When had he become so understanding, so in tune with her feelings?

He reached across the table and trapped her nervous hands under his. "Nobody's perfect, Christie," he said softly.

Of course no one was perfect. She'd never expected anyone to be. Then why did she feel a sense of relief at his words? Had she always expected her mother to be perfect? Or Sam? Or herself, for that matter?

She looked up, unseeing, as she stood on the border of unexplored feelings. Just ahead she sensed a crossing, shimmering under a mist of uncertainty. Could she give up her old way of thinking and move forward on just the hope that the ground beneath her would be solid?

Quietly, Sam returned the untouched order of rolled tacos and an enchilada to the bag, watching her with questioning intensity as he did.

She knew he waited for her to say something, but she needed to think before she could even begin to put her feelings into words. They returned to the Jeep and drove to the house in La Jolla. On the way, Christie grew more reflective and Sam silent. After he parked in the driveway, Christie got out and went inside. Sam followed.

She picked up their conversation when the door closed behind him. "I loved my mother, Sam."

"I know, honey," he said, staring at her from across the foyer. "Nothing should ever be able to change that."

"You think I expect everyone I love to be perfect, don't you?"

"No, Christie. All I'm trying to say is that whatever we find out about your mother doesn't have to have anything to do with you. It doesn't have to change the way you felt about her. We're going to be turning over a lot of stones, and there might be a few bugs under them. That doesn't mean your mom was a bad person or that you failed her or anything. Okay?"

She felt herself go very still as the full impact of his words hit her. "You think my mother was involved in something illegal, don't you, Sam?"

He took his time answering. Waiting, the knots in her stomach pulled tighter.

"Yeah, I think so. But I don't think she planned it that way."

"Meaning what?"

"I think she got trapped. Conned. I can't fill in the details because I don't know them. But it's my guess that DC got her in over her head and Beth found out."

"Beth?"

"Yeah. Something about Beth's story didn't sit right with me."

Christie exhaled loudly. "You sure took your sweet time about saying something. What's wrong with Beth's story?"

"I can't even put my finger on it. But I don't think she busted DC smoking in the john," he said, shaking his head. "He's too smart for that. I think she caught him at something all right, but it was a hell of a lot more serious than smoking some weed."

"Like what?"

"I don't know . . . tampering with records? And this house-trade story we just heard. I don't buy it."

"Come on, Sam. You're not buying anyone's story. So far, you think Pfeiffer's a gangster, Beth's a liar, and Mrs. McClowsky's what . . . a real estate tycoon? You're being just a bit suspicious, don't you think?"

He raised his brows. "So you believe that DC was your mother's assistant?" he demanded.

"No, but there's probably a reasonable explanation for Mrs. McClowsky to think he was. Maybe my mom didn't want to introduce him as the janitor—"

"Why would she introduce him at all? Think about it, Christie. You don't introduce your janitor to your clients—"

"He wasn't just the janitor to my mom—"

"So? He still had no place working with adoptive parents. Besides, didn't Mrs. McClowsky say that DC approached them about the second adoption?"

"Yes, but maybe my mom told DC about them and . . . and . . ."

"And what? He felt charitable and decided to help? I don't think so."

"Maybe he wanted to get back at Beth for something."

Sam paused, thinking about that. "Okay, keep going."

"Well, maybe he and Beth had already had a confrontation over his involvement with my mother, or his work ethic—I don't know. With DC anything's possible. Maybe he saw helping my mom open her own clinic as a way to stick it to Beth and ensure that he'd have a job with my mom."

"That's pretty good. But this house scam. That's a pretty expensive house, Christie. I'm still having trouble swallowing the fact that they just *gave* it to her. I mean, obviously a baby's worth more than money, but how much can the adoption have cost?''

"I wondered that myself.''

"Unless it was illegal.''

"What?''

"Black market, Chris. I think DC sold that baby to the McClowskys.''

"Wait just a minute, Sam. You had me for a while there, but I absolutely will not believe that my mother would be involved with black market babies.''

"I wonder how we could find out where the McClowsky baby came from?'' he said after a pause.

"You mean her real mother? Those kinds of records are sealed. Why? You weren't thinking of dragging *her* into this were you?''

"I guess not. If what I'm thinking is true, that wouldn't do us any good anyway. If the mother sold her baby, she wouldn't talk to us about it.''

"Mrs. McClowsky didn't seem like the kind of woman who'd buy a baby, Sam. She seemed too open and friendly.''

"She said herself that her husband and DC handled all the details. Maybe she doesn't know.''

"Back to maybe again. Maybe we're crazy.''

"You heard how hard she'd tried to get a baby through legal channels, Chris. She sounded as if she'd been desperate.''

"Desperate is one thing. What you're talking about is criminal.''

"Maybe she doesn't see it that way. If the real mother was willing to sell, McClowsky did the baby a favor by buying. You know that child's got a better life with them than she'd have had with a mother who would sell her.''

"But, Sam . . .''

"I know it's hard for you to understand wanting a

baby that badly, Chris, but the McClowskys aren't the first or the last to pay big bucks for a kid.''

"Why do you think it's hard for me to understand that?"

"Well, you never wanted kids yourself—"

"Who told you that?"

"You did."

"I never said that," she protested.

"Yes, you did."

"I never said I didn't want children, Sam. I'll listen to your theories about my mother, myself, my psychosis, but don't put words in my mouth."

"We did talk about it. But I guess it doesn't make much difference now, does it?"

"We talked about it once, Sam McCoy. And as I recall it, we weren't talking. We were fighting—as usual."

"We were fighting about whether or not to have kids."

"Why are you bringing this up now?"

"You're the one getting worked up about it."

"I just didn't want my child to be raised without a father, like I was."

"What are you saying? Did you think I'd get you pregnant and skip town?"

"I wanted to be sure we were going to last before we brought children into it."

"No, Chris. You were already convinced we weren't going to make it. Right from the start."

"And I was right, wasn't I?" She shook her head, brushing her hair from her eyes. "Nothing's changed between us, Sam. Look at us! Just when I think things could be different, we start fighting again. Sometimes I don't even know what I'm fighting about. You keep telling me to put the past behind me, and then you bring it up."

She turned away, rubbing her arms with her hands. Sighing, Sam stared at her back in confused silence.

Finally, Sam said, "You're right. I shouldn't have brought it up. It's just been bothering me, all this time. And then thinking about the McClowskys and everything they did to get their baby . . . whatever it is that they *did* . . . It just got me going."

Christie sat on the bottom step of the staircase and stared up at Sam. "I would have wanted them," she said softly. "If things had worked out for us, I would have."

He joined her on the step, taking her cool hand in his. "Are you going to give us another try, Christie?"

She looked up, into eyes as dark as night. Eyes that waited for her to say more. Slowly she shook her head, her gaze still locked to his.

"I don't know, Sam. You hurt me. I'm afraid to give you the chance to do it again."

"That's not the chance I want," he said softly. Watching the golds and greens of her eyes mingle and change as she stared back, he shifted his weight until he was kneeling between her knees, his lips level with hers. The sound of their breathing seemed to echo in the empty house. He kept her gaze captured.

The heat of her body burned through the thin material of her shirt. He nuzzled her ear, inhaling the familiar scent of her perfume and the memories it recalled.

He pulled back and tried to reclaim her gaze, but she looked down at his shirt. Gently he tilted her face back up to his so she could see the fierce light that he knew burned in his eyes. "Why are you confused, Christie? Because you still love me?"

She shook her head but the answer in her eyes told him more than any words. He caught his breath and leaned closer.

"Maybe," she whispered.

Her soft voice broke the invisible chain that held him back. Frustration, confusion, and fear had accented their every move from the start. Still those emotions weren't strong enough to dominate this one driving need for each other. He kissed her.

She tasted sweet and salty, her lips the softest things he'd ever touched. Her hands moved, whispering against his chest before coiling around his neck. She pulled herself tight against him and he tucked her close. Her breasts felt soft and heavy, flattened against the muscles of his chest, muffling both of their heartbeats. She squeezed his sides with her thighs, moving in a reflexive and rhythmic motion, heat radiating from her.

It had always been like this with them. Anger and laughter. Passion and tears. Never calm. Never boring. The only predictable thing about Christie was that she would drive him to the brink, which is exactly where he wanted to be.

With her body arched against his, he felt hot and alive with sensations. He took a deep breath, fighting for control over the rock-hard tension that fused him to her. This wasn't the best place to be doing this. He'd sworn to himself that he would protect Christie and here he was letting his feelings for her jeopardize his judgment and her safety. She opened her beautiful eyes and blinked at him.

"Come on, Christie. Let's go home."

20

Kathy hugged the passenger door, silently congratulating herself on her victory. While she was with him, Mike Simens would think of nothing but Jessica. She knew it. Once he realized she meant to keep her word and stay out of the way, he would work twice as hard and he would find her daughter.

For now, though, he'd retreated behind a pair of sunglasses and drove in silence. The radio alternated between news and country music and she relaxed for the first time since DC Porter—if that was the bastard's name—invaded her life. She was doing something.

Her frightened neighbors had already banded together to distribute flyers with Jessica's picture on them. With Mike on her side, Jessica would soon be back in her arms. She didn't doubt it for a minute.

Mike consulted an address scrawled on a scrap of paper and turned onto a still street. Twilight glittered through the trees, dappling the street with golden drops of shimmering shadows. He pulled to the side and got out. She popped her door open and scrambled to follow.

Her stomach clenched as she viewed the house. With each step closer the fast-growing shadows added menace to its crumbling decay. Could her baby be inside this horrible place? Hope battled rage at the thought.

Mike broke the silence with his deep voice. "I wish I had a warrant."

"Do you think she's in there?" Kathy whispered.

He shook his head. "No. Not here. But I'd still like to get inside."

He walked up the driveway. Kathy hurried to keep up, scanning the wasted yard for the clue that made Mike seem so certain. He glanced her way but didn't order her back to the car.

Finally, she asked softly, "Why don't you think she's here?"

"I don't know. A feeling. Hunch. Whatever. She's not here."

Disappointment washed over her. Had she hoped to ring the bell and simply ask for her daughter back?

She sighed, spying a yellow cat scratching his back on the roots of a tree sprouting in the dirt yard. Another fat feline sat on the spiky scrub, cleaning its paws and face with disdain.

Wild cats. What were they eating? Thoughts of rats inched her a step closer to Mike's side. He looked at her in surprise.

"What?" he asked.

"Nothing."

Dark windows framed either side of the front door. The one on the right was cracked, masked with electrical tape that had peeled back, leaving a sticky, black scum outline. Cupping his hands around his eyes, Mike peered through a gap. Kathy waited impatiently for his observations. He shook his head and silently continued, checking the door leading to the garage as he circled to the back. Kathy stayed close behind him. Once he looked over his shoulder at her and she thought she detected a small smile, but she was probably wrong. It must have been a frown.

Another cat popped from the weeds clustered around the patio and hissed at them. Kathy became Mike's shadow, bumping into him when he stopped suddenly. They exchanged wary glances and moved on. *This place would give a corpse the creeps,* Kathy thought.

The sliding door was also locked, but the picture window with the cockeyed screen looked promising. Mike yanked off the screen and tossed it behind him. The window slid open with a rusty squeal.

He glanced back and winked as he hooked a leg over the sill and climbed through. Kathy debated for half a second before following. A jagged piece of metal sticking out of the window frame snagged her arm, drawing blood. She bit back a pained yelp, quickly applying pressure to the cut. She tried not to think of tetanus shots and bacteria. Mike would send her home if she started whining about a scratch.

She followed him to the entrance of a dark hallway. Pulling his gun from its holster, he reached his arm behind him, and tucked her close to his back. The protective gesture made her feel safe in an unexpected way, even if he hadn't intended it to.

They checked the bedrooms, empty but for a stained mattress on the floor of the last. In the kitchen, an upside-down bucket served as a chair to an overturned wooden crate. The counters were scatterd with beer cans, an empty bottle of bourbon, and a few pizza boxes. On the counter, a sleek black rat shared the leftovers with a swarm of shiny bugs. A cat watched from the windowsill outside with mean, hungry eyes.

"Oh, my God," Kathy gasped.

Without a word, Mike unlocked the sliding door and shoved Kathy outside. Gratefully she inhaled gulps of hot, pungent air that felt fresh after the sealed up rot in the kitchen. Sitting on the edge of the patio, she watched for bugs or rodents while Mike banged around a bit in the kitchen. He came out looking a little green himself. In his hand he clutched a grease-stained file folder that had been gnawed in the middle.

"What's this?" she asked.

He held it up for her to see the large block letters that spelled Jessica's full name.

"What is this?" she repeated, touching it with a sense of dread. "What does this mean?"

He shook his head, squinting in the growing gloom. "It means he's got Jessica. It means he's got her for a reason. It means maybe she's got a chance."

"Chance? Reason? What do you mean?"

He put his hands on his hips, legs spread wide. Slowly, he shook his head. "I don't know yet," he said, staring at her with narrowed eyes. "Are you okay?"

"Yeah," she lied. "Thanks for getting me out of there."

He grinned and extended a helping hand. His palm was rough with calluses and she wondered what he did that made it that way. He released her as soon as she was steady and they walked away. He swaggered a bit. Like a cowboy hero with guns holstered low. Mike wouldn't let anything happen to her daughter.

At the car, they spotted a woman across the street watching them. She had an undernourished look about her, emphasized by the baggy T-shirt and leggings she wore. She had short black hair and pale skin that seemed to glow in the fluorescent streetlight. She held a glass of wine in one hand.

"You looking for DC," she called. "I hear you're looking for DC?"

"You seen him around?" Mike answered, crossing the street. Kathy stayed close to his side.

"Yeah, he's been here. Gave me this," she said, pointing at her swollen mouth. "He took all my money and left a couple hours ago."

"Where was he going?"

"Do you think he'd tell me?" she demanded coldly.

Mike gave her a serious look. "I don't know. Would he?"

"No. The bastard. Why do I always meet the bastards?"

"You're having a relationship with him?" Kathy asked, barely keeping the surprise from her voice.

"Relationship is too nice a word," the woman said, her breath heavy with wine and her words slurred. She looked curiously at Mike's blue jeans and cotton shirt. "Who are you, anyway?"

"Mike Simens, San Diego Police," he said, flashing his badge and his smile. He didn't introduce Kathy and the other woman gave her a speculative once-over.

"Police, huh?" she said, taking a gulp of her wine. "What do you want him for this time?"

"He's wanted for questioning about a kidnapping."

"Kidnapping? So that's what he's been up to."

"What do you mean?"

"He came pounding on my door yesterday. He'd just found out about Mary Jane and he took it kind of hard. Course that didn't keep him from coming on to me."

Mike pulled a tablet from his pocket and flipped a page. "Is that Mary Jane Collins?" She nodded. "What did he find out?"

"That she's dead. He was gone when it happened. I guess he didn't know."

"What makes you think he's been up to something? Did he tell you—"

"Oh, no. He'd never talk to *me* about something like that. I'm just a pit stop for him. He wanted to know about Mary Jane's house, though," she said, glancing at the shambles over Mike's shoulder. "If it'd been sold. I told him I didn't think so. He didn't stay very long after that. I did see him back at Mary Jane's around two in the morning." She stopped suddenly and scratched her nose. "Not that I watch him. I work the weird shifts over at The Pancake House. He was in and out. He's always like that. There for an hour and gone again."

"He ever have a kid with him?"

"Not that I saw."

"How about a large bundle or bag? Something he might be carrying her in?"

"No. I mean I might've missed something. Like I said. I wasn't watching him."

"Why'd he come back today?"

"He started telling me lies about how he's always wanted me and now that Mary Jane's not around he wants to get to know me. Bullshit. He wanted my cash, and when I wouldn't give it, he smacked me around and took it."

"How much?"

"I had all my tips from the week. He took over a hundred bucks."

"What time was that?"

"I told you, a couple hours ago."

"Who told you we were looking for DC?"

"Del," she said, nodding at the house next to the one they'd just left.

Mike consulted his tablet again. "Delmont Ives? Is he around?"

"It's his bowling night. I saw him leave in his lucky shirt about an hour ago."

Mike showed her a mug shot of Porter. "Is this the man we're talking about?"

She studied it for a minute. "Not a very good picture. I've got a better one—not that he looks the same anymore. But yeah, that's him all right."

"You have a better picture of Porter?" Mike asked.

"Sure. We used to hang out together before Mary Jane died and my husband ran off with a bus driver. Life's a bitch, huh?"

"Can I see your picture?"

"Sure, but like I said, he's changed. Told me he'd been in a motorcycle accident. The doctors patched him up damn good. He looks a hell of a lot better than he used to. Maybe I should try, huh?"

As she spoke, she led them to a slightly better version of the house that Kathy and Mike had just been in. Two giant palms shedding leaves like hair coats dominated the tiny yard. A rusted aluminum lawn chair with magazines stacked beside it occupied the front porch. Kathy's guess was that this woman spent a lot of time in that chair, tending her bottle and her neighbors' business at the same time.

She babbled on the way, introducing herself as Sissy Norman before launching into a story about her husband's desertion, telling them in a confidential tone that the bus driver he'd run off with had been fat and had missing teeth. Could they believe it?

Her house smelled like fried eggs and wine. A dog that looked like a mangy horse snoozed on a braided rug in the living room. It opened its eyes when they entered but couldn't be troubled for a bark.

Sissy stopped off in the kitchen to fill her glass, sloshing some over onto the floor in the process. She didn't bother to wipe it up, but the horsey dog decided that spilled wine was worth moving for. He lapped up the puddle and then hobbled back to his rug.

"I know I just saw that picture because I was planning on cutting Fred out of it." She paused, taking a drink. "I know where it was!"

Pouncing on a stack of yellowed newspapers that towered unsteadily in the corner, she began sorting.

"Aha! I knew it was there. I think I decided to burn it." She shrugged, draining her glass. "Here. Take it."

Mike studied the photo before handing it to Kathy. The recent shot was a close-up of Porter with another man. His smiling face seemed but a shadow of the man who had attacked her. Except for the eyes. The eyes were the same and they made her tremble with anger.

"What about his car?" Mike asked. "Do you know what kind it is?"

"Sure. I even know his linus ... license plate numbers because they're almost the same as my birthday."

A smile spread over Mike's face. "Now that would be helpful."

Kathy watched Mike write down Sissy's information, hoping the woman wasn't too sauced to know what she was talking about.

"Can you think of anything else?" Mike asked, looking up.

She shrugged. "He eats a lot of pizza."

So do his rats, Kathy thought.

Mike ripped a page from his tablet and wrote down his phone number, handing it to the woman.

"Would you give me a call if you see him again? Doesn't matter what time it is—day or night."

"Yeah, sure."

Thanking her for her help, they said good-bye and walked back to the car.

"What now?" Kathy asked.

"I'm going to find a phone and call a buddy of mine at the station. I want an APB on his car and this picture in circulation right away."

"She's right, though," Kathy said, nodding at Sissy's house. "He looks different."

"Can you describe how?"

"Yeah. Seeing that picture brought everything back."

"Listen. I'll drop you off at the station. You talk to Lou Mitchell—he'll do a computer composite from what you tell him. Between the picture and the composite, we'll find him."

"Won't you get in trouble if they find out what you're working on?"

Mike shook his head. "He'll call it an anonymous tip based on a sighting. That ought to shake things up."

"What if they find out, Mike? You could lose your job."

He smiled at her. She didn't think she'd ever seen him smile without the taint of cynicism or sarcasm distorting his features. The difference that humor made was incredible.

"It's a little late to be worrying about my job,

Kathy,'' he said. Then, seriously, ''Who knows, maybe it's time for me to move on anyway.''

''You mean leave the police department?''

He shrugged. ''I'm getting too old to deal with bullshit.''

''Like the FBI coming in and taking over?''

''Yeah, that and other things.''

''Like?''

''You don't really care.''

''Sure I do,'' she said, surprising herself by meaning it.

He stared at her, as if judging her sincerity. ''I've been banging heads with the brass every time I turn around. Then last year a suit was investigated by Internal Affairs and I got called to testify against him. Didn't do him any harm but probably ruined my career.''

''That's discrimination. Sue the department or something.''

Mike laughed. ''I might as well just blow him away and be done with it. He can make my life a worse hell than it is. Twist things around. Play dirty. He can sling as much my way as I can his, and if he doesn't have enough on me, then he'll make it up. It's a dirty business, Kathy. Believe it or not, dealing with the street scum is the easy part.''

He reached over and turned up the radio, effectively tuning out their conversation. Kathy, for once, took the hint and settled back in her seat. At least she felt as if they were doing something. Following a lead, searching out clues. Finding her daughter.

On the radio, Alan Jackson crooned about midnight in Montgomery and whiskey in the air, and Kathy let him soothe her nerves. She'd barely slept since Jessica had been ripped from her life. Now the comforting motion of the car lulled her into a light doze. The song changed to a commercial, followed by the news. A part of her mind registered the fact while another part drifted

down the sweet avenues of memories, fragrant with
baby powder and apple juice and happiness.

"... where a body identified as that of Melanie
Blackwell was found earlier today. Stay tuned for
weather and sports coming up next on KSON."

Kathy jerked upright in her seat. "What did he say?"
she demanded of Mike.

"Who?"

"On the radio. About Melanie Blackwell. What did
he say?"

"I wasn't listening. Why? Do you know her?"

"She owned the preschool I sent Jessica to. I thought
he said she was found dead."

Mike hit his brakes and pulled over to the side of
the road. He turned the dial on the radio, searching for
another report on the story. No luck.

Kathy gave him directions to the preschool, her fists
clenched into painful balls in her lap. It was late and
everyone at Palm Valley might have gone home already. Fortunately, they weren't far away and in a matter of minutes they pulled into the lot and parked.

Mike followed Kathy as she rushed to the door. The
entryway was hushed and dim, all of the children safely
at home, but the door was unlocked, so someone must
be around. Kathy tapped the bell on the front counter
and they waited for a response.

A few moments later Alice Wender lumbered in. Her
eyes were red and had streaks of makeup below them.
She clenched a wadded tissue in one hand and a box
of them in the other. She stared at Kathy for a moment
as if she didn't recognize her, and then she made the
connection.

"Oh, Mrs. Jordan. Did you hear?"

Kathy stepped forward, touching the other woman's
shoulder with concern.

"I only heard part of what happened, Alice. Is it true
that Melanie is dead?"

Alice nodded, apparently just noticing Mike. Stopping, she stared from him back to Kathy.

"This is Detective Simens, Alice."

A weary frown turned down the corners of Alice's mouth. "I've already told the police everything I know," she said to Mike. "They had me for hours and hours. I just don't know anything else."

She began to cry, mopping at her eyes with the wad in her hand before cramming it into her already-stuffed pocket and reaching for a dry tissue.

"Mike's here with me to help find Jessica, not about Melanie."

The reminder of Jessica made Alice cry harder. She fumbled her way to her chair and plopped down in it.

"Has the world gone crazy?" she moaned. "First that sweet girl of yours and now Melanie . . ."

Kathy leaned against the counter, fighting to keep control of her own emotions and not join Alice in an emotional breakdown.

"What happened to Melanie, Alice?" Kathy asked softly.

"It was terrible. Terrible. Who would do such a thing to her?"

Silently Kathy shook her head. Mike seemed to fade into the background, letting Kathy take over.

"They discovered her body last night. This morning. A drunk driver . . . They might never have found her."

Kathy blinked. "She was killed by a drunk driver?"

"No, she was killed someplace and then dumped out by where they're building Highway 57. A drunk driver thought the construction was finished and took the exit right off to nowhere. They were clearing away his wreck when they found her."

She sprouted fresh tears, cramming yet another clump of tissue into her pocket and reaching for a fresh one.

"I'd been calling her ever since she didn't show up for work. She's always here. I called and called. No answer." She blew her nose. "At lunch I even went to her house. I looked in the windows and nothing seemed out of place, but when I got back, I was worried, so I called the police."

She looked up long enough to glare at Mike. "They don't count a person missing until it's too late."

"Do they have any ideas about what happened to her, Alice?"

Alice gave her a blank look. "She was murdered. Raped and murdered," she said, as if explaining the facts of life to a child. "I had to identify her. Her throat had been cut ear to ear. Ear to ear, Mrs. Jordan. It was terrible."

Mike rested his elbows on the counter, looking down at the pathetic figure Alice made, slumped in her seat like a sack of potatoes bulging at the seams. Alice sniffed into another tissue; crumpled balls overflowed from her pocket onto the floor.

"When was the last time you saw Melanie Blackwell?" Mike asked.

"Right before she left on Wednesday," she answered, nodding to herself. "I was cleaning up a mess in the Blue Room, so I was here late. She popped in and said good night. That was the last time I ever saw her. Alive, I mean."

"What time was that?" Mike asked.

"Between six and six-thirty."

"Did you notice anything peculiar about her that night?"

"Peculiar?" She thought about this for a moment. "No."

Something in the back of Kathy's mind caught and stuck. Like a record skipping on the same word over and over. Peculiar. Peculiar.

"Wait a minute," Kathy said. "I remember something. When I came to pick up Jessica . . . Melanie was putting on makeup. Like she had a date."

Kathy and Mike looked at Alice expectantly. Alice shook her head.

"She didn't say anything to me about it if she did and, as far as I know, she wasn't seeing anyone. She was a lonely woman, Melanie. No family. I don't think she got out much."

"Can I see her office?" Mike asked.

Alice gave him a once-over that she must have honed from years of subduing toddlers with just a look. Realizing he was not to be intimidated, she finally hauled herself to her feet and shuffled from around the corner.

"The police have already been through it all. Don't you guys ever talk to each other?" She didn't wait for an answer as she opened the door and let him in. While he looked around the bright room, she turned to Kathy.

"Have they had any luck finding your little one?"

Kathy shook her head. "Not yet, but Mike's helping me. We'll find her."

Alice nodded as if she didn't believe a word of it but had decided to keep her opinion to herself. She stared back at Mike, watching as he opened desk drawers.

He turned to the filing cabinet, giving Kathy a look from across the room. Pulling the top drawer out, he let his fingers walk across the assorted tabs poking up. He pushed it shut and pulled out the second.

"Does every child who attends have a file?" he asked.

Alice nodded. "That's where we keep their medical information. Who to contact in case of an emergency. That sort of thing. We get that before we'll take the child."

"Does Jessica Jordan still have one?" he asked.

"Of course. Well, I mean, I didn't pull it and Melanie hasn't been back . . ."

She sniffled bravely and marched over to the filing cabinet. She flipped through the folders, paused, and started again.

"Well I know she had one. I made it myself when she started." She looked at Kathy. "You did fill out emergency information, didn't you?"

"Yes. I remember doing it. Melanie was a stickler for procedure."

Alice nodded, blushing. "I do remember she was upset about your tardiness, Mrs. Jordan. Maybe she pulled it out for some reason." She began sorting through Melanie's desk, mumbling to herself.

Mike moved to Kathy's side, whispering that he'd be right back as he went out the door. Kathy stared around the room while she waited. Jessica had loved this place. Called it fairyland.

Jessica, where are you now? Don't give up. Mommy will find you.

Mike returned. In his hand, he had the file folder he'd found in Porter's house. Silently he held it out for Alice to see.

"Is this the folder?" he asked.

She recoiled, taking it from him with obvious hesitation. Holding it by the corner between her thumb and forefinger, she stared at the grease and chew marks. "That's it. That's my writing on the label."

Mike nodded. "I thought so."

21

DC stepped from his car, tucking his chin low on his chest. He'd traded his dress shoes for boots and his trousers for blue jeans that chafed when he walked. His hair was tucked under a cowboy hat that kept his eyes in shadow.

He opened the door to Hookey's Bar and walked in. Nervously, he checked out the two big guys playing pool. A fat bartender with dimpled arms and bloated breasts asked him what he wanted. Moments later she put his change in front of him, sloshing it with beer from a dripping mug.

With marked casualness, he took his beer and sauntered to the phone, stuck between doors marked "men" and "wo en." His palms were sweaty and he nearly dropped the slick mug on the way. He felt buzzed, hyped by the adrenaline shooting through his system. Setting his beer on the top of the phone, he dialed the long-distance number from memory and deposited two dollars in change.

"Fort General Hospital," a nasal-voiced woman answered.

"Greg Gainer," DC said.

He waited, nervously scanning the bar. The pool game ended and the players racked up another. Finally Greg answered.

"It's me," DC said.

''Where you been, man?''

''Working on our deal,'' he answered, keeping his voice low and cool. He didn't want Greg to know how uptight he felt. ''I've got it.''

A lengthy pause stretched across the miles and started a quake in the pit of DC's stomach. Something was wrong.

''That's good. That's real good, man,'' Greg said, lowering his voice to a whisper. ''But you got to sit tight, you know? Things are too hot right now.''

''What are you talking about?''

''Listen up. The place is crawling with FBI. Somehow it leaked out, man. I gotta keep low. You too, man. Wherever you are, stay there.''

''FBI?'' DC repeated, turning his back on the bar.

''Yeah, man. It leaked, I'm telling you. I don't know who. I think it was a nurse. Now they're checking all the records looking ... you know.'' Greg cleared his throat. He sounded panicked. Worse, he sounded frantic. ''Don't worry, though. I'm working on lining things up somewhere else.''

''Where?''

''Don't worry about it. I'll let you know when it's time. You just sit tight.''

DC heard voices in the background on the other end. Greg muffled the mouthpiece and talked to them for a moment. DC spent the time collecting his thoughts. What the hell was he going to do now?

Greg came back. ''Sorry, man, I gotta cruise. You got the girl, right?''

''J. Jordan. Heart donor.''

''Shit man, not on the phone,'' Greg hissed. ''Listen up. Keep it cool, man. Stay low. Call me next week and I'll give you the drop.''

''I can't wait that long. Things are hot here, too. They're looking for her.''

''So don't let them find her. Next week.''

DC nodded to the dial tone. Next week? How would he last that long?

He replaced the receiver, trying to maintain composure. In the gritty men's room, he closed the door and splashed cold water on his face, staring into a rusted sink. Now what? He wouldn't last another week without getting caught. He knew it.

Back at the phone, he retrieved his beer and downed it. From his back pocket he pulled a folded sheet of paper with Jessica Jordan's emergency information on it. He dialed the home number. The phone rang twenty times before he hung up.

Cursing, he returned to the bar for another beer. The five o'clock news was playing on a TV tucked under a ceiling beam. Feeling as if the worst had already happened, he watched in horror as his picture, subtitled *Dwight "DC" Porter* appeared on the screen alongside a composite picture that looked as good as a photo. Shit!

A grim newscaster described the alleged abductor's car, complete with plate number. The police had connected Jessica Jordan's kidnapping and Melanie Blackwell's murder to him! How the hell had they done that so quickly?

Christie McCoy. Her name popped into his head. It wasn't enough she had his house. Now she wanted his freedom.

He rubbed his hands on his jeans and wiped his sweaty face with his sleeve. Taking another gulp of his beer, he winced as he forced the swallow past his constricted throat muscles. The broadcast took a commercial break. Grateful, DC stood. Pulling the brim of his hat low on his forehead, he went back to the phone. He called Kathy Jordan's number again.

This time she answered. "Hello?"

"Listen, bitch," he said, impressing himself with his cold steady voice. "You want to see your daughter again, you listen and do exactly what I say."

He felt her terrified silence leap across the line. She took a couple of short breaths. He could picture her face. Empowered, he stood straighter.

"Where is she?" she demanded. "Where's my daughter? I want to talk to her—"

"You're not in a position to want anything. Shut up."

She made a funny little noise, then covered the receiver with her hand. She was talking to someone in the background. The cops?

"Listen to me!" he snapped. "You sure as hell better not be talking to the cops, lady. And don't bother trying to trace this call. I won't be here that long."

"Let me talk to Jessica now."

He didn't answer, letting her stew in his silence.

"What have you done with my daughter?" she pleaded.

"Nothing yet. I've decided to give you a second chance."

"Second chance?"

"Yeah, but don't fuck it up, *Kathy*, or you'll be seeing your baby girl in pieces next time."

"I swear to you, if you've hurt her, I will hunt you down and—"

"What? What will you do?"

She didn't answer. He could hear her crying.

"That's what I thought. I've been thinking about you a lot, *Kathy*. I had a good time the other night. Let's do it again. Maybe this time we'll let Jessica watch. That way she'll see how much you like it."

"You're sick."

"Two hundred thousand dollars and you'll get your daughter back."

"Two hundred thousand? Two hundred thousand? I don't have that kind of money. I barely have two hundred dollars."

"That's a shame. Two hundred thousand or I tell Jessica her mommy puts out on the first date. Maybe

I'll show her how it's done." His laugh had a maniacal edge to it. It scared him. Made him feel out of control.

"Please don't hurt her," Kathy whispered. "She's just a little girl. A kid. She doesn't understand."

"Make it twenties and fifties. Or I make her understand."

"I don't—I don't have it. How am I going to get that kind of money!" she cried.

Slowly he replaced the receiver, staring at his shaking hands. His face was now covered with sweat.

Shit, this was screwed. He knew she was telling the truth. He'd seen how she lived. Kathy didn't have anything he wanted, but Christie did.

Slowly he lifted the receiver again. He'd deal with Christie soon, but first he had to get rid of the kid.

His next call went to his mother. She answered on the second ring.

"Beth McClain."

22

As soon as they climbed into the Jeep, Sam grabbed Christie's hand and flattened it against his thigh, binding her to him both physically and emotionally. There'd be no retreat for her this time.

His blue jeans felt soft beneath her fingers, his leg hard with tensed muscles. Her gaze kept drifting to his profile, studying the straight nose, the sexy curve of his firm chin. The dimple that winked in and out of his cheek as he nibbled on his bottom lip. He turned and gave her a look that smoldered. She knew the same expression burned in her own eyes.

She rolled down her window and tried to concentrate on the scenery instead of Sam. The sun dangled low in the western sky, giving the few puffy white clouds gathered around it a peachy hue. The evening air felt warm and thick. It rushed through the window, wrapping them in a seductive allure.

Her gaze was drawn back to Sam.

He squeezed her hand, his fingers circling her wrist and rubbing the sensitive pulse that pounded there. The trembly feeling he started raced up her arm and through her body. The dimple appeared again. He knew exactly what he was doing to her.

A gust of wind blustered through the window and billowed his shirt, giving her a glimpse of his bare chest, lightly scattered with baby-soft hair. She remembered how it felt pressed against her breasts, beneath her fingers. Her heartbeat tripped up.

She felt fiery and liquid, alive like a drop of oil dancing on a sizzling skillet. It had been too long since she'd felt like this. Felt so *female*. A seductress in control. They spoke with sideways glances and feather-light caresses. How much farther to Sam's house?

He stopped at a red light, leaning over to capture her lips in a stolen kiss while silent mechanisms controlled nonexistent traffic. No such signal existed inside Christie to monitor the rush of emotions that raced unchecked just under the surface.

Finally they turned onto his street, then into his driveway. She followed him up to the door and inside, waiting as he ordered the dogs outside, locked the door, pulled the blinds, and then turned to stare at her.

"Are you sure?" he asked softly. "You didn't change your mind on the way, did you?"

Shaking her head, she whispered, "You have to know your mind to change it, and all I know is what I feel. I feel right."

His lips closed over hers, warm and firm and soft as suede. A light bristle of beard roughened his cheeks and chin and she rubbed her fingers against it, shivering with remembered awareness, trembling with anticipated intimacy. Inhaling, she allowed herself to be submerged in his scent and feel. His chest was hard, his belly flat as a board, and she took her time exploring each familiar muscle there. She teased herself, yielding to the desire to touch his skin, but only permitting brief caresses.

Slowly, he began unbuttoning her blouse, letting the material fall away from her skin a bit at a time. She felt powerful and provocative, centered like a glittering opal in his fixed stare.

Tucked close to the heat of his body, enveloped in his scent and embrace, the past seemed as real as a movie. The here and now was so much more important.

He nibbled on her lips, taking his time with slow deep kisses that went on and on until she felt as weightless as light. His big hands caressed her back and hips, roved over her flat belly, dipping lower, then straying up to the lacy cups of her bra. His touch was gentle here, rough there. He touched her as if she was his and she responded as if he was right.

She pulled his shirt from his pants and thrust her hands under, shivering with sensation as his hot skin touched her palms.

He undressed her with sensuous reverence, looking at her as if she were a work of art, something to be admired and touched with the utmost respect. And then his lips were on her, his tongue teasing her nipples to hard points, sending hot shivers over her body.

She kissed him feverishly, showing him what she could not say, begging for what she was afraid to ask. But he understood. Every signal she sent he answered, moving in perfect rhythm to her needs, giving and taking with such fine balance that she could no longer distinguish which was the giving, which was the taking. The only thing that existed was Sam.

He pulled her into that dazzling room of passion, thrusting her under the light of dizzying heights and sensation. She clenched her eyes against the brightness and let go to the spiral of hot, liquid excitement that whirled her back to the floor. Slowly she opened her eyes and looked into his. She saw the same surprised aftershock in his gaze that she felt in her own.

Who knew what danger or terror waited for them outside. Looking into Sam's eyes, Christie didn't care.

In a husky voice, he said, "We shouldn't have quit on us, Christie."

23

DC sat on the counter, tapping his hunting knife on the edge of the Formica top. It made a tinny sound. A hollow sound that matched his mood.

The girl was huddled on the floor in the corner, watching him with eyes wide and full of fear. Her fists clenched and unclenched over the edge of the blanket she'd pulled around herself. She looked like she was trying to disappear under its folds. She was terrified.

As she should be.

The knife tapped away. His foot, crossed over his knee, waggled in time with it. He shifted his weight so he could reach the faucet. He added it to his drumming. The mismatched clanging competed with the alarms sounding in his mind and the brain-splitting headache pounding on his brain. He didn't care. At this point torture was preferable to the nagging fear clouding his vision, impairing his judgment.

Things were going from bad to totally screwed. Mary Jane was dead. Forever gone, while his mother, as usual, survived. And, as usual, his mother had the power to help him but wouldn't. He ceased his banging, tilting his head to the side. Was that her car he'd heard? The faint hum thinned and vanished as it moved on.

Shit, he was in deep. He had half a mind to do the kid and get the hell out of town. But he'd come too far to scrap it, and he had a lot invested in the deal.

Everything was tied to the deal. He had nothing left but the hundred bucks he'd lifted from Sissy and a lot of trouble to his name.

Jumping to his feet, he chucked the knife into the sink. It clattered around, startling the kid. He scowled at her, watching, as she cringed into the corner.

"You want any more?" he asked, pointing to the open pizza box on the counter.

She shook her head, pulling the blanket, like a cloak of armor, around her slim shoulders. For some reason the gesture made him a little sad, but he crushed the emotion.

Looking at his watch for the tenth time in as many minutes, he began to wonder if his mother would stand him up. Even though he knew he had her backed into a corner, he couldn't erase the feeling that she would somehow ditch him. Hey, it wouldn't be the first time. Heartless bitch.

As if summoned by his thoughts, her car sounded in the driveway and, moments later, the front door opened and closed.

The girl watched from the floor, still as death.

"Go to the bathroom," he commanded.

Without a word she raced down the hall and shut herself in. Feigning a relaxed position, he slouched against the counter and waited for his mother to find him.

She'd come straight from work and when she rounded the corner, a swirl of navy blue silk and expensive perfume followed her. When he was little, before he'd come to the realization that she'd abandoned him to his brutal caretakers and wasn't coming back, he'd thought she was beautiful. While he lived with his grandparents, DC had dreamed of seeing his mother's sweet, pure face on the day she would come to rescue him. His memory had kept every detail intact.

She slammed her suede purse on the counter and glared at him.

"Hello, Mommy. Good to see you."

"Let's get one thing straight," she snapped, wagging a red-tipped nail at him. "You don't ever call me at work again. Understand?"

DC popped the top on a beer, watching her over the rim as he swigged the entire can. Finished, he wiped his mouth with his sleeve and belched.

"You're drunk," she accused.

He wasn't, but if it pissed her off, he'd pretend. "I'm *fucked up,* Mommy dear."

"Quit calling me that, you bastard." She turned and glared at the pile of pizza boxes and beer cans on the counter. "You're still a filthy pig," she said with disgust. "Everything you touch, you destroy. Well, let me tell you, you're going down with this one, DC. Down."

He cursed the hot flush that raced up his face. He didn't give a shit what she thought about him.

"Down?" he repeated. "I'll take you with me, Mommy. You taught me everything I know."

"I don't think so. I've been a fool, but it's over now."

His palms felt sweaty, his stomach sour. Pushing away from the counter, he looked out the back door, hiding his face from her. At times like this, she reminded him of his grandpa's dogs. He didn't dare show fear or she'd rip him limb from limb.

She picked up the scent anyway, and gave a cold, knowing laugh that turned him to face her. Her smile revealed perfect, white teeth that gleamed in the harsh glow of the kitchen light. Like fangs, DC thought, immediately wishing he could snatch back the thought and with it, the terrifying images that snarled through his subconscious.

"You're a little confused, Mommy," he sneered, trying to match her frosty composure. "It's not over. It's just starting."

"If that's the way you want to play it, maybe it is. But I'm out of it, DC. If you have half a brain, you'll get out, too."

"I gotta dump the kid. Help me out and I'll leave. I'll vanish. *Poof,* like magic."

She shook her head, frigid grin unchanged. "I don't believe you. I can't help you. You've locked yourself in, DC. The only way out is to run."

"You sound concerned, Mommy. I'm touched."

"I don't give a damn what you are, DC, unless it's gone."

He groped desperately for an edge. "How's your son?"

"It won't work. I covered my tracks, DC. No one can ever take him away from me."

"I wonder what he'd think if I told him the truth though?"

"He wouldn't believe you," she said, a nervous twitch ticking the corner of her eye.

Finally, a chink. DC pressed.

"I think he would. He'd be pretty upset, too, once he found out that he could have had a perfectly good family if it wasn't for you."

"Shut up, DC."

"*Pissed off.* That's what he'd be once I told him how I snatched him away from his family, just because you wanted him. He could have had a real mother, instead of you. God knows I'd be thrilled to hear it, but James will be mad, I bet. And what about your hubby? Think he'll come visit you in prison?"

The delicate balance of power shifted silently in the tense quiet that hung between them.

"What do you want, DC?" she asked finally.

"I told you. I need to unload the kid."

"What happened to your big deal that was going to make you rich?"

"There's been a delay. I don't have time to wait. I want to get rid of the kid now."

"A delay? Don't take me for a fool, DC. Your *deal* won't work. It just took you this long to figure that out."

He glared at her. "It will too work. I've even done it before. Twice, in Kansas. You of all people should know that once you get the little guy on your side, anything will work. All it took was a cooperative ambulance driver, a little help from the admissions clerk—"

"I don't want the details, DC. I could care less, so screw your wonderful plan. There's nothing I can do for you. Every cop in the state is looking for her. I'd be stupid to help you," she said.

She shook her head, her expression one of total revulsion, as if just looking at him could make her sick. The taut knot of anger in his gut pulled tighter.

"People are looking for her. They're on every street corner, handing out her picture. Handing out yours with it."

She was right. It pissed him off to admit it, but she was right. He cleared his throat.

"I told her mother I wanted two hundred thousand dollars," he said. "As soon as I get it, I'll leave."

"And do you honestly think she'll have it? I checked her out. She doesn't have a pot to piss in."

"Your roots are showing, Mommy," he said, getting some satisfaction from her angry flush. "She'll get it. If not, I'll dump the kid. I'm working on the house anyway."

"The house? Are you insane or just too stupid to get it? You're going to be in jail."

"I'm not stupid and I'm not going to jail."

"Did you know that your picture is in today's paper?"

"Big deal. It's on the news, too. I saw it. So did the three other people there with me. Nobody noticed. A picture's nothing."

"Get out while you can. Do something right for once. I'll get you the money I promised. Take it and leave."

DC opened another beer that he really didn't want to drink and forced himself to take a swig. He wanted to take her offer. He knew she was right. But he'd cut his own throat before he'd admit it.

"Take your money and shove it. That's not even pocket change."

She shook her head, distaste on her face, disgust in her eyes. Snatching her purse off the table, she stomped to the door.

"You're a fool, DC," she called back.

"And you're a bitch, *Mommy*."

The door slammed behind her. As the sound echoed through the deserted rooms, DC's rage doubled back on him.

Who the fuck did she think she was?

He screamed his frustration and kicked the wall. The plaster chipped away, leaving a dent in the smooth surface. He pounded it again and again until the hole went through to the skeletal structure and his foot felt like a ball of fiery pain.

Why was this happening to him? How could it be that Mary Jane was dead? That her slut daughter owned his house? That he was stuck with a snot-nosed kid he couldn't unload? And, once again, he was at the mercy of his mother's whims?

He hollered to the ceiling, venting his anger at the walls.

He'd make them pay for this. All of them.

In his mind he pictured Mary Jane's face. She had loved him. The one and only person in his life to care, and she was dead. The image of her smiling face faded into that of her daughter's. From day one, Christie had looked at him like he was dirt. Worse. Like he was something to be scraped off the bottom of her shoes.

He slammed his fist, then his head, into the wall, aiming for her imagined face. He would even that score, too, before he left.

He would make them pay. All of them, starting with Christie McCoy.

24

Standing to the side, Mike waited for Kathy to quit fumbling with her keys. Finally, he took them from her and unlocked the door himself. In her quick glance he read appreciation and resentment. She was so proud. Too proud. It must have damn near killed her to have come to him in the first place. But then she'd come for Jessica, not herself. For Jessica, Kathy would do anything.

She tossed her purse on the low table just inside the door and stood hesitantly in her small living room, silent, as she'd been most of the day. Mike was still having trouble accepting this side of a woman who used to enjoy taunting and nagging him. Making him feel like a giant idiot.

She didn't even seem like the same woman anymore.

She acted shy about having him in her house. He looked from the worn sofa to the scratched-up coffee table, remembering how it had looked when he'd first arrived on the scene. He'd been stunned to learn that the victims were Kathy and Jessica.

The carpet was stained near the kitchen, the spot a dark maroon that could only be blood. In the corner a big plastic toy box overflowed with stuffed animals and plastic things molded in bright colors and strange shapes. A doll perched on top, looking lost without a little girl. He looked away, saddened by the sight.

Crime scenes had that effect on him. Seeing everything put back in place . . . a Teddy bear patiently waiting on a small bed, or a bicycle returned to the garage without its rider . . . the images swamped him with depression. To him, it said that no matter how normal things seem to be, crime and violence were always lurking around the corner. He wandered to Jessica's bedroom, looking, searching, for the clue that must have been missed.

Where is Jessica? he silently asked the fluffy stuffed cat curled in perpetual satisfaction on Jessica's pillow. How could he even hope to find her? Where did he get off giving Kathy false hope?

He touched the pretty little-girl things that littered Jessica's dresser. Miss Fancy perfume, nontoxic and even edible, caught his eye. He opened the lid and took a whiff, recognizing the scent that had sweetened Kathy's skin today.

He capped the tiny bottle, giving the room another look. In his mind he could hear the laughter that he knew these walls had once contained. Over the imagined sound, he heard the screams that had scarred the small Jordan family and the violence that had separated them.

He had to find Jessica. He had to.

Returning to the living room, he found Kathy in the same place, quietly absorbing Jessica's features from the framed pictures. She looked bewildered, her vacant gaze at odds with the determined angle of her chin. She stood, shoulders back, ready for battle, while soft, warm tears trickled over her lashes and careened down her cheeks. She cried silently, her pain so great it seemed hollow, without sound.

Gradually her gaze refocused on the room before her as she regained a consciousness of the present. Mike shuffled awkwardly, not sure what he should do. Not quite sure what was expected of him.

"Sometimes it's just too much, Mike," she murmured softly. "Sometimes I feel like I can't even breathe. Like I don't even want to try. To think of her out there, scared . . . hurt . . . who knows what. . . ."

Another, more painful silence gripped them. He felt the need to say something positive, but his jaws felt like forged steel and his tongue like an oblong ice cube that refused to melt no matter how hot his face got.

"You did a good job today," he offered finally, feeling ridiculous as soon as the words passed his lips.

She looked at him as if trying to determine what language he was speaking. "What?" she said with a frown.

"At Sissy Norman's house. You kept quiet and didn't crowd. We got a lead."

"A lead? Is that what you call it?" She smiled without humor. "So what, Mike? It's not going to matter. He's probably not even in the country anymore. Who knows if Jessica's even alive?"

"Hey, I can't believe this," he said. "You can't give up."

She stared at him a moment, as if considering his words. Her gaze drifted back to Jessica's smiling face, peering from a golden-leafed tree. As she stared, the corners of her mouth tightened, her fists opened and closed. He watched as she collected her thoughts, storing her grief behind closed doors to be dealt with later. When she spoke her voice was low and strong.

"Give up? No way. I won't ever give up."

And I won't either, he swore to himself.

Their exchanged look sealed an unspoken pact, an unvoiced promise. Breaking the contact with a shaky smile, Kathy rubbed her arm with her hand. For the first time, he noticed her blouse was torn and blood speckled her sleeve.

"What happened to your arm?"

She shrugged. "Nothing."

Moving closer, he pushed her hand out of the way

to see the jagged scratch under the torn sleeve. It was
an angry red and looked sore.

"When did this happen?"

"When I crawled through the window at Porter's
house," she mumbled, looking down at her feet.

"*What?* Why didn't you say something?"

"I didn't want you to make me wait in the car."

He sighed, shaking his head. "Do you have something to clean this with? Hell, who knows what germs
the rats brought in."

The mention of rats turned her skin even paler. Silently he cursed his big mouth. He always managed to
say the wrong thing around her.

"There's a first aid kit under the bathroom sink,"
she said weakly. "I'll get it."

"*I'll* get it," he said standing. He gave his watch a
quick glance. "Why don't you turn on the TV? The
news just started. Maybe we'll hear something new."

He returned with the kit, catching the tail end of the
recount on Porter. The composite looked good. He gave
Kathy an encouraging look just as the phone rang.
Smiling, she answered.

An ominous silence told him something was wrong.
She clutched the phone in a white-knuckled hand. Her
face was pale and her eyes looked like huge, blue chips.

"Where is she?" she demanded of the caller, meeting Mike's gaze across the room. She gestured to the
police recorder set up on the counter. Mike hurried to
switch it on. Cupping her hand over the receiver, she
whispered, "It's *him!*"

Mike listened to her voice, watching with a feeling
of impotence as emotions of terror and anguish fought
for control of her features. She begged to talk to Jessica; the plaintive plea was painful to hear. Mike
watched helplessly, wanting nothing more than to jump
down the phone line and shove his gun right up Porter's
ass. Instead he consoled himself with the knowledge

that as long as DC Porter thought Kathy was alone, they had the advantage.

She hung up, shaken and pale, looking as if she'd just learned there would be no tomorrow. Mike replayed the tape, listening to the voice of DC Porter.

"Where am I going to get that kind of money?" she whispered, staring up at Mike.

He shook his head, not realizing that he intended to pull her into his protective embrace until he felt her fingers gripping his shoulder and her tears burning hot through his shirt. Her sobs rocked through her, her agony vibrating against him. He couldn't remember when he'd ever felt so powerless as he did now, listening to her weep and knowing that if he'd had the support of the department, he might have been able to locate Jessica already. Then her mother wouldn't have to endure this suffering.

Finally, she sniffled and pulled away from him. "I don't have time to cry. My baby needs me, and I don't care if I have to pound down every door in this city, I will find her."

Her words triggered some switch in the back of his mind that started a tiny brain-buzzer humming. He was missing something, something of vital importance. What? He chased it around his head for a moment, but it eluded him, niggling, like an itch that couldn't be reached.

Kathy went around the kitchen counter, whipping off a paper towel to wipe her nose. She ran some water over her fingers and pressed them to her eyes, splashing some more on her face.

"Let me take a look at your arm, Kathy," he said, reluctantly backing off from the worrisome tick gnawing on his mind.

"There isn't time," she snapped. "I've got to get moving."

"Moving isn't going to do you any good if you drop

dead from blood poisoning. It's only going to take a second, then we'll come up with a plan.''

''Plan? Plan? What the hell kind of plan?'' Her voice rose with hysteria, her cheeks flushing from deathly white to heart-attack red. ''What good is a *plan* going to do me?''

She hiccuped, staring at him with wild eyes. He waited her out, letting her hurl angry words his way until she ran out. Slowly, she recovered her composure, straightening her shoulders, raising her chin. She mumbled an apology, staring at him through eyes that gleamed a dull and troubled gray.

He gripped her shoulders lightly between his palms, startled again by his initiation of physical contact with her, but feeling that nothing less than touching would get through to her. She looked into his eyes.

''We're going to find Jessica,'' he said, holding her until she gave him an agreeing nod. ''Now, let me look at your arm.''

She plopped into a chair and unbuttoned her blouse far enough to ease her arm out. Pretending an intense interest in the first aid kit, Mike tried to keep his gaze from the creamy skin of her shoulder and soft curves below.

The gash was deep and painful-looking, dried blood trailing from shoulder to elbow. It must have ached all day. He felt another spark of admiration gleam its way through his murky preconceptions about her. She could take it as well as any man.

He cleaned up the wound and crisscrossed bandages over it. The end result looked childishly inept, but it would do. When he finished, she turned her arm to see. A grin tugged at her lips and thawed her eyes a little.

''Thanks.''

They sat in silence for a moment longer, either too tired or too uncertain to move. His stomach growled loudly, the sound echoing in the quiet room.

''You're hungry,'' she said.

"Aren't you?"

"No, I can't eat. I can't keep it down."

"You should try. You can't live on pain, Kathy, it'll run you into the ground. Let's stop on the way and get something."

"On the way where?"

He shrugged. "If we're going to pound on doors we gotta start somewhere. I'll swing into a drive-thru—"

He froze, the nagging thought racing circles in his head suddenly stopping and becoming crystal clear.

"Better yet, let's have pizza."

25

"I'm hungry," Sam said, dropping a kiss on Christie's nose as he stood.

"We just ate."

Grabbing his pants, he headed for the kitchen. "All that exercise worked up an appetite," he said.

Wrapped in the warmth of lovemaking, Christie went upstairs to change into a pair of worn blue jeans and an oversized cotton pullover that ended mid-thigh. When she came back downstairs, Sam was whistling. He looked up from the refrigerator with a sexy grin that left her feeling quivery.

The sight of him, barefoot, bare-chested, and rumpled, made her smile. In his hands he balanced a container of assorted deli meats and cheeses with a bottle of wine tucked under his arm. Plopping it all on the counter, he grabbed her around the waist and kissed her.

He turned away, reaching for a loaf of bread, but she grabbed him by the belt loops and pulled him back for another kiss. When she finally let him go, she felt light-headed and totally pleased with herself.

"I was looking over the trust agreement while you were changing," he said. "Your mom's house in La Mesa didn't go to DC. It went to Beth McClain."

"What?" Christie asked, returning reluctantly to grim reality. She perched on the barstool. "I can't believe I didn't notice that," she murmured.

"Yeah, well, why would you suspect Pfeiffer? Like you said, there was a lot going on at the time."

He opened the wine and poured them each a glass. She sipped at hers, watching while he cut an onion and tomato, placing the slices on a plate.

"I was thinking," he said, popping a piece of cheese in his mouth and cutting another for her. "Let's drop by and see Pfeiffer. Unannounced. Give him a little surprise. Maybe if we rattle his cage, we'll get some straight answers out of him."

"You and your surprise attacks, Sam."

He looked up, grinning again. "I am getting into this investigation stuff, aren't I?"

"I'd say so. There's one thing you didn't think of, though. It's after business hours. He's probably gone home already."

Sam's self-satisfied grin widened. "I had my pal look up his home address."

"You're not suggesting we go to his house, are you?"

"You bet. On the way, I want to stop by my office. I've been thinking about that business card of mine that we found in the gym locker. The more I bounce it around in my head, the more convinced I get that I've met this guy. His face isn't familiar, but from what you say, it shouldn't be. I usually don't remember faces anyway."

"What's that got to do with your office, Sam?"

"Well, I make everyone who stops in fill out a contact card."

"So?"

"So, I'd like to look through my files and see if I find one on him. Maybe it will ring some bells."

"*You* have files?"

He looked up from spreading mayonnaise on bread. "Yes, *I* have files."

"The circular kind, right? Like the kind the trash man picks up every week?"

"For your information, I have very organized files,"
he said defensively. "Alphabetized and everything."

She took another sip from her glass, watching him
over the rim.

"Okay, okay. A client's daughter does the filing."

"I didn't say a word."

"You didn't have to."

He rolled ham, turkey, and roast beef slices into
cones and neatly arranged them on thick bread, topping
them with crispy bacon. Next went cheddar and jack
cheese, lettuce, thick slices of tomato and onion, then
salt and pepper. Finally, he added a light dressing of
olive oil and Dijon mustard. Cutting the two-inch mas-
terpieces with a giant serrated knife, he passed one over
to Christie.

She took a bite, remembering other nights spent in
this kitchen eating Sam's creations.

"I missed your sandwiches, Sam."

She ate half of the giant sandwich before reluctantly
turning back to the matters at hand.

"Okay, assuming we will actually find this contact
card in your *files,* tell me what good it's going to do
us."

He swallowed a bite before answering. "Well,
mostly it's questions about physical activity and exercise they're used to. I like to cover my ass on that kind
of stuff. Some people don't think of golf as a sport and
don't think they have to be in shape to do it. Heart-
attack scenarios. Other than that, there's an address and
phone. If I have a card on him, it'll be interesting to
see whose he uses. I don't know that we'll get anything
else useful from it, but it's worth a try."

"And? That's not all, is it?"

"And, I want to pick up my gun."

"Gun? No way, Sam. You know how I feel about
guns. A gun is an invitation to get killed."

"I knew you'd react this way. That's why I didn't
want to tell you. I want to have it—just in case. I feel

antsy, Chris. Like something's about to happen. If that's the case, I'd rather not wait for it."

Finished with their sandwiches, they restored the kitchen to order.

Sam gave her a questioning look. "Ready?"

She shrugged. "As ready as I'll ever be."

The last wisps of sunset faded from lavender to black but the evening still held the day's warmth, hugging the thick air close like a woolen blanket. As Sam locked the front door, Christie stared at the shadowed trees and shrubs, motionless silhouettes against a moving gray backdrop. The moon gleamed through the misty veil, silently tracking their steps. She felt exposed in its glow, at the mercy of shifting clouds.

"What's wrong?" Sam asked, turning away from the door.

"I don't know. I'm paranoid, I guess. I always feel like I'm being watched."

"You are," he said, hooking a thumb behind him. "Look."

She turned to see Snort and Bear, paws to the window, watching them from inside. They looked alarmed at the prospect of being left alone. Christie wished she could go back and comfort them, but she didn't think soothing words would disguise her jangled nerves.

Turning her back on them, she climbed into the Jeep beside Sam and closed her eyes as he drove. Sam grabbed her hand and held it, his touch reassuring.

"Quit worrying, Christie. We're not doing anything illegal."

"I guess not, but I'm still as crazy about the idea of having a gun as I am about popping in on Leonard Pfeiffer unannounced. What if he calls the cops or something?"

"I'll leave the gun in the car when I talk to him. We're only going to visit him, Christie, not gun him down. If he asks us to leave, we will."

After a few minutes of driving, they parked in the

deserted Padre Trails lot. Submerged in shadows that rustled with still life, the green oasis looked like a photo negative of the picturesque daytime scene. Trees towered with deathly-looking limbs. the grass glimmering like black quicksand.

Close to the shore, the golf course stretched below an ocean mist that coated the sky. It acted like an acoustical ceiling, muffling and distorting the night's sounds. Christie heard a car in the distance and the hoot of an owl, both noises seeming to come from just over her shoulder.

They crossed the silent blacktop that bordered the rolling greens. In the distance, the *chicka-chicka* of a sprinkler kept pace with their footsteps. Her clothes blended with the night and her white hand seemed to float, unconnected, as Sam grabbed it and guided her to the shedlike office bordering the driving range and the pond. He unlocked the door. Reaching inside to flick the switch, he flooded the doorstep with bright illumination that blackened everything in the periphery. The screen door banged shut behind them.

The inside of Sam's office was small and cluttered, fragranced with the scents of leather and coffee. Christie stood in the narrow space beside a junior-sized basketball net with a strategically placed wastebasket beneath it.

Sam grabbed a club that leaned against his desk and one of the balls scattered over its surface, tapping it across the mini putting green that hogged half of the room. Returning the club to its resting place, he went to the desk, sidestepping more sports paraphernlia with practiced ease. He pulled open the bottom file drawer and removed a folder. Staring over his shoulder, Christie saw that the folder was marked ''Prospects.''

He caught her questioning look. ''These are the ones that don't sign up after they come in. When it's slow, I go through them and touch base. Give them a little push if they seemed serious to start with.''

She'd never thought Sam organized enough to recruit clients, picturing him, instead, as taking it as it came. This simple plan for keeping business going tipped some scale in her mind, revising an opinion she hadn't even known she'd possessed.

As he sorted through the stacks of cards, she wandered to the window, now shut and locked. A tickle raced down her spine, chasing goose bumps across her skin as she looked into her reflection superimposed against the black fabric outside. Her own eyes stared back at her, but she couldn't shake the feeling that someone else's did too. She closed the blinds.

"I wonder if that bastard used his own name or made one up?" Sam mumbled. "There's nothing under Porter. I'm checking the addresses for your mom's."

"Here, let me have half," she said, reaching for a pile.

Together they scanned the cards, the room silent except for the shuffle. Finally Christie paused, staring at the card in her hand.

"Sam, look."

He took the card from her and read the name. "Dwight Calvin McClain."

They stared at each other as, outside, a mockingbird's song suddenly stopped and the silence seemed deafening. Christie looked up, her gaze trying to penetrate the dense blackness beyond the screen door. From somewhere close, she heard a thud. As if someone had kicked a rock or stubbed a toe on a root. Across the desk, Christie met Sam's gaze and knew he'd heard it too.

26

"**D**id you hear that?'' Christie asked.

Sam looked up, not sure what he had heard. Christie stood and moved to the open office door, staring out at the inky blackness beyond.

"Sam, did you hear that?'' she repeated.

He listened harder, nodding his head. "It must have been a squirrel, Chris. You're psyching yourself out.'' He turned back to the contact card he was studying. "Guess who DC listed as his employer? Leonard Pfeiffer. I'm not surprised.''

A sound, or maybe it was the lack of sound—her silence instead of her answer—*something* warned him. He jerked his head up, spinning around in his chair to face her.

Sam didn't need an introduction to know that the man with the knife to Christie's throat was DC Porter. DC jerked suddenly, turning on Sam as if he'd caught sight of some slight movement, but in the split second that passed, Sam had been too shocked to move. DC's sudden spasm cut a nick into Christie's neck. A scarlet drop of blood dribbled over the knife's edge. The sight of it honed Sam's surprise into cold, hard anger.

"Let her go, DC,'' Sam said, putting his hands in front of him in a deceptively placating gesture.

DC's gaze darted around the room in a continuous circle. It was apparent that the shadows made him nervous.

"Get outside," DC ordered.

With the blade on Christie's neck, DC took a step inside the office and waited for Sam to lead the way out.

Sam stalled for time, his searching gaze finding the putter propped against his desk. Keeping his hands palms up in front of him, he stood.

"You don't want to kill her, DC. You'll never get the house then."

DC stilled, staring at Sam. "What do you know about it?"

"I know you and Mary Jane meant to do business. What happened, DC? You blew it, didn't you?"

DC grabbed a handful of Christie's hair and gave it a violent jerk. "She fucked it up for me. Always acting like a fucking queen. Too good for me."

"You let a woman come between you and business?" Sam asked, clicking his tongue reproachfully. "How could you do that?"

DC turned red with angry embarrassment. Too outraged to speak, he flapped his lips like an air-breathing fish and sputtered disjointed curses.

Sam inched around his desk but DC caught the action, jerking him to attention with another vicious yank on Christie's hair. Sam froze.

"I said outside," DC snapped.

"Easy, man. I'm going," Sam said, knowing he wouldn't get an opportunity to overcome DC. He'd have to make one.

With that realization, everything slowed to a minute ticking of emotion and reaction. His glance ricocheted off the putter leaning against his desk. He saw the look of astonishment in Christie's eyes as she realized what his intentions were. He felt the warm night air breeze through the open door and brush against his flushed and heated face. His palms felt like they were coated in Vaseline. DC spewed a string of curses at them, unaware of the changing tides.

Sam drew even with the club and, hiding the action from DC with his step, wrapped his fingers around the familiar grip. In one fluid movement, Sam pivoted his body, swinging the club as he turned. It hissed through the small space separating them, screaming with friction as it parted the thick air. Christie lunged to the side while surprise momentarily froze DC. With all Sam's weight behind it, he slammed the club full speed at DC's head, but at the last moment DC acted with quick reflexes, jumping to the side. The club glanced off his shoulder and sent the knife flying across the room.

"Christie," Sam yelled. "Run."

She ducked away from DC but, instead of running, she lunged for the knife. Sam stared at her for an incredulous split second. Damn her, he'd said run! She never listened.

Sam swung the club again but, with incredible strength, DC wrenched it from his hand. Hurling his body at DC without hesitation, Sam propelled them both into the screen door. It snapped back on its hinges, spilling them out of the office. They hit the hard ground with a force that knocked all the wind out of Sam and left a dark veil of stars over his eyes. Somehow he'd landed on the bottom with the weight of DC shifting on top of him. Frantically he blinked his eyes, peering through the star-studded blackness just in time to see DC throw a punch that smashed into his nose and obliterated everything but a screeching pain that rendered him sightless again.

Striking out blindly, Sam's fists connected with DC's body. He pounded with all his strength. Pinned by the other man's weight, Sam still managed a lucky shot that clipped DC in the face and knocked him off-balance. Locked in battle, they rolled to the shore of the still pond between the first hole and the pro shop.

Sam's vision began to return and the hazy image of DC loomed into focus. Scrambling to his feet, Sam had just a second to brace himself before the weight of DC's body slammed him backward, into the pond.

They shattered the icy surface, the shallow oily waters sucking them into the muddy slime. The shocking cold cleared Sam's mind instantly, narrowing his fight strategy into one simple impulse. Kill.

Pushing off the floor of the pond, he locked his hands around DC's throat. DC fought, clawing at his throat, trying to peel back Sam's fingers to let in even a breath of air, but Sam held tight. The feel of DC's cold, slippery flesh beneath his fingers fed the consuming rage that tore through Sam, demanding blood. Demanding vengeance.

Gasping, DC's body flopped forward. Pathetically loose-limbed, he sagged from the neck down like a giant rag doll. Sam kept his fingers around DC's throat, watching with chilly satisfaction as they seemed to disappear under the folds of purpling flesh.

"Sam!" Christie called from the lighted entranceway to the office. "Sam!"

Her voice penetrated the haze of his rage like a buzzing fly in a closed room. He wanted to swat the sound away and concentrate on choking the life from DC Porter.

"Sam!" she cried again, this time with panic. "Sam, stop it! You're killing him! Sam!" she screamed.

He felt her terror as he had when DC's knife was pressed to her throat. But now it was he, Sam, she feared. The note of fright, hanging between them in the total silence, jerked him from the grips of murderous insanity. He stared in horror at the head dangling limply on DC's neck. As if burned, Sam snatched his hands back. DC crumpled. The black water absorbed him up to his chest, his face safely out of the water.

Heart pounding, Sam stared for a moment as DC gasped through unconsciousness for air. He'd nearly killed him. The realization left him feeling queasy and shaken.

"Sam?"

Christie had moved into the shadows, her voice a terrified quaver. Swaying from DC's beating, Sam turned to face her but suddenly DC moved, grabbing Sam around the ankles. As Sam struggled to keep his balance, DC maneuvered himself from the pond and, in one swift movement, kicked his feet upward, connecting with Sam's jaw, striking him with a force that rocked his head back on his neck.

Still off-balance, Sam was defenseless against the vicious kicks that slammed into him again and again. With each staggering blow, DC gained more control and Sam's tenuous grip on consciousness faded. He heard the peals of Christie's screams but he could no longer see anything beyond the black veil that obscured his vision.

With terror he felt himself slip away and knew he was about to pass out. Still, DC pounded Sam's face, the pain becoming one giant sensation that sucked up all but his last thought.

I should have killed the son of a bitch.

27

Purpose rejuvenated Kathy. She sat up straight in the passenger seat as Mike pulled from the parking lot. Kathy scratched a name from their list and read Mike the address for the next pizza place. Earlier, they'd rechecked Porter's house for a name or address on the pizza boxes they'd seen there. But the boxes had been generic, claiming "fresh hot pizza." That, at least, eliminated the major chains and their hundreds of outlets.

Now, after visiting four independent pizza parlors with no luck in finding anyone who recognized Porter, hope still burned inside Kathy.

The ache in her arm had diminished with the cleaning and bandaging Mike had given it. She smiled, thinking of the crazy patchwork he'd left on her arm. His gentleness had surprised her. Whatever the reason for his kindness, she was grateful to receive it. She needed a little strength right now. Her own reserves were painfully depleted.

On the left they passed DC's street and headed two blocks up to a tiny pizza parlor tucked away on a quiet corner. Stepping from the car, Kathy crossed her fingers and prayed.

Scorletti's Pizza was set up for carryout and delivery only. It didn't have tables for diners, only two orange plastic benches set against the wall. It was deserted but for the cooks clowning around in the kitchen and the aroma of sausage and onions and pizza sauce.

The door sounded a bell as it closed, alerting the cooks to the presence of customers. A swift silence from the back was immediately followed by the appearance of a young man dressed in white with a tall poofed hat on his head. Pizza sauce was smeared on the front of the apron that covered a double-breasted shirt. He looked to be about seventeen, his face scarred with acne eruptions.

"Help you?" he mumbled, shooting a smile over his shoulder as the voice of his coworker delivered some parting gag understood only by him.

Mike showed the kid the picture of DC. "Have you seen this guy?"

Surprise widened the boy's eyes and elevated his brows, which disappeared under a greasy thatch of brown hair that hung low on his forehead.

"Are you a cop or something?" he asked, taking the picture.

"Yeah or something."

Having this confirmed, the kid grinned and studied the photo with care. Finally, he shook his head.

"I don't recognize him. Hey, Steve, com'ere."

Another lanky boy appeared from the kitchen, shuffling and blushing as he made his way to the counter. He wore a uniform of jeans and a polyester shirt. A machine-embroidered oval patch with his name was placed just above a flying pepperoni pizza with *Scorletti Pizza* on its middle.

The cook handed Steve the photo.

"Yeah, I've seen him. Pepperoni and sausage," Steve said.

Kathy felt as if the air had been sucked out of her lungs. Her ears rang as her mind replayed what he'd said.

Yeah, I've seen him . . .

"Where?" Mike was asking.

"Over on Mesa Ridge. I deliver there a lot. Guy never tips."

Mesa Ridge ... the rat house.

"When was the last time you were there?"

"Yesterday."

"Have you seen him anywhere since? Maybe he's stopped in?"

The kid shook his head. "No. Just there."

"This guy's a suspect in some kidnappings. You heard about them?"

The kid exchanged a wide-eyed glance with his friend.

"I don't know anything about him," he rushed to explain, as if knowledge of DC would somehow make him a suspect too. "I just know that he gets pizza a lot."

"You haven't seen a little girl around when you deliver?"

"No. I don't go in, though. Just wait on the porch for him. The place gives me the creeps anyway. All those cats."

Mike played twenty questions for a while longer, but the kid didn't know anything else. What had they expected? It had been a lame shot anyway.

"Well, listen," Mike said, scrawling down his phone number. "If you hear anything from him, give me a call. There's a reward."

"Sure," both boys said at once.

In the wake of the anticlimactic knowledge that DC had been seen, but not found, Kathy wasn't sure what to think or feel. Numb, she followed Mike out.

28

The trunk of DC's car reeked of gasoline and blood and terror so intense it lingered long after the victim ceased to fear. Knowing she was not the first to do so, Christie prayed that her last memories would not be of the awful stench inside.

She thought of little Jessica Jordan and realized she must have made the same terrible journey to an end that could only be worse. Christie hoped the girl's imagination had been too innocent to conjure the horrifying images her own flashed against the white numbness of her brain.

She heard herself calling Sam's name in humming rhythm with the engine. Closing her eyes, she pressed her trembling lips together. Was he alive?

The wheels hit a bump, jarring her backward into a piece of metal that dug into her side. She concentrated on the pain instead of thinking about Sam. She'd come completely unhinged if she even considered a world without him.

The tires slowed, crackling over loose gravel before idling for a few intolerable seconds. With a roar, the car jumped forward a few feet and then shut off.

Christie's ears began to ring as she listened to the sudden quiet, trying to piece together tiny sounds with actions.

A door opened. Footsteps followed.

Oh, God, why hadn't he simply killed her? She waited with the same confused hysteria a mouse must feel, clutched in the talons of a hawk circling its nest. She whimpered, pressing her face into her shoulder.

The garage door banged closed behind the car and then keys jangled against the trunk seconds before it popped open. DC reached in, grabbed her by the front of her shirt, and hauled her up. She scrambled to get out, fearful her shirt would tear under his rough hands and leave her stripped and vulnerable. On her feet, she stumbled as he shoved her through a door that led inside the house.

She groped in the darkness, using the soft glow of an outside light spilling through a window to guide her. The atmosphere inside felt tense. Watchful. As if the house itself was a silent participant in the unfolding drama. She turned to face her assailant, knowing she could show no fear.

"Okay, DC. You got me here. Now what?" Her words echoed in the empty rooms, sounding defiant and courageous.

He shrugged, the gesture appearing too casual to be genuine. She noted the tight strain on his bloody face and the jumpy way his gaze bounced around the room. "That depends on you," he said.

She forced her voice to bypass the clenched muscles in her throat and the dryness in her mouth. "What depends on me?"

His fist connected with her mouth so quickly it took a moment for her to feel the sting of pain that rushed to her swelling jaw and the taste of blood that filled her mouth. She lifted a hand to her face and touched the place where he'd struck her. With a savage grunt he grabbed her by the hair and shoved her down the hall to a closed door with a padlock dangling from its hinged lock. With one hand he fumbled for his keys and opened the door. He shoved her through.

Christie stumbled into the small bathroom, tripping

over the child who huddled on the floor. Incredulous, she met the wide blue gaze of a little girl she knew had to be Jessica Jordan. Fear had cast dark shadows under Jessica's eyes and washed her skin to a paleness that bordered on translucency. She communicated her desperation to Christie without a word or a movement.

Suddenly, Christie knew the stakes in the game she played with DC had just gone up.

DC towered in the doorway, staring at her as she gripped the edge of the sink for support.

"Try anything and you can watch me kill the kid," he said, slamming the door. The sounds of the lock clicking shut echoed in Christie's heart long after DC's footsteps retreated down the hall.

"Are you Jessica?" she asked the girl.

Jessica nodded in response.

"Are you okay?"

Another nod. "Is my mommy dead?"

"No, honey. She's alive. She's looking for you. Everyone's looking for you."

"Did he kidnap you, too?"

"Yes."

"He's bad."

"Yes, he is. Very bad."

Pale and terrified, Jessica stared at Christie as minutes ticked by. They could hear DC in the other rooms, banging cupboards open and shut. His footsteps returned to the hallway.

Christie sat on the closed lid of the toilet, reaching a hand down to grip Jessica's small, icy fingers. Gently she squeezed as much reassurance as she could manage into her touch. Jessica responded, but her eyes seemed to swallow her face as the lock clicked again.

DC banged the door open, a wild-eyed nervousness ticking at the corner of his lips. He threw a towel and soap into the room.

"Get cleaned up."

"Why?"

"Because I fucking said so. The kid too."

Carefully, Christie picked up the towel and wet it in the sink while trying to gauge the pressure points of this volatile DC. Motioning Jessica over, Christie helped her onto the counter and began dabbing at the dried blood and dirt on her face.

"You're not going to get away with this, DC," she said.

Did every hostage in the world say that? It never did any good, even with fictional villains.

A chilling light gleamed from his blue eyes. "I'll get away with it all right."

"How? What are you going to do with us?"

"You ask a lot of questions."

"What are you going to do with us?" she repeated in the same, level tone in spite of the trickle of insane fear dribbling down her back.

"You ask too many questions."

"Every cop in the city is looking for her. You take two steps out that door with her and they will gun you down where you stand."

He laughed, as if the very notion of his being caught were ludicrous.

"That's what you're for." He snapped his fingers in Jessica's face. "She's Mommy and I'm Daddy. Got it? We're getting out of here and that's the way things are going to be from now on."

Christie met his gaze in the mirror. "I don't think so, DC. I'm not going to play your make-believe game."

With a cold grin he stepped inside the room. His smell rushed at her, cloaking her in its greasy tide. He pulled his hand back, flashing the back of it like a salute. Christie braced herself for another blow, but it was Jessica that he struck. Christie gasped, reaching to catch the girl as she teetered on the edge of the counter. Jessica clutched Christie, burying her small face against Christie's shoulder as terror trembled through her.

"Lesson number one," DC said.

Christie nodded disconnectedly, lifting Jessica up and setting her back on the counter. This time she stood between DC and the girl.

"You're Mommy and I'm Daddy. You do anything stupid and I kill our daughter."

Christie looked into his eyes and what she saw there was more terrifying than the attack in her house, than the ride in the trunk. DC did it for the thrill. He hurt people because he liked to.

She had to think fast, be smart.

"It won't work, DC. No one's going to buy a child the whole country is looking for."

His eyes widened and his skin color grayed to the sickly shade of cold oatmeal. He tried to speak, but for a moment, could only sputter. Finally he broke free of his angry amazement and began to curse. Christie fought the urge to cower as his anger ricocheted off the tiles and mirror.

"Who told you that?" he demanded. "Who told you about selling her?"

Christie measured his reaction in silence, holding her meager hand of cards close and playing them carefully. "Who else?" she replied, feeling as if she were striking a match while standing in gasoline. "You know damn well who told me, DC."

Her bluff narrowed his gaze to a penetrating laser that sizzled across her features for interminable seconds.

"When did you talk to her?" he asked.

"Not long ago," Christie answered, wishing feverishly she knew who they were talking about. "She told the cops, too. Everyone. Even the newspapers. The news." The match in her mind burst to flames, as she took a chance. "She betrayed you, DC, so give it up."

He slammed a fist into the wall. "NO!" He pounded again. "NO! I'll kill her! I'm going to kill her!"

"Give it up. You can't get away. Not with the girl. Let her go and you stand a chance. Let her go, DC."

He stared at them for a long minute, his gaze taking in each detail of Jessica's pale face before switching to Christie, searching for her plan with the high-beam intensity of a prison light. Christie watched as emotions seemed to war on his features. Indecision, resolve, black rage, inconsolable self-pity. The expressions flew in and out of focus before one finally stuck.

Impaled by the clear cruelty in his eyes, Christie knew that whatever piece of DC she might once have been able to reach was gone. His brain had gone into overload, sizzling components, frying transistors, melting everything into one smoldering hunk of brutality.

"Do you think I don't know?" he yelled suddenly, making Christie and Jessica both jump. Christie shifted her body closer to Jessica's, acting, without thought, as a human shield to DC's monstrous wrath. The girl's small hands clenched her arm.

"Let us go, DC. It's your only chance."

A sheen of sweat glistened over his face and ringed his armpits like a brand of ownership, its sour scent cloying in the tight quarters. His suspicious glare darted around the room, lingering on the window. His fingers danced against his thigh, popping, snapping, clenching into tight, fierce fists.

"You think I don't know what you're trying to do?" he demanded.

He sounded somehow childish, brandishing his anger like an armor against the unknown. But the child in DC was imprisoned by the body of a cold-blooded murderer.

Christie could see no escape for any of them.

29

Sam felt the darkness pressing against his eyelids and puzzled at it for one hazy second before his memory rushed over him, sucking him up like a wave full of gritty sand and spewing him ashore.

Christie.

He sat up too quickly. The blood pounded at his temples and blackness swam behind his eyes. No, he wouldn't pass out. The ebony wave retreated to the edges of his consciousness.

Sam eased himself to his feet, swaying like a drunk toward the gaping door of his office. He squinted in the bright light, afraid to look in case he saw her body abandoned in the mess. Relieved, he reached for the phone, the decision to place an anonymous call to the cops already made. If he identified himself, the police would want him to wait around and answer their questions. He didn't have time for that. He had to get Christie before DC killed her.

He thought of the cop who had visited Christie, Mike Simens. His number was in her purse. Sam found it quickly and dialed, waiting impatiently while the seconds ticked like long, agonizing hours, each one possibly the last that Christie would survive. In moments, Simens answered and, talking fast, Sam filled him in.

"How long ago?" Simens asked.

Sam peered at the shattered face of his watch. "I

don't know—maybe ten minutes ago. He knocked me out, cold. When I came to they were gone.''

"Where are you?"

"Padre Trails, but don't bother to come here. I'm not hanging around. I've got to talk to someone who might know where he's taken her.''

"Did he say anything about the little girl? Jessica?''

"No, but I'd lay money he's your guy. He's got some kind of black market scam going on. Check out the house on Mesa Ridge. I don't think he'd go there, but—''

"I know the house. I'll get someone on it right away.''

"Another thing, Mike. I didn't call the cops—''

"Don't worry, I'll take care of it. Where are you going?''

"To see a lawyer.''

"I'll meet—''

"No, you go see DC's old boss, Beth McClain.'' Sam gave him her business address. "I don't know where she lives—''

"Don't worry, I'll get it when I call the station and brief them. If you find anything out, call Jackson at the station and tell him. I'll check in with him after I speak with the McClain woman.''

"Got it.''

Sam hung up and grabbed his gun from the locked supply cabinet, cursing himself for not having done it first thing. The pounding in his head beat to the rhythm of his feet against the uneven ground as he raced to the car. His tennis shoes sloshed, making sucking noises with each frenzied step.

He was on the road in seconds, shaky and numb from the pain in his ribs and the jarring agony that used to be his jaw.

Pfeiffer lived in a luxury condominium complex off Friars Road, not far from the golf course. Sam squealed into the parking lot and raced on foot to the security door.

He thumbed the door buzzer down and held it for the count of five.

A voice box showered him with white noise and then Pfeiffer answered, ''Yes?''

''Pfeiffer? Sam McCoy—''

The static interrupted him seconds before Pfeiffer's voice.

''I have nothing to say to you,'' he said in a cold tone.

''Well I've got a hell of a lot to say to you. DC just kidnapped my wife. Either you give me some answers or I talk to the cops about what you and Beth McClain have been up to.''

More white noise that grated against Sam's nerves. He buzzed again. ''Pfeiffer! Goddammit, he'll kill her.''

Another pause and then the door buzzed. ''Third floor, 302.''

Sam punched the elevator button, waited two seconds, then vaulted up the stairs, taking them two at a time until he stumbled, whacking his head against the concrete. He felt the *whoosh* of the blackout covering him in its blanket again, and then he was on his feet, pushing it back.

Pfeiffer waited in his open door, barefoot, and looking as if he'd been sleeping between his mattress and box springs. His hair stood up in perfect forty-five degree angles to his head and his worn sweats were twisted and wrinkled.

His eyes widened when he saw Sam, bloody, wet, and smelling of pond water. He sputtered uselessly as Sam brushed passed him and marched inside. Pfeiffer's place had a temporary feel to it—as if the occupant didn't plan to be around long enough to bother with pictures or knickknacks. Or maybe they'd all been packed away in anticipation of a hasty disappearance.

A kitchen counter doubled as a bar and Sam made his way straight to it, gripping the edge as another tidal wave of unconsciousness played chicken with his equilibrium.

"You're bleeding," Pfeiffer said, pointing as if Sam would need the guidance to locate the blood.

"I'm goddamn dying, asshole."

Decanters of liquor lined the bar like soldiers in formation. Sam flipped a matching glass right side up and poured from the first one his hand touched.

"Help yourself to a drink," Pfeiffer said resentfully.

Sam sloshed some more into a second glass and passed it to the attorney.

He shook his head but reached for it anyway. "I don't care for bourbon."

Neither did Sam, but its warmth traveled through him, chasing back the pain, stinging his brain into gear. He sucked air through his teeth, biting down on the screaming raw nerves that reported from every bone in his mangled body.

"Where did he take her?" Sam demanded.

"I don't know."

Sam gave him a look that bordered on physical violence.

"I'm telling the truth! I don't know."

Sam slammed his glass on the counter, pacing his words for the ultimate impact. "Well, let me tell you what *I* know. How about I start with black market babies?"

"I'd be fascinated to hear what you have to say, of course, but I don't see how it pertains to me."

"You don't? I traced the house in La Jolla back to its original owners, Leonard. I'm sure you remember the McClowskys. They remember you."

Pfeiffer took a swig from his glass. "I'm sorry to disappoint you, McCoy, but I'd have to check my files. I have many clients—"

"That's not what Beth McClain tells me."

"What?"

"Beth said she was your only client and you were her only attorney. Intimate relationship. She said she keeps you busy with her business."

Pfeiffer cleared his throat. "I have handled many of her adoptions, but I assure you—"

"All of them, according to Beth," Sam bluffed. "Even the ones that had to be done in the middle of the night."

Pfeiffer paled and emptied his glass.

"Where'd he take her, Leonard?"

"I told you, I don't know. Why don't you ask Beth?"

"The cops are on the way there now."

Pfeiffer winced at this news. Sam pressed on.

"Why do you think Beth would know where DC took Christie? Would he go to her for help?"

Pfeiffer began to bounce on the balls of his feet. His hands searched his pocketless sweats for someplace to hide. Finally he crossed his arms, stuffing his trembling fingers under his armpits.

"I didn't say she would help him."

"You're a lousy liar, Pfeiffer. How'd you ever make it as a lawyer? Why would Beth help DC Porter?"

Pfeiffer sank to the couch behind him, rubbing his hands over the thick shadow of his beard. It rasped in the electric silence.

"You can tell me now or wait for the cops. It's all going to come out anyway. Either you fill me in on what the hell's going on, or you keep it to yourself and become an accessory to Christie's murder. Probably Jessica Jordan's too."

Just saying the words put a painful lump in Sam's throat. He wanted to reach across the room and choke the life out of Pfeiffer, as he should have done to DC. His only chance of finding Christie, though, was in finding the facts and following them. Like it or not, Leonard Pfeiffer was his one source at this point.

"Who are you protecting, Leonard? I hope it's not Beth, because she already spilled her guts about you."

"You're bluffing."

"Am I? Take a good look at me, Leonard. Do I look like I'm bluffing?"

Sam could see his own reflection in the window behind Pfeiffer. Dried blood caked around his ears and hair, its smear tinting his skin a rusted shade. His clothes clung to his body, still uncomfortably damp and slimy feeling. A fierce light gleamed in his eyes and he aimed his glare at Pfeiffer. The taut silence stretched for another moment before the lawyer finally spoke.

"Beth is DC's mother."

"What?"

Pfeiffer held out his glass and Sam refilled it, leaving his own glass, still half-full, on the counter.

"It's a long story, and I don't know all of it, but Beth gave DC up when he was a child. Later, he came looking for her."

"When?"

"Fifteen years ago."

"I don't give a damn about fifteen years ago, Pfeiffer. I want to know where DC's taken Christie tonight."

"I'm telling you everything I know."

"Okay. She dumped him—he came back. Why?"

"Revenge? Money? Who knows why DC does anything?"

"Why would he want revenge?"

The lawyer shrugged. "He claimed to have been abused by his foster family."

"Claimed?"

"Beth never believed him."

"She sounds like a caring mother. How about you? Do you believe him?"

Pfeiffer sipped at his drink and then, as if making some monumental decision, he gulped down the rest.

"Yeah," he said. "I believed him. He's not normal. Something had to make him that way."

''What did Beth do when he came back?''

''She was just starting her business. Things weren't going well. Her first adoption fell through. The second baby died in delivery. She was broke and desperate . . .''

''So she started stealing babies?''

A sweat had formed on Pfeiffer's face, giving it a shine, like a glazed donut.

''I don't know what you're talking about now. You'd have to ask—''

Sam crossed the room, pressing his face close to Pfeiffer's. The smaller man smelled fusty, like a damp cloth that had been forgotten under a rock. He cowered back, cringing from the coldness in Sam's face.

''I thought they were legal,'' Pfeiffer blurted out. ''I swear, I thought they were legal.''

''So you were a victim. Is that the way you want it to read? Keep talking. Who set who up? Did Beth talk DC into it, or the other way around?''

''I never knew. In some ways, they're a lot alike. I'd say it's a fifty-fifty bet either way.''

Sam nodded. ''Once you figured out what was going on, why didn't you get out? Report it to the cops?''

''I'd already involved myself.''

''Bullshit. You could have turned her in and not been incriminated.''

''By then she was my only client and I needed her.''

''So you did it for the money. You're in deep shit, Pfeiffer.''

''It wasn't just that.''

''Then suppose you tell me what it was?''

''I did a couple of adoptions. The first was a Hispanic infant girl that went to a couple in New York. The second one was also Hispanic, a boy that Beth adopted.''

''Beth stole her own son?'' *Jesus this is nuts*. Sam checked his watch, wishing he could hold the passing seconds back, but they ticked by without regard to his feelings. He looked up, glaring at Pfeiffer, who began to talk faster.

"Beth couldn't have children. She damaged herself while trying to abort DC. She'd never told her husband about DC and didn't think he'd understand."

"I wonder why," Sam said sarcastically.

"He's a doctor," Pfeiffer said, as if explaining that a businessman might have understood.

"How do *you* know all this?"

"I had an affair with her."

A disbelieving curse slipped past Sam's swollen lip. "*Had?* When did it end?"

"Four months ago."

When Christie's mother died.

Sam shook his head incredulously, wondering how all this would help him find Christie. "I can't believe this shit!" Speechless, he stood staring at Pfeiffer. "Back up for a minute, just so I'm sure I've got this right. You're telling me that you and Beth have been doing the bump-and-grind while her son was out stealing babies? And this has been going on for *fifteen years* without any of you getting caught?"

"Good Lord, no. Not all that time. Only that first year, but by the time I realized what was going on, I'd handled over twenty illegal adoptions."

"Twenty? Twenty? How could you not know? You can't be that stupid, Pfeiffer."

"I know it sounds hard to believe, but I swear it's the truth. The babies always came from Mexico. Not Tijuana or Ensenada, but farther south and never from the same town. We didn't hear their news. There was no way for me to make the connection. Beth always had the mother's paperwork in order . . . How was I to know?"

"Then why did you stop? I'm assuming she never got caught."

"That's right. Maybe she wouldn't have stopped. I know this won't mean much to you, but Beth thought she was doing those children a favor. Her clients were very wealthy and the babies came from impoverished families—''

''More bullshit. She stole babies from their mothers. Don't try and ice it with anything. Answer my question, why did she stop?''

Pfeiffer sighed, his eyes suddenly bright with unshed tears. He rubbed them and sniffled. Sam clenched his teeth, the pain shooting through his jaw distracting him from his angry desire to box Pfeiffer's ears.

Slowly, the lawyer began to speak. ''One time DC decided not to go to Mexico. He found a homeless mother and her child living on the streets here in town. He snatched the baby and murdered the mother. We'd already handled the adoption by the time the body was found and the story hit the papers. An autopsy showed the woman to have delivered shortly before her murder. A massive search went out for the baby.''

''Jesus, I remember reading about that.''

''Beth was furious. She sent DC away and told him never to come back. I was there. It was not a good scene.''

''They never caught her? How did she get away with that?''

''She was never a suspect.''

''Jesus. Wait a minute—why was DC helping her in the first place?''

''Who knows? I always thought he was trying to . . . win her over? Prove himself to her?''

''Still bullshit.''

''Maybe he did it for the money, too.''

''So what's he doing back now?''

''DC will always come back.''

''Where do Mary Jane and Christie fit in all this?''

''After DC left—the first time—Beth went legitimate. Things settled down. We both started making money off her legal transactions at the clinic. We have years and years of honest work making families, McCoy. Something good. Something to be proud of—"

"Something to make you forget all the families you ripped apart."

He went on as if Sam hadn't spoken. "Business became so profitable that Beth hired Mary Jane. But then, DC came back again. We told him things were straight now. He went on the rampage, accusing Beth of using him the first time—"

"Which was true."

"Yes. He threatened to tell everything if she tried to send him away again. So she offered him a job."

"As custodian?"

"She hoped he'd throw her offer in her face and leave. But he took it."

"And started working on Mary Jane."

"Yes."

"And then he did it again."

"Yes. This time the murdered girl was only fourteen and the baby only a few days old. He'd followed them home from the hospital and broke in while she was alone with the baby."

"I read about that, too."

"They didn't find the mother's body for months. DC had plenty of time to convince Mary Jane that he was helping a young girl in trouble and use her to get the paperwork through me."

"The McClowsky's baby."

"That's right."

"Did McClowsky know?"

"Only after."

"Why didn't he turn DC in?"

"And risk losing the baby? He and his wife had been trying for years to get a child and the baby's natural mother was already dead. He made the only choice possible for him. He paid."

"You know this story well."

"Yeah, well, I just talked to Dr. McClowsky tonight.

You and Christie shook him up pretty good with your visit today.''

''What did he say?''

''Nothing much. Just that if he went down, I'd go with him.''

''Is that why you're spilling your guts?''

Pfeiffer shook his head, draining his glass again. He gave the decanters a longing glance before he began to speak. Sam watched him with narrowed eyes.

''I know you won't believe this, but I never intended for things to go so far. I kept telling myself that one day I'd come clean.''

''You're breaking my heart.''

''I just don't want to see your wife end up like her mother did.''

Sam stilled, feeling his breath catch in his sore chest. ''What do you mean?''

''Mary Jane died in her car, but it wasn't an accident. It was murder.''

''Jesus,'' Sam whispered. ''I knew it. Was it DC?''

''No, it was Beth.''

''Beth?''

''When they found the body of the young mother that DC murdered, Mary Jane put the pieces together. She planned to go to the police, but first she went to see Beth.''

''Mary Jane knew about Beth's underground business?''

''No, she went to confess. She thought Beth would be ruined when the truth came out. Mary Jane felt she had to tell her in person.''

''And Beth killed her for it.''

Pfeiffer nodded. ''Beth came to me afterward, crying and insisting it was an accident. Said she meant to flag Mary Jane down, not run her off the road.''

''You didn't believe her?''

''Beth doesn't make mistakes. In fact, DC is the only

one I can think of. If Mary Jane ended up dead, it was because Beth wanted her that way. End of story.''

He looked up, his eyes full of emotion. He seemed to be asking Sam for forgiveness. But forgiveness wasn't Sam's to give even if he'd been inclined. Which he wasn't.

''I'm just relieved it's all finally over,'' Pfeiffer said.

''Not over, Pfeiffer. Just beginning. You're going to help me find Christie.''

''I don't know where she is, I told you that.''

''What about Jessica? Why did he take her? Is he planning to sell her? Has he contacted you?''

Pfeiffer shook his head, giving his face another vigorous rub. ''Beth called me,'' he said. ''Earlier this week. She told me what DC had done and warned me not to help him. As if I would.''

''You with your high standards? Or course not.''

''She told me he had some big plans, but she didn't know what they were.''

''Any guesses?'' Sam asked, glancing at his watch again.

''Not until tonight, when I talked to Dr. McClowsky. He told me his office had been vandalized around the same time DC came back. His files were stolen.''

''So?''

''Jessica Jordan was a patient of Dr. McClowsky's. Her records were among those missing.''

The files they'd found in that gym locker had to be McClowsky's. Sam stared at his own bloody reflection in the window, sorting through the facts, searching for the missing piece that would make it all make sense.

Sam shook his head, confusion adding its own special agony to the pounding in his head. ''I don't get it. What did he want with the files?''

Pfeiffer dropped his face into his hands.

''Why did he want the files?'' Sam demanded.

''He means to sell Jessica, all right. Piece by piece.''

''*What?*''

Pfeiffer rushed to explain. "Do you remember hearing about the little boy who needed a heart transplant? Do you remember the battle launched when his parents tried to buy a heart from a family with a brain-dead child on life support?"

"Yeah, the parents offered half a million dollars to the family if they'd pull the plug and donate the heart."

"DC was very interested in the case. I think when he left here four months ago, he had already made contacts to sell organs."

"That's insane. How would he do that?"

"It wouldn't be that difficult to handle the administrative side of it. All he had to do is find someone within the system to forge the paperwork once he presented the donor. I don't know the procedures, but it could be done."

"You're telling me he kidnapped that little girl to hack her up and sell her like a scrapped car?"

"If there's a market to buy, there are men like DC looking to sell."

"But who would buy black market parts?"

Pfeiffer gave him a level look. "If I've learned anything in this business, Sam McCoy, it is to never underestimate what someone will do to—or for—a child."

The phone rang, jerking both men from the sudden thick silence that fell between them. Sam followed Pfeiffer into the kitchen, glaring at the lawyer as he sputtered into the phone.

Sam couldn't control the fear that quaked through him as he replayed Pfeiffer's words in his mind. What if DC had the same plans for Christie as he did for Jessica? Jesus, he had to find her soon.

Pfeiffer looked up at Sam, mouthing, "It's Beth."

The attorney's end of the conversation consisted of monosyllables. Sam listened while he stared at the clock with a feeling of panic in his gut.

How long had he been at Pfeiffer's? Fifteen? Twenty minutes? It was time for Sam to get moving, but to where? For all he'd learned, he was still no closer to finding Christie.

Pfeiffer hung up the phone, looking pale and shaken. "DC is using Beth's rental," he said. "I've got the address."

Sam snatched the scrap of paper from Pfeiffer's hand and started for the door.

"How'd you find this out?" Sam asked as he stepped outside.

"She's on her way over. She wants me to go with her and assist in murdering DC."

"What are you going to do when she gets here?"

"Be gone. I'm almost finished packing. I won't be sticking around for the trials. Good luck, Sam McCoy."

30

Beth hung up the phone and stared at it for a long, quiet moment. It seemed she'd come full circle, back to the place she'd begun. Now she only waited for the appropriate ending to the pathetic cycle of her life. She looked up, catching sight of herself in the mirror. In reflection, she looked younger, as if she'd slipped back to yesterday instead of stepping forward to tomorrow.

Hadn't she always sensed that she would end here, squared off against DC, while staring into her own image with disgust? What did it matter? She'd already lost her freedom, her husband . . . her son.

What a good laugh fate must be having. She'd abandoned a son she detested and, because of him, she would lose the son she loved. James would hate her when he found out what she'd done . . . what she'd paid for his life.

Dragging a chair from the lighted vanity table, she went to the closet. It only took her a few minutes to find what she was looking for. In a shoe box, in the back.

Her palm cupped the small pistol, her fingers caressing as they slipped around the grip to test the trigger. Years ago, when she'd bought the gun, she'd done so for protection. And now she would use it for that very purpose, to protect herself from DC and the destruction he brought with him. She grabbed extra bullets from the shoe box and loaded the gun.

Slipping it into her purse, she went downstairs. She passed James without noticing him.

"What's with you?" he demanded.

She stopped short, wincing at the resentment burning in his eyes. For a moment she thought he must have discovered her treachery, but then she realized that wasn't possible. Not yet.

"Where are you going?" he demanded.

She shook her head, wondering when James had last spoken to her in a civil tone.

"I'm going out."

"Is Dad going with you?" he asked.

"Dad is still at work."

"You're going out alone?"

A note of uncertainty cracked his voice. She saw the insecure boy behind the belligerent adolescent for just one second.

"James?" she asked, ignoring his question.

"What?"

She reached out to touch him but he jerked away, leaving her fingers dangling in the space between them. "Do you know I love you?"

He frowned, not liking the turn in conversation. "Yeah, sure."

"And you know I would never do anything to hurt you?"

"I guess. What are you getting at, Mom?"

She sighed, smiling sadly. "Nothing. I just want you to know that. I love you. I always have."

"Yeah, right. Got it."

"Do you know that when you were a baby, I used to go into your room and wake you up just so I could care for you?"

"So? What do you want me to say? Thanks, I guess."

" 'Thanks, I guess'?" she repeated, shaking her head. "Maybe it was selfish of me."

"Mom? Are you okay?"

She kept her smile steady. "Yes, honey. Mommy's fine. But just promise to remember what I said. Okay?"

He turned his palms up to her, shaking his head. "Sure. Okay. You love me."

"More than anything in the world."

She waited for him to repeat it.

"More than anything in the world."

"Thank you," she said softly. "Now I'd better go before I'm late."

"Late for what, Mom?"

She let the door close on his question and hurried to her car. She drove to Leonard's on autopilot, finding herself at his door with no memory of the ride.

She'd always come to Leonard when she needed help. He'd always been there for her. But she knew he couldn't solve her problem. Not this time.

She'd come full circle and there was no way out. Full circle.

She used her own key to unlock Leonard's door and opened it quietly, dropping her purse on the sofa. She could hear his movements from the bedroom and followed them. As she drew even with the bar, she noticed the glasses. Two of them.

She felt the chill of betrayal grip her heart. Who had been drinking with Leonard? Silently she continued down the hall.

A suitcase, opened and full, sprawled over the unmade bed. Leonard stood with his back to her, yanking his clothes from the dresser drawers and tossing them into a giant trash bag behind him. He'd worked up a sweat and his T-shirt clung to his back.

"Going somewhere, Leonard?" she asked softly.

He jumped, spinning around to face her with a look full of guilt.

"Beth! You scared me."

She wandered in, clearing a space on the bed to sit. "Am I so terrifying?" she said.

"No, no. I mean, not at all."

"You didn't answer my question. Where are you going? You seem to be in some hurry to get there, wherever it is."

He mopped at the sweat on his face with a handful of clothes. "I thought it might be for the best if I left town after tonight."

"For how long?"

"I don't know. A couple weeks."

"You're sure taking a lot of clothes."

"I like to be prepared."

"Hmmm," she said, examining her nails. "You didn't tell me you had a visitor when I called."

"What visitor?" he said.

"Am I mistaken?"

"You're talking in circles, Beth. I don't understand."

Slowly she stood and approached him. She could sense his retreat from her, though he didn't move. A sheen of fear glistened in his eyes. Fear? Of her?

A twitch jerked the corner of her eye in rhythm to the pounding in her head. She stared at his suitcase. Was he planning to leave her holding the bag? The last threads of her unraveled cloak of control separated and fell in tatters at her feet.

"Who have you been talking to?" she whispered, touching his face with her fingertips.

He stood transfixed in her stare for a heartbeat of time before dumping the clothes in his hands onto the pile on the floor. He backed away from her, sidestepping around to the door.

She followed down the hall, watching as he fixed a drink, which he swallowed in a gulp. It was her turn to fear.

"Who, Leonard? Who?"

"Sam McCoy."

"No . . ."

"Your renegade son has abducted Sam's wife now. I had no choice."

She stared at him, shaking her head in disbelief. "So you betrayed me?"

"Beth, we're at the end of the line. It's time to get out. Get away. You should be home packing, too."

"Do you think I can just *leave?* Do you think *I* can just *run away?*"

"I don't think you have a choice."

She felt a cold fury wash over her at his words. No, she didn't have a choice. She never had. But neither did Leonard. If he thought he could simply cut and run, he was crazy.

"And what of my son, Leonard. What of him?"

"Leave him behind. This is all his fault anyway."

"I'm not talking about DC, you fool. What about James?"

Leonard crossed to the bar and poured another drink. She noted the unsteadiness of his hands, her ears tuning to the slur in his words.

"He's not your son, Beth. That's the trouble."

His words stung her voice away. Painfully, she cleared her throat.

"What about your records, Leonard? At the office?"

"I've destroyed everything."

"When?"

"After McCoy left my office today. I knew it would be only a matter of time before . . ."

"Before what?"

"Before they tracked DC to you and me. We've done enough damage to people. I didn't want it compounded with the chaos that those records would bring to our clients."

"How noble of you. Yet you didn't think twice about selling me out. What about the chaos that James will go through?"

Leonard lowered his drink and gave Beth a look of disgust. "Maybe you should have thought about that before you started your business."

"I beg your pardon? Don't you mean *our* business?"

"You tricked me into working for you. I had a future. I had a career. You stole that from me."

She laughed, shaking her head in amazement. "I *made* you, Leonard Pfeiffer. You had nothing before me."

"But I was someone."

"Oh, please. You were someone who wasted his time with dime-a-dozen petty criminals. You'd still be in that hellish office in El Cajon if it wasn't for me."

"Maybe you're right, but I wouldn't have spent my life looking over my shoulder wondering when I'd get busted."

"If that's the way you feel, I suppose it's pointless for me to be here. You had no intention of helping me clean up, did you?"

"If it was just DC, maybe I would help. But I know you, Beth. It wouldn't stop there."

"Meaning?"

"Meaning there's still Christie McCoy and Jessica Jordan to deal with. There's no way you can *clean up* them. Not now."

Shaking with anger, Beth retrieved her purse, comforted by its weight. With her back turned to Leonard, she opened the clasp and reached in. The gun felt cold and solid, its presence an anchor, keeping her steady in the fast-moving waters of indecision.

"I intend to take care of them the same way I'll take care of you," she said, turning with the pistol aimed high and sure.

Leonard looked at her, surprise contorting his face. "Beth? What are you doing? Beth? Beth? Don't do—"

She pulled the trigger.

31

DC slumped against the kitchen counter, a bottle of bourbon in his hand. Slowly, methodically, he took long drinks from it, but the liquor did no good. The sizzling charges of panic and fear inside doused the fiery alcohol, canceling even the most generic buzz. Unwanted thoughts cluttered his aching mind. Like a movie playing backward, the events of his life slipped before his unseeing eyes. Outside, the neighborhood dogs began to bark again.

The sound slowed the flashing pictures. Suddenly, he was back at his grandpa's. It was the week before his thirteenth birthday and the dogs were barking. They woke him a second before he heard the floorboards squeak outside his door.

Grandpa? Of course. Come for another of his nightly visits.

The old man slithered into the room, his stink wafting like a siren before him. DC's nostrils flared with repugnance. Not again.

He stayed very still, holding his breath, praying Grandpa would move on. But in all his years there, that had never happened. DC was a fool to think it would this time.

He felt the hand, rough and smelling of beer and smoke, press against his throat. Then his Grandpa moved closer, levering his body into bed beside DC.

DC felt rage begin to simmer at his toes, rising up like a belching black cloud of smoke until it erupted in flames of fury. Roughly, he pushed Grandpa away, twisting his body so the older man could not pin him. Still holding DC's neck, Grandpa squeezed. He would not be overpowered.

Neither made a sound. Neither wanted to wake Grandma and bare this awful truth to her.

The silence made DC strong. He had endured this for eight years. He could take it no more. He fought, twisting and turning. His resistance took Grandpa by surprise. Usually DC lay still, letting Grandpa do what he would, crying in silence as the old man shot him full of filth and disgust. Afterward, Grandpa would call him dirt. Call him trash for tempting him this way. It was, after all, DC's fault that Grandpa did this to him.

DC wrestled Grandpa to the floor, grabbed him by his ears and pounded. Only when blood poured from his grandpa's ears did DC realize he'd pounded the old man senseless.

He froze, thinking suddenly of his grandma. Panic chilled the sweat on his skin.

Grabbing Grandpa by the arms, he dragged him out of his bedroom, out of the shack. As if sensing the violence they'd been unable to witness, the dogs began to bark louder.

"Get back," DC yelled at them. Surprisingly they did.

DC opened the cage and shoved his grandpa in.

Back inside, DC quickly dressed, then snatched Grandpa's keys from the rusted hook in the kitchen. He didn't know how to drive, but this was a good time to learn. As he steered away from the house, he heard the dogs begin to snarl and fight.

As if over a bone.

DC blinked the memory away, but nothing could banish the dirty smudge it left on him, like a decaying souvenir. He took another drink of bourbon, then hurled the bottle at the wall. It exploded on impact, permeating the air with the pungent aroma of booze as the amber liquid splashed against the white paint.

It was time to move.

DC locked the bathroom door again and left. With stunned relief, Christie heard the garage door bang open and closed, then the roar of his engine fading down the street. He was gone.

She spun, facing the bathroom as a warrior faces battle.

"Jessica? We have to get out of here."

The young girl nodded.

"Did you check this place out? Is there anything we can use?"

"It's empty."

Christie scanned the room, frantically looking in the cabinets anyway. Her gaze ended on the small window. She climbed into the tub and tested it. The thick cover of paint sealed the seams around it. Bracing herself, she tried to force the window up. Sweat beaded her upper lip as she strained, but it wouldn't budge.

Back on the floor, she turned in a circle, feeling like a caged animal. There had to be a way out. She studied the small room again, her search bouncing from the mirror to the tub to the window again.

There had to be a way. Her gaze shot to the sink, then to the toilet where it stayed for a stunned second.

So simple. So obvious.

The lid to the tank.

Moving quickly, she yanked the oblong piece of porcelain from the top of the toilet. It felt cold and heavy in her hands.

"Jessica? I'm going to throw this at the window and break it. There's going to be glass everywhere, so you'll need to protect yourself. Do you think you'll fit in the cabinet under the sink?"

Jessica nodded and scampered to obey. Tucking herself easily into the small area, she peered out and asked, "Do I have to close the door? I don't like the dark."

"The dark is not what we have to fear, honey. I'll need your blanket."

The girl considered this for a second, then handed it over with a solemn look. As soon as Christie took it, Jessica started to squirm. As if the blanket had been her only security and now she'd given it up.

"Okay?" Christie asked.

"Okay," Jessica answered, closing the cabinet door.

Making a hood from the blanket with the ends trailing over her shoulders, Christie shifted the position of her arms. She hoped she was strong enough to heave the tank top through the window. Staring up at the frosted glass, she hoisted the piece of porcelain to her shoulder. A frantic prayer moved her lips in a silent plea as she chucked it at the window. Instinctively she stepped back, curling into a protective ball under the shield of the blanket. The tank lid hit the wall two inches low with an explosive crash.

"Damn!"

Cursing under her breath, she stomped to the tub and looked in. A triumphant smile curled her lips as she saw that the tank top had smashed into three parts. She picked up the medium-sized piece, hefting it in her hands. Not what she'd planned, but no complaints.

"Christie?"

"It's okay. Didn't work, but hang in there one more minute."

Biting her lip, Christie climbed onto the side of the tub. Blanket in place, she balanced herself against the wall as she took aim, this time able to control her missile. The chunk sailed from her hand like a bullet from a pistol, whistling through the air.

It shattered the window, showering Christie in a lethal storm of a thousand sharp little pieces. Gasping, she took an instinctive step for cover. Too late, she remembered she stood on the tub. Caught in the folds of the blanket, she teetered on the edge before crashing to the tile floor. Her skull cracked the enameled edge of the toilet and black-and-red stars danced behind her lids as the hot rush of unconsciousness clutched at her brain.

Outside, a dog barked, startled by the sound of the exploding glass. Christie grappled through the darkness, latching onto that sound.

Bark! Bark!

If she let go, they'd be dead for sure. If she allowed herself to slip into the comfort of never-never land, DC would come back and discover her. Discover her attempted escape and punish her and Jessica both for it. Kill them both.

Woof, woof!

Another dog joined in. She concentrated on them. The darkness turned gray, receding as rapidly as the tide. Behind it, Christie became aware of the pain. Excruciating agony throbbed through her head and arm. She moved her legs. They, at least, seemed okay.

Slowly, carefully, she opened her eyes. The bathroom glowed dimly in the moonlight, but the room seemed incredibly bright without the frosted glass to filter the light. Fresh air streamed through the shattered window. Christie filled her lungs, feeling the sting of tears in her eyes. Until that moment she hadn't realized how convinced she'd become that she would never smell the softness of a night breeze again. She sat up, wincing as she jarred her arm.

Jessica cracked the cabinet door and peered out. "Christie? Are you okay?"

Biting her lip, Christie fought down the pain. She thought she might have broken her left arm but she couldn't be sure. She'd never broken a bone in her life and had nothing with which to compare this hurt. Gently she turned her wrist. Nothing seemed to be grinding. Honestly, she didn't know if that was good or not. She did know that if the arm was broken, the fingers didn't move. Or was that the spine? She shook her head.

"Yeah, I'm okay."

"There's blood on your head," Jessica said, pointing.

The floor glittered with brilliant pieces of glass. Trying to touch as little as possible, Christie struggled to her feet and shook out the blanket. She swayed with a sickening lurch of nausea, fighting the black waves. She saw a bloodstain on the blanket and some more splashed on the base of the toilet. Afraid to know, afraid not to know, she turned to the mirror and inspected her head.

A gash on her forehead. Nothing too bad. If they stuck around here much longer she'd get a lot worse.

She faced the window, pushing her misery to the depths of her mind. Long, jagged edges poked up through the wooden frame like wicked blades. Using the blanket to protect her skin, Christie stood on the side of the tub again and punched at the shards of glass, knocking them out. She draped the blanket over the window ledge, put one foot on the soap dish and the other on the faucet sticking out of the wall. Gripping the shower head, she balanced herself between the two. She could only hope the fabric would protect them from any glass still poking through the frame.

Sending up a silent prayer, she pulled on the shower head and pushed with her feet until she could get her armpits hooked on the sill. A second cry caught in her throat as her throbbing arm protested the strain. Sweat beaded her forehead and tears careened down her cheeks. Biting her lip, she forced herself on. Her feet bounced against the wall as she hung like a fly. Grunting, she walked her rubber soles up the tile, pushing off the wall and inching her body up until she was half-in, half-out of the window.

Below her was a shrub and, beyond that, grass that

looked black in the night. She squirmed back in and dropped to her feet.

"Jessica, this is our plan. You and I are going through that window."

Jessica nodded.

"Now, I can help you get up there, but you're going to have to jump out on your own. Can you do that?"

"I'm a good jumper."

"Well, I'm glad to hear that, sugar, because you're going to need to be."

"Are we going to get away?"

"Yes—"

"Really? I mean, he's not going to just get us again?"

"Come here, Jessica." Jessica shuffled over. Squatting to her eye level, Christie asked, "Are you scared?"

"Yes."

"I'm scared too. But I'll tell you what. I'm more scared of being here, than of being out there. You just have to remember, on that side of the window we can get help."

"Okay, Christie. I'm ready."

"That's my girl. Let's get out of here before he comes back."

Christie climbed back in the tub and squatted, so Jessica could crawl onto her shoulders. Standing, she willed her unsteady legs to support them. Her heart pounded so hard her chest hurt. Her legs trembled and her arm screamed pain.

She felt the press of responsibility for the child on her shoulders. It colored her emotions a swirling gray of unknown. She'd never been responsible for another living soul before. It scared her.

Somehow through the years she'd convinced herself that she couldn't be accountable for anyone but herself. That because her mother had been incapable of giving unselfishly, Christie, too, would be unable. But here she was, escaping and saving a child in the process. It charged her with a new and unexplored feeling.

Maybe she could have made Sam happy if she hadn't been so certain that he would leave her. Thinking back, she had forced him to the door. She prayed she would see him again so she could tell him she loved him. She prayed he was still alive.

Balancing Jessica on her shoulders, Christie murmured a silent pledge to get them both out of this and away from DC Porter. She *would* protect them. She would not give up.

And after this was all over, if Sam still wanted her, she would go back to him. This time, when he wanted to talk about children, she wasn't going to freeze up inside. She would explain her fears and face them. No more hiding. No more running.

If Sam was even alive.

She shoved the thought to the back of her mind.

As soon as Jessica grabbed the window ledge, Christie took hold of her legs and pushed her up. On the ledge, Jessica looked back, her eyes questioning and reassuring at once. Christie sent the same message back. *I know it's scary, but you can do it.* Jessica jumped.

Immediately, Christie followed. Clearing the bush, she hit the grass. The impact jarred her arm and head, but she hardly noticed. Rolling with her fall, she looked for Jessica.

"Okay?" Christie whispered.

"Okay," Jessica answered.

They ran.

32

The headlights of Mike's car picked out the sprawling white hacienda as he pulled into the circular drive and parked. In the backseat, Rookie whined, pressing his nose to the window. Mike didn't question the impulse that had motivated him to bring his dog. Rookie was the best backup he'd ever had.

Through the darkness his gaze met Kathy's. The ordeal she'd suffered lined her face, adding years to her appearance, but nothing could take away from the quiet beauty that molded her features. He reached over and squeezed her hand as she moved to get out.

Mike rang the doorbell, listening to it echo through the house. They waited in the glow of the porch light as the last notes faded. He rang again, peering through the narrow stained glass window. Inside, he spotted a teenage boy ambling down the hallway toward them, in no hurry to answer the door.

Mike bit back his frustration. How was the kid to know the importance of this visit? How was the kid to know that time was running out?

Finally the door opened and the boy stared at them with belligerent eyes. "Yeah?"

Mike identified himself as a police officer and asked to speak with Beth McClain.

"What do you want her for?"

"Is she here?"

"Nah. She's gone," he said, pushing the door closed.

Mike stopped it with his foot. Too tired to deal with the kid's attitude, he forced his questions through clenched teeth. "When will she be back?"

"You got a warrant?"

His patience snapped. "You got a problem? I'm looking for Beth McClain. Right now I don't plan to arrest her, but if you aggravate me any more, I'll find any reason I can to haul her in. Now when's she going to be back?"

Blinking his surprise, the boy shrugged. "I dunno. She just left a few minutes ago."

"Okay, that's a start. Where did she go?"

"I dunno. She didn't tell me."

"What's your name?"

"James."

"You're her son, right?"

James nodded, shifting his weight from one sneakered foot to the other. His hands were jammed deep into his pockets and his shoulders slouched forward. His expression grew less aggressive, more unsure, the longer Mike stared down at him.

"All right, James," Mike said, pulling out the picture of DC. "How about this guy? Have you seen him around?"

"Yeah," James mumbled. "I've seen him here talking to my mom. She was pretty pissed when he left."

"What were they talking about?"

"I don't know."

Mike stared at the kid for a moment. James was scared. Mike sensed his fear under the smartass facade.

"Can we come in?"

James opened the door wider. "I guess. My dad should be home later, but he probably doesn't know anything either. They never talk, unless they fight. Are you going to tell me what's going on?"

"We're looking for the guy your mother was talking

to. He's wanted for kidnapping and murder. Do you know how she knows him?''

James paled, blinking his eyes rapidly as Mike's words sank in. ''No. I only saw him that one time.''

''When was that?''

''A few days ago. I was upstairs listening to my stereo. When I came down he was in the kitchen with Mom. He left after he saw me. Mom said he was a client, but he didn't look like one. He looked like he'd been in a fight or something.''

''Did you hear any of their conversation?''

''No, I told you.''

''And he hasn't been back since?''

James shook his head. ''But I think he just called.''

''When?''

''I was on the phone when you rang the bell.''

''What did he say?'' Kathy spoke for the first time, leaning forward with anxiety.

Mike placed a comforting hand on her shoulder, explaining Kathy's presence to James. ''We believe he's kidnapped Kathy's daughter. She may not have much time left.''

With his confusion clearly written on his face, he told them, ''He asked for my mom. I said she was gone. He called me a liar. Said he'd just talked to her. Then he called me a bastard and hung up. What does he want with my mom?''

''Good question. He used to work for her. Ever hear her talk about her employees?''

James shook his head again. ''I don't know anything. I swear.''

Mike exhaled, looking at the kid's anguished expression. ''Okay, James. Thanks for trying. Where's your phone?''

While Mike called the station, he watched Kathy sitting in numb silence, staring sightlessly at James. They both seemed absorbed with their own questions, their own misery. His call connected to Jackson and he turned his back to the room, listening to what he had to say. When he hung up, Mike was ready to move again. He met Kathy's gaze, motioning for her to come with him as he headed for the door.

"McCoy hasn't checked in," he said, "but Jackson says some kid from Scorletti's Pizza called. DC was just in, using the phone."

James looked up. "Scorletti's in El Cajon?"

"Yeah, that's the place. Why?"

"We've got a rental house out there."

Sam checked his watch again, his curses echoing in the closed cab of the Jeep. He was still a good ten minutes away. He'd wasted precious time trying to get through to Jackson at the station. First, an endless busy signal. Then, terminal hold. He couldn't delay any more. He had to get to Christie.

He dodged between lanes of traffic, flashing his brights into the rearviews of those who wouldn't get out of his way. For once, he wished the cops would see him. God knew he could use the backup. But flying across the blackened freeway, only Sam's fear for Christie chased him.

He had to find Christie.

Christie and Jessica ran down the dark street as fast as they could, cutting across yards as they went door to door, pounding on each. None opened to let them in.

Christie choked back her frustration. It was late, the neighborhood seedy, the city crazed with crime. Who could blame the occupants for remaining safely barricaded behind their closed doors?

Legs pumping the ground, hearts pounding in their chests, they kept moving. Sweat burned Christie's eyes and her spit tasted hot in her mouth. She pushed harder, half dragging Jessica along with her.

The neighborhood was quiet with only a few dogs peeking from behind fences to witness their escape. She didn't know in which direction she ran, didn't know where she was going. She just moved.

Turning a corner, they tried another house without luck, then darted onto the connecting street. From behind her, Christie heard a car. Terrified that it was DC, she dived behind a bush that scalloped the sidewalk, pulling Jessica down with her. Moon shadows played with her imagination. Darting images of horror danced across the lawns and bent through the trees.

But nothing was more horrifying than what she'd left behind. She bit her lip as the car cruised by. An unfamiliar face glowed like a small moon behind the wheel. The car turned the corner.

Christie and Jessica bounded from their hiding place and kept running. She would get to a phone. That was her plan. Her only plan. Get to a phone.

Sam . . . are you still alive?

With a renewed burst of strength, Christie pushed on.

As the scenery whipped past them in a jerking blur, Christie searched for a phone. When she finally saw one glowing from the parking lot of a deserted gas station, she couldn't believe her eyes. They raced to the lighted booth.

Christie grabbed the receiver and punched out the three numbers that would connect her with help. She waited, but the call didn't connect. Jarring the hookswitch up and down, she listened to the flat silence that should have been a dial tone.

Frustrated rage bubbled up inside her. She glanced over her shoulder, scanning for a different phone, feeling far too exposed in the small booth. Another set of headlights gleamed from the street, becoming bright as they moved closer.

Christie squeezed Jessica's hand, tensing to run as she tracked the car's progress. It was moving fast and it passed them quickly before the rear lights flashed as brakes screamed.

Christie dropped the phone, yelling, "Jessica, run!"

The two turned, heading for the back of the station as the reversing engine thundered in the dark. It stopped ... doors opened. Christie's heart felt as if it would explode, her scant reserves of adrenaline hitting her bloodstream with little effect. As hard as she tried, she could not push her feet to pump faster.

Ahead, Jessica faltered, looking back at Christie.

"Go—" Christie commanded.

"Jessica!" a woman's voice screamed from behind them. "JESSICA!"

The girl froze, stopping so suddenly she stumbled over her momentum. "Mommy?"

As the whispered word left Jessica's lips, Christie heard her name, too. Who was calling her? She dared a look over her shoulder, shock widening her eyes as she recognized Mike Simens behind her. Confused, Christie's gaze swiveled to the woman-sized version of Jessica Jordan racing at his side.

Too pumped by terror to conceive the idea of rescue, Christie slowed gradually as Jessica ran to the outstretched arms of her mother. The two Jordans collided in an embrace that went beyond physical. Kathy's moan carried on the dark breeze, sounding inhuman in its depth.

Slowly, Christie sank to the ground.

"Christie? Are you okay?" Mike asked as he knelt in front of her.

She stared at him, trying to put meaning to his words. What was okay? She shook her head and asked, "Sam?"

"Sam's alive. He's okay. He's looking for you."

The wake of relief left her teeth chattering and her body shaking. It was no use trying to pull herself together when she'd been blasted so far apart. Her gaze moved to Jessica, wrapped in the haven of her mother's arms. Suddenly, the longing for the warmth of her own mother overwhelmed Christie.

Then she realized that she did feel her mother, within

her, holding her tight, putting the scattered pieces of her daughter back in place. She felt her arms, her hands stroking Christie's hair, brushing away her tears. Caressing away the hurt.

"Come on," Mike said, rising. "Let's get out of here before Porter finds us."

Kathy nodded, sniffling through her tears. Wrapped in a cocoon, insulated with shocked relief, Christie rose to her feet. Her gaze met Jessica's across the space that separated them and she knew instinctively what the girl was about to say.

"Aren't you going to go get him?" Jessica asked. "If you don't get him, he'll come back. He'll come back for us."

"Jessica's right," Christie said reluctantly. "He's going to run when he finds out we're gone. Disappear, so you'll never catch him. But he'll come back for us. I know it."

"I know it, too," Mike said. "And as soon as I drop you off at the station—"

"NO!" all three of them cried at once.

Mike continued as if they hadn't spoken. "I'm going after him. But we've got to get moving. Every second counts."

Kathy shook her head, reaching out an imploring hand. "Mike, if you take us to the station, we'll be answering questions for hours. Jessica's not up to that. I'm not up to it, either."

"If it's not the station, Kathy, it'll have to be the hospital. She's got to be checked for injuries and evidence."

Kathy paled at the implications behind his words. Tears filled her eyes as she looked at her daughter.

"I don't want to go to the hospital. I want to go home," Jessica pleaded.

"I know, sweetie," Kathy said, hugging her close. "Me, too. But we . . ." She paused, searching for words. "They . . ."

Her helpless gaze met Mike's.

"I don't think he touched her," Christie said softly. "Jessica and I talked during ... She said he just hit her and locked her in the bathroom."

Mike squatted down to Jessica's level and put his big hands on Jessica's small shoulders. "Jessica, did he touch any other way?"

"You mean give me bad touches?" she asked.

Mike looked at Kathy. "She learned about good touch and bad touch at school," she explained.

"Yes, Jess. I mean bad touches."

Jessica shook her head. "He hit me here," she said, pointing at her face. "But he didn't do bad touches."

Kathy's relieved sigh carried on the night. "Jessica's been through enough for one night already, Mike. Take us home."

"I've got to find Sam," Christie said. "After you drop them off, I'm going with you."

Mike stared from one determined face to another with exasperation. Finally, he let out a frustrated breath and began herding the group into his car.

"I'll take you *all* to Kathy's house, then I'll track down Porter. Christie, Sam will be checking in. Let him find you. You could spend the whole night looking and never find each other if you are both on the move."

He faced Jessica. "Don't worry, honey. I promise you, I'll get him."

Lights were on. Lights on in the house. DC pulled into the driveway of his mother's rental house and jumped out of the car. His heart felt like a jackhammer, wreaking havoc through his body. He stormed to the bathroom prepared to kill, but the destruction inside stopped him short. His mother sat in the middle of it, staring glassy-eyed at the broken window and the glitter on the floor.

"Where are they?" he demanded.

She blinked, her glazed eyes turning to him. She

hardly looked surprised at his bloody appearance. "Looks like you're a little late, DC."

"The kid and Christie," he said, fighting to control his red-hot rage. "Where are they?"

She shrugged. "I told you to give it up, but you wouldn't listen." Her gaze traveled up and down his form. "You never listen."

He clenched his fists. "Goddammit, where are they?"

Her brows raised. "Don't you cuss at me." Suddenly, she jumped to her feet and darted three steps across the room to where he stood in the doorway. She jabbed him in the chest with her finger. "Don't you cuss at me," she repeated. "I don't know where they are. I don't know anything anymore."

He backed off, dropping his gaze to the bathroom floor. "They did this?"

"Well, I certainly didn't." She faced the mirror, smoothing her fingers over her face as if to erase the lines that mapped out her misery.

DC stared at her reflection. For the first time he noticed the wild look behind her glassy eyes. The blood drained from his face in an icy wave. He met her gaze, as hard and cold as the reflective glass.

Laughing, she pushed past him. He followed her to the kitchen, yanking his keys from his pocket as he went. She watched him from the shadows, looking eerily like a ghost from his past.

"Where are you going?" she asked.

"Where the fuck do you think? Did you come here to psych me out? Is that what you're trying to do? Is it?"

She shook her head. "I'm just coming full circle, DC. Finishing things up for you and me."

"What are you talking about?"

For the first time he noticed the gleaming weapon in her hand.

"What are you doing? You're going to kill me? Is

that it? You've been doing that since before I was even fucking born.''

He waited for some denial, but she didn't offer one. Just stood there, masked by the striped shadow of the venetian blind, watching him.

''Why?'' he asked softly. ''Why do you hate me so much? Why have you always hated me so much?''

In the silence she cocked the gun.

''Why? Answer me, goddammit! What did I do? Why do you love James so much and hate me? He's not even your own flesh and blood.''

She shook her head.

''Answer me!'' he screamed.

She stared at him, her eyes gleaming coldly through the darkness. ''Because we're too much flesh and blood, you monster. Don't you see?'' The veins stood out on her neck and pulsed beneath the translucent skin on her forehead. ''Don't you get it? We had the same daddy, DC,'' she yelled.

DC blinked, feeling the pieces of the puzzle finally fall into place. The same daddy. The picture became clear and the implications behind her words rolled over him like a giant steamroller, mashing him into pulp.

Too much flesh and blood.

The same daddy.

She would have known, then, when she abandoned him, what was in store for his young life. She would have known, because she'd been through it. And she'd left him anyway, as if it were DC's fault that he'd been spawned by Satan himself.

It wasn't DC's fault, though. It wasn't his fault.

He looked up, perhaps hoping to explain this to her, but she'd reached her own conclusions on the matter. The barrel of her gun was the only solution she was prepared to accept.

She aimed her gun at his head and fired.

DC felt the bullet zip past him as he hit the floor, rolling as she fired a second shot, barely missing him again. He lurched to his feet and tackled her, slamming her back into the counter. Another bullet whizzed across the room and embedded itself in the wall.

He grabbed her arm and jerked it back, wrestling for the gun. She fought him, twisting and kicking. Finally he grabbed her waving hand and squeezed her wrist limp. The gun fell from her hand.

He caught it, turning it on her as she scrambled away from him, cowering in the corner, just as Jessica had.

"You left me," he accused.

His face felt hot and wet. He wiped it with his hand, surprised to find tears streaming down his cheeks. "You left me there when you knew what he'd do to me. You knew and you did it anyway," he cried.

"I couldn't wait to get rid of you. You are his *filth*. When I look at you all I see is *him* and his filthy, dirty ways."

DC shook his head, his pain so deep that sobs shook his shoulders.

"I'm not him. I'm nothing like him," DC whispered. "I hated him as much as you do."

She pointed a finger at his face, hissing, "You are his son."

"That's not my fault," he said, but looking into her eyes, he realized that she didn't believe him. She had branded him filth before he was even born and in her mind, he would never be more.

"Say it," he pleaded in a broken voice. "Say it wasn't my fault."

She laughed at him.

"Say it," he yelled, pointing the gun at her head. "Say it!"

"Trash. That's all you'll ever be. You ruined my life and I hate you. I hate—"

He shot her, feeling the inconsolable chill of destruction race through his body. The bullet tore through her smile and silenced her bitter laughter.

"You bitch," he said. "You bitch."

He shot again, not caring that she was dead already. He pumped the last bullet into her, splattering the walls and his clothes with her blood.

He lowered the gun, staring at the bloody mess, the mangled corpse of the woman who had always refused to be his mother.

"It wasn't my fault," he repeated. "It wasn't my fault."

Kathy cried all the way. Tears of disbelief; tears of relief. She held Jessica close and warm, nestled under her arm. Burying her face in her daughter's hair, she rejoiced in the scent of the child she had brought into the world. Jessica's small arms were wrapped around Kathy's body as she rested her tired little head on Kathy's breast. Rookie sat on Jessica's left, a silent sentry in the moving night.

". . . and then Christie tried to talk him out of it. But he's mean, Mommy. Really mean. She saved us."

Kathy's tearful gaze met Christie's in the dark interior of the car. "Thank you," Kathy said.

"You're welcome."

Simple words that held such complicated meanings. Christie had given Kathy back her daughter, her reason to live. Kathy, in producing Jessica, had somehow managed to give Christie the hope she needed for her own future.

Only moments after Mike had found Jessica and Christie at the gas station, he pulled to the curb in front of Kathy's house and got out. Jessica clung to her mother as they stepped from the car.

Mike made a quick search of the house with Rookie's attentive assistance, but none of them expected him to find DC there.

With her thoughts on Sam, Christie joined Kathy and Jessica in the kitchen while Mike called for backup. The little girl claimed to be starving, but she only nibbled at the sandwich her mother set in front of her.

Exhaustion slumped Jessica's shoulders, but her shadowed, wide eyes refused to close.

Mike found them at the kitchen table, watching Jessica watch her food.

"Are they sending someone out?" Kathy asked him.

"A patrol car is on the way."

"Just one?"

Mike nodded, chewing his lip. "That's all they can spare right now. It looks like they tracked down the other kidnapper and he's holed up with hostages. Everyone who's not already responding to a call is there. Don't worry. If I thought DC would be back here, I wouldn't be leaving you."

"But—"

"I'll have my man guard your door and I'll go on to Porter's."

"Not alone?"

Mike set a hand on Rookie's head and ruffled his ears. "I won't be alone and Jackson will get someone else out as soon as he can. Don't worry."

"Any word from Sam?" Christie asked.

Mike shook his head. "Not yet, but I left word to tell him you're here. Stay put, Christie. Sam will find you."

Outside, they heard a car stop. Mike looked out the window and nodded.

"The officer's here."

On his way out, Mike paused, looking back at Kathy.

"Be careful," she whispered.

He nodded. "I'll be right back."

And then he was gone.

Sam cut his lights and engine, cruising to a soundless stop in front of Beth's rental house. The front door stood wide open, light spilling out onto the doorstep. With panther silence, Sam pulled his gun and crept in.

He smelled the blood on the air as he neared the kitchen, and recoiled from it. His fear felt like a rock in his gut. Christie? Please God, not Christie.

He rounded the corner, gasping when he saw the gory mess that only vaguely resembled Beth McClain. He stepped back, forcing down the acid feeling inside him. Turning, Sam looked into the gray shadows behind him. Cautiously he moved into the hall, stopping at the door to the bathroom. Holding his breath, he pushed it open with his toe.

Glass. Blood splashed on the base of the toilet. The broken window. A blanket. All the details rushed to him at once. Shock and anger shook him as he stepped inside, glass crunching under his shoes. Was he too late? Had DC taken them and moved on?

He heard a sound behind him and spun to face the business end of a gun. The man holding it flashed a badge. Mike Simens.

Sam quietly set his gun on the ground and held his hands up. Meeting Mike's eyes, Sam mouthed "Sam McCoy."

Recognition flashed across Mike's face a second before he lowered the weapon. A huge dog at his feet watched for a command. Mike stayed him with his hand.

Still silent, Mike darted his gaze down the dark hall and back to Sam again. Sam shook his head. He hadn't investigated that far. He didn't know if they were alone or not.

By unspoken consent, they moved together, inching their way down the hallway, opening doors and investigating each closet and corner.

"He's gone," Mike said moments later. "Who's that in the kitchen?"

"Beth McClain. DC's mother."

"His mother? McClain's his *mother*?"

"Was. He must have had Christie and Jessica here—"

"He did. I picked them up a few minutes ago."

Sam's knees wobbled and he grabbed the wall behind

him for support? "What? Are they . . . ? Where are they?"

"They're alive. I left them at Kathy's house with a cop on guard."

Sam's glance bounced to the kitchen doorway and the splatter of blood that extended outside it then back to Mike. The uneasy fear in his eyes sent a message that was clearer than any words he might have uttered.

"Let's go," he said, already out the door.

"I finally got Jessica to sleep," Kathy told Christie as she came from her daughter's bedroom. "She talked nonstop through her bath and then it just hit her. I don't think she's slept since . . ." Kathy blinked back tears. "She was afraid to close her eyes in case she woke up and he had her ag—"

A loud shot cracked the air, obliterating the rest of Kathy's words. Watching Kathy's lips move, Christie couldn't understand what she'd heard. A stunned silence followed and, as if in slow motion, Christie turned her head and saw the splintered wood of the door.

She scrambled to her feet as the second report sounded and another shot smashed through the door. Kathy jumped back, staring with terror-widened eyes at the bullet now embedded in the wall.

"It's him," Christie whispered.

She didn't need to say who *him* was. They both knew. And without a doubt, the cop left to protect them was dead. They were on their own. Backing away from the door, they watched in horror as it shimmied again.

The fourth shot sent the doorknob flying like a saucer across the room and the door crashed back on its hinges into the wall behind. DC stood on the doorstep splattered in blood and wearing a smile colder than an Arctic wind.

"I don't think your friend will be staying for dinner," he said, flashing them a bloody police badge. He shoved the gun into a holster he had presumably lifted with the badge, but the menace he presented only increased.

Kathy gulped and moved away, unaware that she'd backed herself into the corner until the walls cupped her in their trap. DC pushed through the tattered door like a high-speed train, heading straight for her. Christie circled around him from behind and darted into the kitchen.

Pinned to the wall by her own fear, Kathy froze as he grabbed her by her shoulders and jerked her up into his face. A scream that had started full strength at his approach caught in her throat and died when he touched her.

She struggled, fighting for herself, fighting for her daughter, who slept just on the other side of the wall, but her frantic movements only entangled her more in his grip. With lightning speed, he covered her face with his hand and smashed her head into the wall. She felt her brain go soft and hot, but refused to give in to its fuzzy heat. She would not pass out and leave her daughter to this monster a second time.

Hell, no!

The suffocating pressure of his palms covered her mouth, locking her screams in her throat, but forcing her jaws open. Kathy caught the heel of his hand between her teeth and bit as hard as she could, gagging on the taste of his blood. He yelled, jerking his hand back. She dodged under his arm, but he tripped her and sent her flying across the floor.

Moving quickly from the kitchen, Christie hugged the wall to the front room, forcing her frightened shivers to cease. She took a deep breath and held it, gripping the handle of a butcher knife. It felt unreal, as if the hand on the end of her arm belonged to someone else, along with the knife clutched in the bloodless fingers.

She lunged at DC's turned back while he wrestled with Kathy. As if he had eyes in the back of his head, DC dodged the lethal blade at the last moment. But he was too slow. A tear, a red gash, appeared in the center of his shirt. He staggered back.

Beyond fear, beyond rage, Christie closed in on him. He let her, watching through slitted eyes. Unflinching, she stared back.

Seeing an opportunity, Kathy moved quickly, kicking her foot into his groin as Christie shot forward with another jab of the knife. Unfazed by Kathy's glancing blow, DC quickly jumped out of the swinging arc of Christie's blade, somehow knocking the knife from her hand. With a breathless surge of dread, both women watched the knife spin through the air in slow motion, landing and sliding out of reach.

In a crouch, he faced them like a hungry predator, too greedy to let one of his prey go free while he devoured the other. The smile he gave Christie told her more than she ever wanted to know about what he planned.

Suddenly, from outside, the squeal of tires and the slam of a car door thundered in the sudden silence that held them all motionless. Sam charged through the splintered fragments of the front door and, without pausing, drove his body straight into DC, knocking him to the ground.

Another car door slammed just as DC managed to squirm free of Sam's grip and stagger to his feet. DC groped for his gun as Christie watched in frozen horror.

Suddenly a growling beast of fur and fangs shot through the front door. DC's gaze darted to the dog and he screamed, his terror raising his voice to child-like pitch.

Mike cleared the door just as DC's cry pealed through the house. The sound seemed to render them all immobile. For a split second, Christie's eyes met DC's and the beseeching bewilderment and aching desolation she saw in them overwhelmed her.

He lifted his hand as if to reach out to her, as if to seek consolation. Rookie's jaws clamped over the outstretched arm in an instant and, with a powerful wrench, the dog forced DC to the floor.

DC's howls reverberated through the night, at once pitiful and frightening. He scrambled for the door but Rookie would not let go, moving with savage speed from DC's arm to snarl and chomp at his leg. DC managed to gain his footing, but Rookie lunged, determined to bring him back down.

He was no match for a dog trained to kill. Rookie went for his throat with terrifying ferocity and single-minded determination.

DC continued to grope for the gun in his holster, drawing it while protecting his neck with his other bloodied arm. Rookie saw the weapon the instant DC touched it. The dog pounced on top of DC's chest and sank its fangs deep into DC's arm, ripping another wail of terrified agony out of the incapacitated man.

Still, DC would not relinquish the gun. Fighting the powerful weight and forceful tenacity of Rookie, he swung his hand and pointed the weapon.

Christie found herself trapped in his sights as time seemed to stretch and slow. Her gaze shot to a stunned Sam. He called her name and sprang at her in the exact instant Mike's gun took deadly aim on DC.

Two gunshots simultaneously echoed in the small house and Christie braced herself for the searing pain of a bullet. But it was DC's body that jerked back a second before Sam slammed into Christie. She felt DC's bullet part the air above her as she hit the floor.

The sudden silence seemed cavernous, echoing with the gasping breaths and supercharged emotions of the survivors. Unable to stop herself, Christie peered over Sam's shoulder.

DC lay sprawled in the doorway, Rookie sitting passively at his side. The bottoms of his shoes faced her, toes up.

How ordinary the soles of his shoes looked, she thought disjointedly. How like everyone else's. Yet DC had never been ordinary. Had never been like anyone else.

"He's dead," Mike said softly, checking DC's vital signs. Rookie watched the body, at ease yet alert and ready for battle. The sound of police sirens filled the night.

Sam stood and pulled Christie to her feet. "It's over, babe," he whispered with tears in his eyes. His voice cracked. "It's over."

She shook her head. It would never be over for her, but at least it was finished. Staring at Sam through pain-shadowed eyes, she threw herself into his arms.

The flashing lights of the band of police cars gathered in front of Kathy's house lit the street like a carnival. The monotone drone of the dispatcher echoed in the air. Christie stood back, away from the crowd of officials with their high-beamed flashlights and reporters pressing against the yellow police tape. Watching with a sense of detachment that must surely be shock, she paced a small circle, her rubber shoes whispering over the black asphalt in a soothing way.

It seemed that they'd been there for hours, answering questions, repeating the events of the evening. With each retelling, it seemed more and more a fantasy, less and less a reality. How could it have really happened?

She stared at Sam, his features tinged blue, then red, as the spinning lights flashed across his face. He'd saved her life. Without him, DC and death would have run over her, forever erasing her from this world. A tremor rocked through her. She'd gone from making love to meeting death in the span of one night. It was too much to grasp.

Sam had told her about Beth's relationship to DC. About how Beth had killed Christie's mother and, if the police were correct, Leonard Pfeiffer, too. So much bloodshed, so many people gone. All because of DC.

Mike had pulled Sam aside and told him that the

FBI had confirmed DC's connections with a hospital in Arizona. The files they had found in DC's locker belonged to Dr. McClowsky. DC had used them to learn vital statistics so he could search out a donor. What DC had planned for Jessica boggled Christie's mind and made her sick to her stomach.

What kind of person could even conceive such a brutal plan? DC, though, had not only planned it, he had successfully carried it out in another state. Copying an existing criminal pattern in a city, DC had abducted several victims before he'd ever reached San Diego. The horrifying scandal would make headlines for many weeks to come.

She caught Sam's eyes across the way. His bruised face must have made the action painful, but he smiled at her anyway, warming her heart and filling it with purpose.

DC may have left behind a string of victims, shocked and bruised by his violence, but already they were becoming a group of survivors.

Still, as long as she lived, she'd never forget the look in his eyes before he died. The imploring entreaty. She'd never known just what it was he'd wanted from her. Now, she never would.

Epilogue

Jessica had been home for three days and at the end of each one, Kathy thanked God for her return. Neither she nor her daughter seemed ready to let the other out of her sight but that was okay. They had already started counseling and in time they would learn to live as they had before DC Porter shattered their shallow illusion of security.

As she sat on the front porch watching Jessica playing with her dolls, a familiar car pulled up to the curb. Surprised and immensely pleased, she saw Mike step out followed by a benign-looking Rookie.

Kathy hadn't seen him since that night. She'd begun to think she wouldn't see him again. Jessica ceased her play, reaching out for Rookie as she watched Mike make his way to the porch. Rookie trotted over to give her a lick and sniff her dolls.

Dressed in shorts and a T-shirt, Mike smiled at Kathy. "Rookie wanted to make sure everyone was okay," he said.

"Just Rookie?"

"Well, since he couldn't drive himself, I thought I'd check too."

Kathy smiled, feeling suddenly shy. "It's good to see you again, Mike."

"It's good to see you, too," he said, pulling her gently into his arms. "I think it's time for us to be friends."

She wound her arms around his neck, feeling somehow at home in the haven of his arms. "Just friends?" she asked.

Jessica's ecstatic question stopped Mike's lips a second before they touched Kathy's.

"Mommy? Did the Daddy Fairy come while I was gone?"

Christie stretched and rolled over, snuggling into the warmth of Sam's body. He smiled in his sleep. For three days they'd done nothing but eat, talk, and make endless love that left her feeling like a cat on a sunny windowsill with nothing to do but purr.

She had finally made peace with herself. She had finally allowed herself the freedom to live normally. Now it was time to bury the past, once and for all, and look toward the future.

She felt as if her world, which had always been askew, had finally been righted on its axis. She couldn't bring back her mother, but she could hold her memory close and cherish all that she was, instead of lamenting what she had not been.

The children who had been stolen from the love of their real parents could never be returned. Pfeiffer had destroyed all his records. That was the real tragedy. But the past was just that, and she could do nothing to change it or the senseless pain of the victims.

She could give something back, though, and that was the house in La Jolla. She had decided to donate it to San Diego's homeless children. She felt a sense of justice in that.

For now, she would continue to breathe new life into her relationship with Sam. Without the added baggage of yesterday, it was easier to shed the worries and insecurities that had haunted her every waking moment. It surprised her how easy it was to give everything to the man she loved. Gently, she rubbed Sam's chest.

"What are you thinking about?" he asked softly.

She hadn't noticed his eyes open, but now they stared at her with the gently banked fires of a man well loved.

"You, and how much I love you."

"Christie, I'm so glad to have you back."

He pulled her close and kissed her with all the feelings that words could not describe. "I missed you so much."

"I'm glad to be here, Sam. This is where I want to be forever."

She touched the tender line of his jaw, rubbing her fingertips over his lips. Feeling shy, but not unsure, she formed the question that had weighed so heavily on their relationship.

"So how many kids do you want?"